You Are Called to Greatness

Also by Leo J. Trese
from Sophia Institute Press:

*Seventeen Steps to Heaven:
A Catholic Guide to Salvation*

Leo J. Trese

You Are Called to Greatness

SOPHIA INSTITUTE PRESS
Manchester, New Hampshire

Previously published in 1964 by Geoffrey Chapman, London. This 2022 edition by Sophia Institute Press contains editorial revisions.

Cover design by LUCAS Art & Design, Jenison, MI.

On the cover: *The Ascension* by Gustave Doré
(KHCB4K) © Peter Horree / Alamy Stock Photo.

Biblical references are taken from the Douay-Rheims edition of the Old and New Testaments.

Sophia Institute Press
Box 5284, Manchester, NH 03108
1-800-888-9344
www.SophiaInstitute.com

Sophia Institute Press is a registered trademark of Sophia Institute.

paperback ISBN 978-1-64413-722-2

ebook ISBN 978-1-64413-723-9

Library of Congress Control Number: 2022933764

First printing

Contents

You Are Called to Greatness

1

Sainthood Is for You

You probably are accustomed to thinking of yourself as "just an average Catholic." That is not something to be ashamed of. To be an average Catholic in America is to be a very good Catholic. You assist at Mass every Sunday, good weather or bad, headache or no. You receive Holy Communion every week. You go to Confession monthly or more frequently. You pray every day. You attend your parish mission, novena services, and Forty Hours' devotion. You contribute generously to your parish and to the diocesan collections. You helped to build a Catholic school, and you continue to support it. You read religious books and Catholic periodicals, at least occasionally.

In many countries of the world, even in some so-called Catholic countries, you would not be looked upon as an average Catholic. You would be considered to be close to sainthood because, when we talk about being average we have to ask, "At what point does the grading begin?" A youngster who is just average in a school for gifted children will be head and shoulders above the best in a school for slow learners. Similarly, as an average American Catholic, you would rank well above the average in those countries where, for example, less than 20 percent of the Catholics attend Mass on any given Sunday and an even smaller proportion attend Mass every week.

This is not said to encourage you to complacency. If you were a complacent Catholic, you would not be average. It is one of the most encouraging characteristics of the average American Catholic that he feels spiritually dissatisfied. He knows and acknowledges to himself that he is not as good as he ought to be and as he could be. Unfortunately, he often procrastinates in forcing himself another step upward, but at least he does feel some shame that he hasn't yet attempted that step.

The fact is that you are a saint. Not a canonized saint, of course, but a saint in the original meaning of the Latin word *sanctus*: one who is holy. It is in this sense that St. Paul addresses himself to "the saints who are at Ephesus" (Eph. 1:1) and to "all the saints in Christ Jesus, who are at Philippi" (Phil. 1:1). You are a saint because you are in the state of sanctifying grace. Your soul is sharing in God's own life and is transformed by your personal union with God's infinite holiness.

For all your human weakness, you do try doggedly to preserve God's life in your soul—this marvelous divine kinship that was established in your soul at your Baptism. You know that Jesus made you His blood brother or sister (and God's own child) at the cost of the Cross. Even aside from your own self-interest, you recoil from the perfidy of wasting Christ's agony by breaking the bond between yourself and God, a bond forged at such a price.

You are too intelligent to take pride in your sainthood. You know too well that it is not something that you have acquired by your own efforts. You are not proud, but you are everlastingly grateful. You know that in sharing God's life, you possess a gift beside which, by comparison, all other gifts fade into insignificance.

Good health, good job, good friends, outstanding talents, money, success: if you have any of these, you have a little bonus. But, if you have none of these, you still stand ten feet tall; you still are a giant among those who have not grace. Devils envy you with a white-hot hatred; angels bow to you as you pass.

You feel secure, too. You know that no power in Hell or on earth can sever your intimate union with God unless you yourself choose to make the break. You know that God, for no reason that you can discern, loves you with a possessive love. He wants you with Himself in Heaven and is not going to let you get away easily. He all but smothers you with His attention. He dogs your footsteps with His day-to-day helps, trying to nudge you past the danger points and onward. You know that there is no such thing as sinning by accident. You know that you cannot sin "because you couldn't help it," since free and deliberate choice is of the very essence of sin. You know that as long as you honestly keep trying to do your best, God will take up the slack.

It is no wonder that so much of your prayer is prayer of thanksgiving. In every Mass and in every Our Father and Hail Mary, your gratitude is a recurring refrain. You are aware that if you spent every waking hour from now until Judgment Day, saying over and over, "My God, I thank You," you never could pay your debt.

Yes, you are a saint. It is a bit of a tragedy, though, that God has to work so hard on you (and on me) for so little return. He has nursed us along so patiently for such meager fruit. Perhaps now we could make a new effort? We could try just a little harder to deepen and intensify the divine life within us? True enough, we have resolved on this a hundred times before, only to find ourselves back at our starting point. It may be, though, that we relied too much on our own wisdom and strength. Possibly we need to pray a little harder, and with fewer reservations, "Please, dear God, make me to be what You want me to be; help me to be what I ought; help me to be a saint!"

You do not ask, of course, to be a miracle-worker with your picture on a holy card. To aspire to the glory of canonization would be an act of pride. We may be sure that there is no saint in the Church's calendar who ever expected to be raised to the honors of the altar. A true saint is much too realistic (which is to say, humble) to picture himself in a heroic role. He is too preoccupied with the thought of how much better he should be to advert even briefly to a consideration of how good he is.

No, you should not pridefully expect yourself to become a canonized saint. Yet it is very likely that you do wish that you could be better than you are. In some of your more thoughtful moments, you do feel a stirring of shame that you are doing so little for God, who has lavished such love upon you. That is to your credit, too. It is *not* to your credit, however, if at that point you give a mental sigh and resign yourself to mediocrity; if you take the defeatist attitude that spiritual greatness is not for you.

If you reject the possibility of holiness for yourself, it means that you have forgotten two basic facts concerning sanctity. The first fact is that spiritual growth is the work of God, the work of His grace. You are quite right in thinking that you do not have within you, *of yourself*, the makings of a saint. You are ever so wrong, however, if you think that, for you, sanctity is a hopeless quest. Every saint is a miracle of God's creative power, of God's transforming grace. He needs very little to work on. In fact, we might say that God enjoys working with unlikely materials. The more shoddy the human nature with which He begins, the more unmistakably the power of His grace shines forth.

The second basic fact ignored by one who says, "Me a saint? That's a laugh!" is the truth that sanctity is not achieved by great deeds undertaken for God. Such feats as the founding of a religious order or the conversion of thousands of souls are the fruits, not the genesis, of holiness. They are not even the most important fruits. To God, the most precious product of sanctity is the intimate union with Himself of a soul who loves Him with an undivided love.

Now and again, God does pick a particular saint to spearhead some special work that God wants done. But great works are not necessarily a mark of sanctity. Many notable and praiseworthy achievements have been accomplished by persons whose motives were purely natural. Moreover, the saint whom He does use for a specific task is no dearer to God than is the hidden soul whose upward struggle is known only to Himself. There must be a few "big name" saints to initiate important projects, but God needs and wants a multitude of little saints, too—people like you and me.

Since human weakness is no barrier to sanctity (thanks to God's grace) and great undertakings are not a requirement for sanctity, what *is* needed by an aspirant to sainthood?

Assuming that we have the basic love for God that is evidenced by avoidance of grave sin, the springboard to sanctity is a spirit of generosity toward God. This spirit of generosity is rooted in the conviction that, loving us as He does, God never will ask of us more than we are able to give. Or, to put it another way, we know that if God asks anything difficult of us, He always will give us the needed grace for the task. We are convinced, in short, that if we go along with God wholeheartedly, we simply cannot lose. We open our soul completely to the operation of

His grace. We stand before God and say, in effect, "Take me, God; I am all Yours!"

We have said that sainthood is principally the work of God. Obviously, however, growth in sanctity is not a completely painless process; otherwise there would be more saints than there are. Like the rocks and sunken logs that impede the flow of water in a brook, our self-attachments hinder the free operation of God's grace within us. This is where, for us, the pain comes. There will be no big and striking act of heroism. But, a hundred times a day there will be small acts of heroism as we attack our faults and try to clear the channel for God's love.

It is not easy to be patient with the active, noisy children, especially if we are tired. It is not easy to be receptive to God's will when our plans are upset or when someone else's carelessness makes extra work for us. It is not easy to accept criticism in a spirit of humility. It is not easy to make ourselves change the subject when gossiping begins or, if need be, to disengage ourselves from the gossiping group.

It is not easy to hold our tongue when we are tempted to tell that very funny but very smutty story. It is not easy to be charitable toward some of the people we have to work with. It is not easy to be temperate at the cocktail party and be content with one or two drinks when everyone else is having four or five. It is not easy to be always conscientious in our work and to give to each successive duty the best that is in us. Yet, it is out of such small victories as these that sanctity grows.

These self-conquests may not be easy, but you will admit that, taken individually (as we walk, one step at a time), they are not beyond your capacity. Perhaps, for fear of another failure, you hesitate to commit yourself to this adventure in sanctity, to this complete generosity with God. If that is so, it would be interesting to make at least a "trial run." You need not bind yourself to a lifetime of effort. Just undertake to be a saint for a single day. For the next twenty-four hours, live each hour as God would want you to live it. For a single day, be just as patient and cheerful and charitable and unselfish and attentive to duty as you possibly can be.

Inevitably you will have some misses because the truth is that saints are not made in a day. But you will find the experience surprisingly exhilarating, as you exercise spiritual talents that long have lain dormant. The pursuit of sanctity is a highly creative occupation. It can give a new and unsuspected flavor to life. After one day of it, you may want to try a second day, maybe a third, and—who knows?

We shall be more vigorous in our quest for sanctity if we are mindful of the Holy Spirit's presence within us. On Pentecost, the apostles were changed suddenly from bewildered and fearful men to heroes of fiery zeal. The Holy Spirit had come upon them to effect this transformation. Why, then, do we not feel something of this same courage and zeal? The Holy Spirit came to us also, in the sacrament of Confirmation.

If ours is a lukewarm response to the presence of the Holy Spirit within us, this may be due to the fact that we do not *know* the Holy Spirit as well as we should. If He is a partial stranger to us, He will not have, in our religious thinking and in our prayers, the prominent place that is His due. The fire and force of His influence will be to a great extent neutralized because we are unaware of the tremendous power that is at our disposal.

God the Father we know well. The well-loved parent who loomed so large in our childhood has loaded the word *Father* with a wealth of meaning. The very name of God the Father tells us much about the first Person of the Blessed Trinity.

We feel on easy terms, too, with the second Person of the Godhead. The Son of God became one of us. He experienced human pain and human sorrow, human affection and human joy. From the Cross, He hammered into our hard heads the reality of His love for us. It is no wonder that so many of our prayers are addressed to Him.

God the Father is our loving protector and provider. God the Son is our loving Redeemer and compassionate shepherd. God the Holy Spirit, however, is—well, the Holy Spirit. Our path to Him is a bit more difficult. There is no bridge of familiar and human ideas over which we can cross to Him. As a consequence, we give the Holy Spirit a respectful mention at the end of the Sign of the Cross and the Glory Be and feel that we have done our duty by Him.

If our personal response to the Holy Spirit is to be more than nominal, we must probe more deeply into His true identity. This involves an examination of the Godhead in whom the Holy Spirit resides. The nature of the Blessed Trinity is a mystery, of course. Puny human minds cannot hope to probe the infinite depths of God. Still, there is much about the Blessed Trinity that we can know and must know if we are to see the Holy Spirit in true perspective. It may be helpful to review, very briefly, what we do know about the Triune God.

Begin, if you will, by speaking your own name. As you speak your name, *think* of yourself. Picture yourself as the person who you are. The mental image that you have of yourself may be quite defective. It is possible that your friends could tell you things about yourself that would surprise you.

However, even if you are utterly honest with yourself; even if you have learned to know yourself inside out; even if your mind's picture of yourself is a very accurate likeness—it still is not a *perfect* reflection of you. You are a living being. For your mental image of yourself to be a perfect image, it should be a *living* image. Otherwise, it does not completely represent you.

Now let us turn to God. God is infinitely perfect. Everything that pertains to God is perfect to an absolute degree. Consequently, God's knowledge of Himself is a perfect knowledge. The image of Himself that God has in His divine mind is an absolutely perfect image, an exact replica of Himself. Since it belongs to the very nature of God to exist, God's idea of Himself must have an existence of its own. It must be a *living* image; otherwise it would not reflect God perfectly. It *is* a living thought of Himself that God possesses, and this living image is He whom we call God the Son. From all eternity, God has known Himself. From all eternity, He has generated His own living image: His Son.

Let us return to yourself for a moment. When you think of yourself, when you "look at yourself" in your own mind, you probably like what you see. Admitting that there are some directions in which you would like to improve, some faults that you would like to eliminate, it still remains true that on balance you are reasonably content with your image of yourself. You are glad that you are who you are. Indeed, a wholesome self-love (psychologists call it self-acceptance) is essential to mental health.

When God looks at Himself, what does He find? He finds an infinitely good, infinitely perfect, infinitely lovable image of Himself. God's living image, the Son, looks back at the Father (we speak in human terms) and sees the infinite lovableness of the Source from which He springs. Between the two—the Father (God knowing Himself) and the Son (God's knowledge of Himself)—there flows a mutual love. It is a love of infinite intensity, an infinitely perfect love—and therefore a *living* love.

This perfect, living love is the Holy Spirit. It is as simple as that. The Holy Spirit is love. He is God's love—a living, conscious, and eternal love.

We can see how different, how wonderfully different God's love is from human love. Human love is an emotion, an attitude. When you love someone, you experience a feeling toward the other person (a feeling easier to recognize than to define). But, no matter how much you may love, you remain outside the other person. You cannot get inside that person and become completely one with him or her. You may say to someone, "I love you with my whole being!" But really you do not. You cannot.

God, however, can and does do just this. Since God's love is God Himself, this is the only way God *can* love. His love is not an emotion that goes out from Him. His love is Himself, the Holy Spirit. If God loves someone, it means that the Holy Spirit is personally present within the person, uniting to Himself the one He loves. When you whisper to yourself, "God loves me," what you really are saying is, "The Holy Spirit is within me."

God's love, who is the Holy Spirit, comes to us for the first time when we are baptized. It is by Baptism that the soul is opened to God's love so that He may enter there. The Holy Spirit wills to remain with us forever. Whether or not He can do so depends on us. God cannot love except by being present within us. Mortal sin, by its very definition, is a turning away from God, a denial to God of access to our soul. It is awesome that we humans should have such dreadful power over the Holy Spirit: the power to expel Him, the power to nullify His will to love us.

With a better understanding of the true nature of the Holy Spirit, perhaps we shall be more mindful of His presence within us and more scrupulous in safeguarding His abode there. We shall turn to Him more easily and more frequently in prayer. We shall be intent on making more room for Him by the practice of virtue and by growth in goodness.

We shall advert to the impulses of the Holy Spirit within us and identify those impulses more surely. We especially must be more conscious of the Holy Spirit's urgent desire to find entrance, through us, into the souls of others. We even may experience a little of the fervor that the apostles manifested with such abundance after Pentecost. We shall be more alert to the spiritual needs of others and quicker to recognize our opportunities (and our obligation) to be of help to our neighbor.

The Holy Spirit is God's love. Love is a dynamic force. In it is wisdom and courage and power. Pentecost changed forever the lives of the apostles. The fire of Pentecost still burns. It is for us to let the embers within us burst into flames. If we let the Holy Spirit possess our soul to the extent that He wishes, then our lives will be transformed indeed.

If we are to be holy, we must be humble—but let us be clear as to the meaning of humility. There probably is no other virtue so misunderstood. For many persons, the adjective *humble* evokes a picture of a plainly dressed, self-effacing, and self-deprecating individual who will admit to the possession of no talent, take the last place always, and make himself a doormat for everyone else. However, this is not an accurate picture of the truly humble person.

Humility is the virtue by which we achieve a sense of reality and due proportion. It is the virtue by which we view ourselves through God's eyes and see ourselves as nothing except what God has made us. That "except" is a very important qualification, for God has made of us something really great. The whole point of humility is that we do see ourselves as something quite wonderful: immortal beings, divinized by grace and destined for eternal companionship with God. We balance this knowledge, however, with a vivid realization that it is God who has made us what we are and that we dare not take credit for a bit of it.

It may clarify the virtue of humility a little bit if we try to correct some of the misconceptions concerning it. For example, plain clothes are not an essential mark of humility. I remember being told by a young woman who does settlement work in the slums of a large city, "We always wear our make-up and try to dress attractively. We owe this to the poor as a recognition of their dignity as persons. We feel that they are worth dressing up for." This young woman and her colleagues certainly are not lacking in humility.

Self-effacement is not a sign of humility, either, if it really is a bid for notice. Christ's little parable in illustration of the principle that "Everyone that exalteth himself shall be humbled; and he that humbleth himself, shall be exalted" (Luke 14:11) is frequently misinterpreted. Jesus was directing a few barbs at the Pharisees, who loved to put on airs and to lord it over others. Jesus did not intend His illustration to be taken literally. If it were, Jesus would be saying that we should take the last place precisely so that we may be called up higher and given public honor—which certainly was not His meaning. In practice, the truly humble man would just drop into the first chair he came to. He would not be thinking in terms of higher or lower because his mind would not be on himself.

Along that same line, I once read of a saint who, if he was served tasty food, would sprinkle it with ashes so that he would not enjoy the taste of it. Feeling a little guilty at not being edified by this practice, I was relieved when I read of another saint whose mind was so occupied with God that he never could tell, after a meal, what he had eaten. He just didn't notice the food. It is unfair to compare saints, but I would put my money on the second one.

If self-effacement is not a sign of humility, neither is self-deprecation. It is not humility to downgrade oneself falsely. God *wants* us to be pleased with ourselves as we are because we are His work. He wants us to feel, "I'm glad I am who I am, and not someone else." As we have mentioned, this wholesome satisfaction with self also is a good indication of mental health. A person who really feels that he is no good is a sick person. One who *pretends* that he is no good dishonors God, who made him what he is.

Plainly, then, it is not a proof of humility to deny the talents that God has given us. If we have been accorded special gifts, God expects us to be mindful always of their origin; but He expects also that we should use those gifts, when we can, for the benefit of others. It is the most specious kind of humility to say, for example, "Oh, don't ask me to sing; you know I can't sing," if really I can sing; or to say, "Please don't ask me to head the committee; you know I'm no good at organizing," when really I am quite good at it. The falseness of this type of self-deprecation is pretty obvious. It has been termed, "Humility with a hook"—an angling for compliments.

As for being a doormat for others, it unquestionably is an act of virtue to waive one's personal rights and take a back seat in the interests of peace and fraternal charity. However, in this interdependent world of ours, our own rights often are bound up with the rights of others—and sometimes with the rights of God. If surrender on our part means that the welfare of others may be jeopardized or God's honor demeaned, then we well may have the obligation to come out with both fists swinging (figuratively speaking, of course).

No, if you are looking for a humble person, do not look for a hangdog character. Look for a person who is at ease with God, himself, and his neighbor—a person who respects himself as God's handiwork. He does not toady to the rich and famous or patronize the lowly. He has a sense of humor because he has the ability to laugh at himself. He has great patience with the ignorance and stupidity of others because he knows where his own brains came from. He is generous with his time, talents, and money because he knows that he must answer to God for the use of God's gifts. He is compassionate toward sinners because he is ashamed that he has had so much more grace than they—and has used it so poorly. His prayer life is strong (although this you cannot see) because he knows how much he must depend upon God.

It should be evident that the virtue of humility is not restricted to any particular walk of life. A man may be a corporate executive and still be humble; he may be a car washer and still be proud. A woman may be a great actress and yet be humble; she may be an unknown waitress and yet be proud. It is all a question of one's sense of reality and proportion. It is a matter of giving credit where credit is due: to the God who made each of us, lovingly, as we are. He has not yet finished His work on us. It is by giving full rein to His continuing graces that we shall reach the fullness of what He wants us to be.

2

Loosening the World's Hold

Nobody likes mortification—nobody, that is, in his right mind. The most basic instinct of the human organism is to seek pleasure and to avoid pain. A person who seeks suffering for suffering's sake is mentally or emotionally ill. He is either a masochist or the victim of psychological guilt feelings that can be eased only by self-punishment.

However, it is a different story when man frustrates the pleasure-pain instinct in the interest of a noble cause. This is man at his best, demonstrating the gulf that exists between man and lower animals. We think of the hardships undergone and the agony risked by those who fight in defense of their country. And we think, inevitably, of Christians who violate the pleasure-pain principle in order to share the Cross of Christ.

With most of us, mortification is not a popular topic for discussion. One reason may be that we experience some feeling of shame whenever mortification is mentioned. We know that we are much too inclined to dodge self-denial. We love the soft life and would prefer to leave our conscience undisturbed. Aroused, it might indict us as shirkers of Christian duty.

In justice to ourselves, however, we should recognize that our lives are not wholly unpenitential. A person cannot be a good Catholic without practicing self-denial to a considerable degree. Sunday Mass, daily prayer, Friday abstinence and fast days—there is penance in all of these. Even more fundamentally, the keeping of God's commandments involves strict mortification. Every temptation overcome is an act of self-denial. However, it still is true that many of us are much too easy on ourselves, not through lack of good will, but rather through lack of awareness of the importance of penance.

We do know that we must do penance for our sins, here or hereafter. When we truly repent of a sin, God grants His pardon gladly. However, God still expects us to make reparation for the harm we have done—somewhat as the guilty party in an automobile accident, although forgiven by his victim, still must pay for the damage done. When we sin, we not only do spiritual harm to ourselves; we also hurt the Mystical Body of Christ, of which we are a part. There is no such thing as a strictly "private" sin. When I sin, grace is lost to the whole Mystical Body. Every baptized Christian suffers a little because of my dereliction. By mortification, I atone for the damage I have perpetrated on His Body.

However, this is not the only reason for penance. Even if my life had been completely sinless, my love for Jesus still would urge me to do penance. If I love Jesus, then I will love those who are dear to Him—which means every soul for whom He died. The salvation of others will be important to me because it is so important to my Lord. Others need my penances, even if I do not. Often these others will be unaware of their need for penance, or, what is worse, they will not care. By God's design, my penance can substitute for their lack of it. My prayers and penances can be the levers that will open their hearts to God's grace.

It is both a privilege and an obligation that Jesus has accorded me: the privilege and the obligation to share with Him His work of redemption. Pope Pius XII, in his encyclical on the Mystical Body, tells us,

> Dying on the Cross, He left to His Church the immense treasury of the Redemption, towards which she contributed nothing. But when those graces come to be distributed, not only does He share this work of sanctification with His Church, but He wills that in some way it be due to her action. This is a deep mystery . . . that the salvation of many depends upon the prayers and voluntary penances which the members of the Mystical Body of Jesus Christ offer for this intention.[1]

With this thought before me, I shall not contemn mortification even if I can honestly say (and who can?), "I have no need for penance." An endless line of brothers and sisters stretches into the distance, brothers and sisters whose salvation depends upon the pain that I shall bear for them. The salvation of a person whom I never have seen may be accomplished through my acts of self-denial.

I also shall be a better person for having practiced that self-denial. There is a bonus, in the natural order, that comes to us through mortification: we grow in emotional maturity. A person who is emotionally mature ("well adjusted," the psychologists say) directs his life by reason rather than by emotion. Emotional control is achieved by the disciplining of our impulses, and there is no practice better calculated to discipline impulse than the practice of mortification. We all have met the emotionally immature person.

[1] Pope Pius XII, encyclical *Mystici Corporis Christi* (June 29, 1943), no. 44.

"He just never grew up," we say resignedly. The person who evades all self-denial invariably is a person who is emotionally immature.

This, incidentally, is what we are talking about when we say that self-denial strengthens the will. Factually, the will is not a muscle to be toughened by flexing. Our will is a faculty of our spiritual soul and can be strengthened only by grace. When we speak of strengthening the will, we really mean the weakening of impulse, which easily can trick the will into unwise choices. Many sins can be traced to uncontrolled impulse. In self-denial, we have an excellent antidote to temptation and a powerful preventative of sin.

For love of Christ, then, and for love of our own soul, we shall practice mortification. It is good, too, to re-examine our personal program of self-denial. If we tend to think of penance always in terms of *physical* hardship, we may need to correct our sense of proportion. Interior mortification is far more important (and usually more difficult) than exterior penance.

A hot-tempered person, for example, will do better to abstain from his temper outbursts than to abstain from the funnies. A gossipy person will gain more merit from a single day free from uncharitable remarks than by many weeks of dessertless meals. A hypercritical person will please God more by curbing his fault-finding than by taking his coffee without sugar. Some exterior mortification is necessary for us all, but never to the neglect of the more essential interior self-discipline.

Let us not overlook, either, the wonderful opportunities afforded by our inescapable crosses: the splitting headache, the rebuke from the boss, the flat tire, the burned potatoes, the nasty weather. Accepted without complaint and in union with the sufferings of Christ, every little pain and disappointment can be made a precious source of merit.

When we do turn to exterior and voluntary penances, let us remember that a small success is better than a big failure. We have met the heavy smoker who swears off cigarettes on Ash Wednesday and lights up again the following day. His comforting excuse is, "Well, I tried. I just haven't got the willpower." He would do better to resolve, "I shall not smoke a cigarette any day until after breakfast." It would be a small penance, but a possible and effective one. We have met, too, the drinking man who renounces liquor during Lent, then gets drunk on Easter Sunday. He would do better to limit himself during Lent to one beer or highball before dinner or bedtime and to forego the Easter overindulgence. (I am not speaking here of the alcoholic, for whom total abstinence is the only moderation.) For the sweet-lover, it would be better to do without dessert one day a week than to abjure sweets entirely and then begin, little by little, to cheat on the Lord.

God looks to us for some degree of penance the whole year through. One small success will lead to another. We shall grow in fortitude. And God, who asks of us no more than we are able to give, will bless with new graces our evident good will.

It dates me mercilessly to admit it, but I can remember the day when there was no such thing as installment buying. In my childhood, the only credit extended to the consumer was a thirty-day charge account. This was the pre-appliance age. In our home, the only household appliance (if it could be called that) was the kitchen range. Bread was toasted on a wire grid on the range top. The purchase of galvanized washtubs and zinc washboards did not require extended-time payments. There was no easy-payment plan for a horse and buggy.

Fifty years ago, life was more rugged, but it also was simpler. It was much easier to practice the virtue of detachment. There was no Madison Avenue to create urgent wants and artificial needs. Advertising pretty much confined itself to telling where certain merchandise might be bought and at what price. It was only the patent medicine ads that indulged in superlatives.

It seems significant that a steadily increasing divorce rate has accompanied the rise in installment buying. It is the experience of marriage counselors that financial difficulties are the greatest single cause of marital rifts. Yet the tragedy is that such difficulties are almost wholly self-made. Poverty has declined, but wants have mounted. As incomes have increased, covetousness has increased even faster. A spiral of installment payments can be a quick destroyer of domestic peace and happiness.

Much of our covetousness has its roots in sloth. Power lawn mowers, automated kitchens and laundries, remote-control television, and electric-eye garage doors all save time and energy. It is a question, however, of whether we are using our reclaimed time and energy in constructive, creative ways, whether we are enriching our lives by greater service to God and neighbor.

Pride, as well as sloth, can lead to covetousness. Ours is the era of the status symbol. A good wool coat is as warm as mink, but it does not speak as loudly (even if falsely) of affluence. A Ford provides adequate transportation, but it takes a Cadillac to make the neighbors sit up and take notice. Fish bite no better from a cabin cruiser than from a fourteen-foot outboard, but the cruiser is much more ego-satisfying. Comfortable living can be found in an older neighborhood, but "a good address" is important, too. Who can resist the attraction of "homes of spacious elegance in a highly restricted community"?

More and more, modern advertising bases its pulling power on snob appeal. We are moved to wonder why it is that we are so eager to appear better than our friends and neighbors, so eager to inspire envy in others. Perhaps we are defending ourselves against deep-seated feelings of inferiority. Perhaps we seek to escape a sense of inadequacy in our roles as spouses or parents. Perhaps we are surrendering to naked pride.

Certainly we are untrue to our vocation as Christians if we let ourselves be drawn into the vortex of acquisitiveness that swirls around us. Blessed are they who preserve their freedom as children of God and who refuse to be enslaved by "things." Blessed are they who are content with the ordinary comforts and conveniences of life and feel no compulsion to possess the newest or the best. Blessed are they who find their greatest pleasure in the mutual love of family and friends and who feel no need to flaunt (or to pretend) superiority. Peace reigns in the home that is governed by the spirit of detachment.

Thrice blessed are they who restrain their own appetites for superfluities so that they may have more to share with those less fortunate. St. John Chrysostom once said, "I have no right to two coats as long as my neighbor has none."

Detachment, or poverty of spirit, is the virtue by which we view all created things in their relationship to God. Whatever contributes to our progress toward God—that is, to the doing of His will—is good. Whatever retards our progress toward God is bad. The term *created things* refers to more than material possessions. It refers to persons, too. It is possible, for example, to cultivate a friendship that takes us away from God or weakens us spiritually. "Things" also include work and recreation. A man or woman may become so immersed in a job, sport, or hobby as to neglect family responsibilities and religious duties.

There are very few things that, by their nature, are either good or evil. Ordinarily it is the *use* we make of things that determines their moral significance. Ideally, everything in life should have God as its ultimate target. The purpose of our recreation, for example, should be the refreshment of mind and body so as to keep ourselves in condition to fulfill our vocation and to do God's will. We need not advert explicitly to this purpose every time we plan some fun or experience some enjoyment, but this should be our habitual motive. Any pleasure that defeats this purpose plainly would be wrong.

However, we continually are faced with choices in which the use or non-use of a particular thing would seem to be a matter of indifference. Our decision will be neither helpful nor hurtful to ourselves or others. In such instances, we are quite free to follow personal preference. All that God has made is good, and God is pleased to have us enjoy His created gifts. Our appreciation of God's bounty and our gratitude are a part of the honor that we pay to Him.

In the practice of detachment, it is important that we be guided by the virtue of prudence. For an imprudent person, however well-intentioned, the practice of detachment could lead to unhappy consequences. As an illustration, I cite a Catholic couple I once knew, a couple with exceptionally high ideals. They felt that true poverty of spirit would be violated by having a television set in their home. As a consequence, their children spent most of their free time in the homes of friends, watching television. The zeal of this couple is to be admired, but it would have been more prudent to have their children watch television at home under parental supervision.

Besides imprudence, there is another danger to which we are exposed as we try to perfect ourselves in detachment. This is the urge to make ourselves the pattern of our neighbor. We have achieved some degree of self-denial. Perhaps we have given up smoking, drinking, or some other self-indulgence or luxury. We are tempted then to sit in judgment on those who are less ascetic than ourselves. We view them with pity, if not with contempt. We even may try to impose our own code upon them.

It should be evident that detachment has ceased to be a virtue if it has spelled death to humility and fraternal charity. Incidentally, we have here a characteristic difference between a real saint and a pseudo-saint. A real saint, while strict with himself, invariably is compassionate toward and patient with the weaknesses of others. Yet a pseudo-saint is demanding and critical of others. Love for God never can lapse into unnecessary offensiveness to our neighbor.

That, quite simply, is what detachment is: an exemplification of our love for God. It manifests a love for God that goes beyond the mere minimum of abstention from grievous sin. As we grow in love for God, we necessarily grow in the spirit of detachment. "What God wants is what I want. Everything must take second place to Him." This is the attitude that underlies detachment.

Like mortification, detachment is a virtue for all seasons. A few minutes of quiet thought with our eyes upon the crucifix may make us a bit ashamed of some of the values that we have set up for ourselves. We even may be moved to revise our personal list of wants and goals.

Perhaps you are one of the fortunate ones. Your life is completely free from pressure and tension. Circumstances have conspired to cushion you in an environment devoid of frustration. You have an exceptionally attractive personality. You like people, and everyone who knows you likes you. You are much sought after as a guest at social affairs. Nevertheless, you are not dependent upon social activities. You combine a placid temperament with an active and questing mind. You can spend a quiet evening at home with a good book or a symphony album and enjoy every minute of it. Your work is intensely interesting. Your associates at work are congenial and cooperative.

If married, you are blessed with a devoted and understanding spouse. Your wife (or husband) is a totally unselfish person, ministering to your every whim. Your children seem to have been born free from original sin, so thoughtful and obedient they are. Teachers marvel at their intelligence and exemplary behavior. Aside from an occasional cold, you cannot remember when there was a day of sickness in your home. Family income is more than adequate. You owe no bills and have money in the bank.

"What a dream!" you will say, and rightly. The person I have been describing exists only in some of the more old-fashioned romantic novels and saccharine Hollywood productions. While all of us have much for which to thank God, none of us can live long in this world without experiencing our share of frustrations. There will be disappointments, anxieties, pain, sorrow, and sometimes staggering blows. Even if we ourselves are perfect (an absurd fiction), we have to live and work with people who are not.

We can expect, then, a certain amount of buffeting in life. If we are to maintain our emotional balance and preserve our sense of direction through this buffeting, we need some kind of built-in stabilizer and guide. An airplane pilot, trusting only his own sense of direction, easily can drift or be blown far off course. However, modern planes are equipped with automatic pilots. When automatic pilots were introduced as a navigational aid, the heart of the technology was a gyroscope, a perpetually spinning top that can sense even the least deviation from course and automatically sets in motion the necessary corrective measures.

We have a gyroscope, too, for our progress through life—and we are fools if we do not use it. Our spiritual gyroscope is the practice known as abandonment to the divine will. Abandonment means that, without any evasion or compromise, and with utmost sincerity and 100 percent commitment, we identify our will with God's. What He wants, we want. Nothing else matters, as long as His will is done.

This abandonment can develop only from certain basic convictions. The first such conviction is that God is infinitely wise. He knows always what is best, including what is best for me personally. The second conviction is that God is infinitely powerful. There is nothing that He cannot do and nothing that can happen unless He chooses to permit it. The third and the most important conviction is that God loves me. He loves me personally as an individual, with what we almost might call a hungry and possessive love.

It is comparatively easy to accept these truths on a theoretical level. As Catholics, we have to accept them—or be guilty of heresy. However, to give intellectual assent to these truths is not quite the same as holding them as unshakable personal convictions. To achieve abandonment, these principles must be imbedded "in our very bones." We must *feel* them as well as believe them.

The principle we usually find hardest to absorb is the reality of God's personal love for each of us. Admittedly, the scope of infinite love is hard for finite minds to grasp, despite the assurance of Jesus, "Are not two sparrows sold for a farthing? And not one of them shall fall on the ground without your Father.... Fear not, therefore: better are you than many sparrows" (Matt. 10:29–31). I reflect that there are almost three billion people in the world. I am one tiny speck on a tiny planet in the great universe of planets and stars. My human mind almost balks at the idea that I am as intimately present in God's mind, as exclusively an object of His attention and love, as though I were the only creature that He ever had made.

Knowing myself as I do, and my own pettiness, such love on God's part seems quite ridiculous. It is ridiculous from the human point of view. We could not believe it at all if God Himself did not give us the grace to believe. Even then, we have a tendency to hedge, a tendency to discount the truth that we profess to believe.

"Yes," we say in time of temptation, "I know that God says (or "the Church says," or "the priest says") this is wrong, but there is no other way out for me. It's all very well to say that this is a sin, but I've just got to do it. The cost to me is too great to do anything else." What we really are saying is that, when the chips are down, we don't fully trust in God's care and love. We assume that God is willing to stand by and see us crushed in the very act of doing His will. Or, alternatively, we do not really believe that God is infinitely wise. This time, we feel, we know what is best for us better than God does. We must do it our way rather than His way. And so, like a man who ignores the barrier at a washed-out bridge, we drive on to our own destruction.

At other times, our mistrust of God takes the form of self-pity, perhaps even despair. We suffer a great loss, sorrow, or failure. "If God loves me, how could He ever let this happen to me?" we demand. "How can any good come of this, for me or for anyone else? It doesn't make sense!" Yet, even as we rebel, God's compassionate love broods over us; His encircling arm supports us.

Because the idea of God's intimate love and care for each of us seems so fantastic, we have to remind ourselves of it often. We need to pray often, too, for the grace to overcome our incredulity, our slowness to understand, our mistrust. Our aim is to realize vividly, right down to the tips of our toes, that God does know best, always—and that God does love *me* with an insatiable love.

Then we are ready to throw ourselves unreservedly into His arms. We are ready to abandon ourselves to His will.

Abandonment to God's will does not mean that we become completely passive. We are not to surrender all initiative, to drift like a leaf on the river's current. God has given us gifts of mind and will, and He wants us to use those gifts. He wants us to think for ourselves, to make decisions in the light of the reason He has given us. The only restriction is that we make God's will the measuring stick of all that we do. God's guiding grace, unseen and unfelt, will be at work.

Sometimes God's will may seem obscure. We cannot be sure what He would prefer under particular circumstances. We must depend upon our human wisdom for a decision. Yet, even in such instances, our choice is bound to be the right one. God will see to that, since we have abandoned our will to His. Even if, by human standards, our decision proves to be the wrong one, it still will be the right one from God's point of view. It still will be the best choice in the long pull, even though we may have to await eternity to discover the why and the how.

"Take me, God, and use me as You see fit. Help me always to do Your will. Joy or sorrow, health or sickness, success or failure—I have no fear, just so that I do Your will. I know that You never will ask of me anything beyond my present strength. And if I should prove stubborn, dear Lord, please *make* me do Your will, whether I want to do it or not. I do not demand always to know Your will. I do not ask for the merit of resignation or of voluntary choice. Just so Your will is done, blessed God, nothing else matters."

When we can pray in this vein and mean it with all our heart, we have reached the point of abandonment. We have learned the secret of mental peace amid external turmoil. We are on our way to confident, constructive, and happy living. With our hand in God's, we know that we cannot lose.

3

Faith Is Basic

If you aim at a vocation that calls for special skills, you first must obtain the necessary training. Specialized training calls for time and effort. Even with time and effort, in every professional school there are many who find the going too hard and decide to quit. In most of these instances, the quitter simply does not have the necessary talent for the work he contemplates. Without manual dexterity, for example, a person will become neither a good typist nor a good surgeon.

Yet there is one vocation to which all of us must aspire. It is the vocation to which God has called us: the vocation to be a saint. This involves a training course that is lifelong. Death is our graduation. It is only then that the diploma is placed in our hands.

We have one great advantage that often is lacking to those who seek a worldly career. We already have the necessary talents for our task. God has given us the requisite abilities. We know that, as long as we maintain our effort, we cannot miss. There is no basis for discouragement. There is no excuse for failure.

It was in Baptism that God gave us the talents we need in order to become a saint. At the moment of Baptism, God infused into our soul the three great virtues of faith, hope, and love. God's gift of these virtues is an indication of His love for us. God is so anxious (speaking in human terms) to have us with Himself in Heaven, that He makes our progress as foolproof as possible. He does not leave us to struggle toward Him as best we can, at the mercy of our merely natural capacity for faith, hope, and love. God provides us with a supernatural facility in the practice of these virtues, to bring us more surely to Himself.

From the fact that the Greek name for God is *Theos*, faith, hope, and love are called the *theo*logical virtues. Their immediate object is God Himself: to believe in God, to trust God, to love God. Other virtues, which are called moral virtues, have intermediate objectives. Such virtues as justice, truthfulness, and chastity, for example, concern our neighbor and ourselves.

A virtue is defined as a habit that perfects the powers of the soul and inclines one to do good. A simpler description of a virtue would be to say that it is a spiritual talent.

A natural talent, such as a talent for music or art, is an inborn skill. Such a talent does not necessarily make one a musician or an artist. An individual might be born with a great artistic talent. Yet, if he had no lessons in art and never had a paintbrush in his hands, his talent might lie dormant and unused.

Similarly, the spiritual talents that God infuses into our soul at Baptism may remain unused. Having been baptized, we have a supernatural facility for believing in God and His teachings, trusting in God's promises, and loving God. However, if we never had received any religious instruction, our talent for believing would remain unrecognized and unused. Since hope and love follow upon faith, these virtues also would remain uncultivated.

If someone were to ask you, "What is your most precious possession?" would you answer, without a moment's hesitation, "my Catholic faith"? That should be your answer. Nothing that you have—family, friends, health, or material possessions—can compare in value, even faintly, with your religious faith.

Faith is the very foundation of your spiritual life. It is faith that gives meaning to your present existence. It is faith that is your passport to Heaven.

Without faith, *right* and *wrong* are empty words. Morality is a matter of convenience. Suffering is an unmitigated disaster. Self-sacrifice is stupid, and whole-hearted selfishness is the most sensible course for a man to pursue.

We who have been Catholics from infancy tend to underappreciate our faith. Never having known what it is to live without religious convictions, we take our faith for granted. We do not thank God often enough for this most basic gift. We do not fortify our belief often enough by making conscious acts of faith. We even may grow careless in protecting our faith and may expose it to unnecessary dangers.

In Baptism God infused into our soul the *virtue* of faith. This means that we have a special ability, a supernatural talent for believing. We shall not lose our faith easily. We shall not lose it, except by our own fault.

It is almost inevitable that we should be afflicted with temptations against faith. Ours is a limited and imperfect intelligence, trying to cope with the limitless depths of God. An ant, if it had a mind, could more easily understand the world of humans than we humans can understand the infinite reaches of God. If religious belief were a body of self-evident truths, always in plain harmony with every other facet of human knowledge and experience, faith would be no problem. In fact, faith would not even exist.

By its very definition, faith is belief in divine truths on the authority of God who has made those truths known to us. If the truths were demonstrable, such as the truth that a straight line is the shortest distance between two points, there would be no need to invoke the authority of God. There would be no need for faith—no merit in it and no reward for it.

We expect, then, that we are going to meet with temptations against our faith (although, as Arnold Lunn has observed, the intellectual difficulties of a believer are as nothing compared to the intellectual difficulties that beset the unbeliever). However, it is important that we do not increase our temptations by courting unnecessary hazards. Unwise reading, for example, easily could pose a threat to our faith.

Authors of books, like university professors, have about them an aura of learning that frequently far exceeds their actual attainments. We tend to over-respect their opinions and pronouncements. Thus, when we read a book or hear a lecture by an eminent "thinker" who loftily assumes that no intelligent person today really believes "the outmoded dogmas of medieval minds," we squirm a bit at being convicted of lack of intelligence. For we still do believe that God created the universe and that Jesus Christ is God. We then begin to wonder whether we may not be mistaken.

If we deliberately expose ourselves to very much of this high-level sniping, the day may come when it is too late to run for cover. We may find that our faith is shattered and that we cannot put the pieces back together again. This is more likely to happen if we neglect to seek the answers to our difficulties. If we but have the humility to ask, any priest easily can puncture the sophistries that trouble us.

Of this we can be certain: a faith cherished will never be lost. It is only our own neglect, our own needless exposure to peril, our own intellectual pride, or our own abuse of grace that can rob us of this priceless gift.

There is a difference between the virtue of faith and the act of faith. The virtue, which is a state of readiness to believe, was infused into our soul at Baptism. Most of us received this virtue as infants. However, there could be no exercise of the virtue until we reached the age of understanding. Only then did we learn that there is a God and that He has made certain truths known to us. Only then could we give free assent to the truths of God and say, meaningfully, "I believe."

No one can make this act of faith without God's help. That is why we speak of faith as a gift of God. A person can prepare himself for an act of faith by learning about God and about the truths of religion. For the final step, however, when with mind and heart we unreservedly accept God and His revelation, we must have God's assistance. This is the *grace* of faith, as distinguished from the virtue of faith. If we were baptized in infancy, we received first the virtue and later the grace of faith. Those who became converts in later years received first the grace of faith and then, in Baptism, the virtue.

Occasionally we meet with a non-believer who says, "If I were to join any church, it certainly would be the Catholic Church. It all seems so reasonable, but somehow I can't seem to make up my mind." This is a person to whom fullness of the grace of faith has not yet come.

Since faith is a gift of God, it is something to be prayed for. The person in search of faith who, with complete sincerity, asks God for this gift, certainly will be given it. However, there are millions who do not even know of their own need for faith. In our love for Christ, a big intention in our daily prayers should be, "for the conversion of unbelievers."

Another daily intention will be for an increase in the depth and strength of our own faith. Faith is not a static attitude of mind. Either faith grows or it weakens—and sometimes dies. We have particular need to pray when, as does happen to most of us, we find ourselves beset by temptations against faith.

We usually think of temptations against faith as arising from intellectual scruples: apparent clashes between religion and science, for example, or difficulty in understanding how God can be present under the appearance of bread. These, however, are easily conquered with prayer and, if need be, investigation.

The temptations against faith that are more often fatal are those that arise from moral conflicts rather than from doctrinal obstacles. A man does not first lose his faith through intellectual difficulties and then marry a divorcée. A woman does not first lose her faith and then begin to use contraceptives. The sequence, most often, is just the opposite.

We humans cannot long sustain an interior conflict. If mind and emotions are at war with each other, we must somehow establish peace. When a person of faith finds himself strongly drawn toward a sinful course of action, he experiences a painful state of conflict. Faith pulls one way, self another.

The sufferer can quickly reestablish peace by renouncing the sin, however painful (for the moment) his renunciation may be. If he is unwilling to surrender his present or contemplated sin, then it is his faith that has to give. He begins to find points to criticize in his religious beliefs, and he begins to manufacture difficulties and see apparent contradictions. Eventually, he finds the peace he seeks, a specious and fatal peace. He loses his faith. This has been the history of the majority of apostates from the Church.

It is not likely that we are enmeshed in grave habitual sin. However, when we find ourselves afflicted with severe temptations against our faith, it will serve us well to do some honest probing. It is possible that we may find self-love, in one form or another, to be the instigator of our temptations.

There is one source of temptations against faith we encounter today that our ancestors did not have to face. This is the ever-widening frontier of scientific knowledge. When our earth was thought to be the center of the universe—with sun, moon, and stars circling around us and ministering to us—it was easy to believe in God's intense interest in us. We were very important creatures.

Now, however, we know that our earth is just one tiny, insignificant planet in the galaxy of suns and planets known as the Milky Way. And the Milky Way is just one of countless other galaxies of suns and planets that stretch through the uncharted reaches of space.

There may be life on other planets, too. There may be creatures superior to ourselves, somewhere between ourselves and the angels. We begin to wonder, "Is it possible that the infinite Power who created all this can be interested in us, little microbes that we are, crawling about on this pinhead earth of ours? Could God possibly have taken a human form and become one of us?"

This is what we might call inverted pride, a specious form of humility. We, who judge importance by numbers and size, attribute our own way of thinking to God. We question God's revelation because we cannot conceive that God could so stoop to us, a little world of beings on a tiny, cooled-off fragment of an exploded star.

We forget that this is precisely what God's infinity means. He is not limited by time or space, by size or numbers. It would be no strain upon God's infinite power to create this unmeasured universe just so that it might produce the one little speck of earth that is ours—a space platform for souls on their way to eternity. A whole universe to produce one puny world? An entire ocean to produce one little pearl? This would not daunt God at all.

It is quite possible, of course, that God has other plans underway throughout the universe. There may be souls in Heaven from other worlds that ended eons ago. There may be planets now inhabited by intelligent creatures who never sinned and who have no need for redemption. There may be other planets, still in the making, destined for occupancy a billion years hence. There is no limit to what God may have done or may choose to do. Undoubtedly, we have some surprises in store for us when, upon seeing God face to face, we see all things in Him.

By all means, let us be humble, but in our humility let us not try to cut God down to our own size. He may have created other beings to love Him and to sing His praises. Nevertheless, a hundred billion others will not distract His love and His attention one single instant from you or from me. God is *infinite*. He is not hampered by quantity. He is not confused by numbers.

Astronomers may continue to probe the universe. Physicists may continue to split the atom. Paleontologists and anthropologists may continue to trace man's history back through millions of years. It still remains true that God so loved this human race as to become one of us and to die for us.

Knowing our own imperfection and pettiness, you and I cannot understand God's predilection for us. It is not necessary that we understand it. It is enough that we know it is so because God has said it is so. It is enough that we concede to God His right to do what He pleases—and to do it in His own way. Boldly, then, and gratefully, we say our Credo.

Loss of faith may result from intellectual pride or from habitual sin. Yet there is another potential danger to faith that may arise from the emotions rather than from the intellect or the senses. This is the danger faced by the person who in childhood has had an unsatisfactory relationship with his or her father. When a father is a cold and rigid sort of person, perhaps harsh and domineering, even brutal, a child almost certainly will develop a feeling of hostility towards his father.

In many instances, the child is afraid to admit this feeling into the realm of consciousness. He represses his hostility into his subconscious mind and on the conscious level assures everyone, including himself, that he loves his father. However, repression does not eliminate. The buried hostility still exerts strong pressure upon the emotions.

Unfortunately, in later life, this hostility is likely to be ventilated toward anyone who presents the image of fatherhood. God, by His very nature, is a father image. The adult who has a submerged resentment against his own father may be tempted to transfer his resentment to God the Father. The danger is more acute if God's law is a barrier to something that this individual wishes to do.

The person may hesitate to rebel directly against God. However, there is a less august father figure close at hand: the pastor. A person with a repressed hostility to his own father will find it extremely difficult to establish a comfortable relationship with his pastor.

He will be hypercritical of the pastor and resistant to the pastor's requests and directives. Unless the priest possesses exceptional tact, the day may come when the parishioner quarrels openly with his pastor, then crowns his rebellion by staying away from church.

There is hardly a parish in the land that does not have at least one man who is an ex-Catholic because he "had a fight with the pastor." Sometimes there is no overt quarrel because there is no personal contact. The rebel still may abandon Mass and the sacraments with the excuse, "I can't stomach that man," (meaning the pastor, of course). This fallen-away Catholic is unaware that he is trying to get back at his own father by "punishing" the pastor—and, ultimately, God Himself.

This does not mean that just because we feel a stirring of resentment against a particular priest, we therefore are suffering from an acute emotional problem. We may have been genuinely hurt by a priest. Profiting by progress in the science of psychology, seminaries make a scrupulous effort to spot any sign of emotional instability in candidates for the priesthood. Good personal adjustment and a fair degree of prudence are high on the list of requisites for a priestly vocation. However, no screening process is foolproof, and a man of unbalanced character may slip through.

Even if this were not so, we priests are human. We have our faults, and we make our share of mistakes. It is not surprising if we sometimes do something that is offensive to a parishioner. Faults aside, there also may be clashes of personality. It does sometimes happen that two individuals, each a fine person in his own right, will find themselves quite incompatible and irritating to each other.

If our faith is basically strong, we do not allow our resentments, whatever their source, to turn us away from God. We do not "punish" God because we are tempted to be angry at a priest. We do not punish our pastor because he reminds us, obscurely, of our own father. With our faith fortified by charity, we do for the disagreeable priest what we would for any person who has offended us: we pray for him and recommend him to God's mercy. In the meantime, we happily continue to fulfill our religious duties. We know that one priest is not the Church—and much less is he God.

4

Hope Gives the Impetus

You are fairly sure that you will get to Heaven, are you not? You *should* feel secure on this score. The divine virtue of hope was implanted in your soul when you were baptized.

You began to exercise this virtue when you became old enough to understand the meaning of God's love for you. You learned that God made you because He wanted you with Himself in Heaven. You learned that God has promised you whatever graces you may need throughout your life in order to come to Him in Heaven. You learned that God is all powerful; whatever He wants to do, He can do. You learned that God never breaks a promise; what He has said He will do, He will do.

You probably were not conscious of any formal chain of reasoning. Yet, at some early point in your spiritual development, you wrapped all these truths together and made an act of hope. You knew then, as you know now, that if you do your reasonable best to cooperate with God, He will bring you safely through all dangers. He will bring you to Himself in Heaven.

It is easy to see why an act of hope is also an act of adoration. By hope, we acknowledge God's infinite goodness, His infinite power, His absolute fidelity. Conversely, we can see why despair is such a grave sin. Despair (even undue anxiety) questions God's power—His ability to help us conquer our temptations—or His trustworthiness. What is worst of all, despair questions God's love and whether He really cares what happens to us.

We can miss Heaven, of course, but if we do so, it will be only because we have neglected to use God's grace. It will be only because we have not really tried. The sole uncertainty there can be is the uncertainty of our own perseverance. It is good to have a healthy mistrust of ourselves and our own strength. We would be idiots to think ourselves incapable of sin. Yet, our mistrust of self is compensated for, overwhelmingly, by our trust in God. He wants us in Heaven far more than we ourselves want to get there. Short of taking away our free will, there is just nothing God will not do to bring us to Heaven.

It is a rare thing for a person to sin by despair. It is a rare thing for a person to decide, "I am lost. I cannot possibly get to Heaven." It even is rare for a person to entertain grave (as opposed to reasonable) fears for his salvation. Such states of mind do occur. However, more often than not, such morbid feelings are symptoms of mental or emotional illness. Rational thought has been blocked or seriously disturbed. In such a state of unwilled depression, the sufferer is not guilty of sin. He needs a psychiatrist much more than he needs a priest.

Against the virtue of hope, sins of presumption are much more frequent than sins of despair. Presumption occurs if we expect God to do not only His own full part in getting us to Heaven, but to do our part as well. Figuratively, we twist God's arm, trying to force from Him graces to which we have no right. We may neglect prayer. We may neglect the sacraments. We may expose ourselves unnecessarily to temptation. We may read books that we should not read, see movies that we should not see, cultivate friendships that can only spell danger. When sin ensues, as inevitably it must, we assure ourselves that God is good, understands our weakness, and will not cast us off. What we really are saying, in such an instance, is that God does not care whether we love Him or not. God will have us on any terms, even our own. In short, we say that God is a fool. This is the sin of presumption.

If God had to make a choice, doubtless He would prefer that we expect too much of Him than that we have no confidence at all. However, the golden mean of hope—secure but not presumptuous—must be our aim and practice. We shall make our mistakes. Spiritually we may dawdle, wander, stumble, and even fall. If we fall a dozen times, still we reach for God's outstretched hand and rise again. We do not give up. That is the important point: we do not give up. We keep trying. We do our honest best and trust God to bring us safely to the end of our zigzag path. He will.

It seems strange that most of us show so little eagerness to get to Heaven. We all have a great desire to be happy. We look forward with keen anticipation to each approaching holiday when, freed briefly from humdrum routine, we can "have a little fun." The thought of Heaven, however, leaves us comparatively unmoved. We experience no stirrings of pleasurable excitement at the prospect of what awaits us after death.

One reason for this impassive attitude toward the joys of Heaven is the fact that to get to Heaven, we first of all must die. For most of us, too, death will be preceded by suffering. Our minds are so preoccupied by the thought of suffering and death that we seem unable to raise our eyes to what follows after. Suffering and death are the grime on the window that obscure our view of the beautiful world that lies outside our present shabby quarters.

It is not discreditable that we shrink from a confrontation with death. God has made us that way. If death were too attractive, we might not take proper care of life and health. We might expose ourselves too easily to physical dangers. Our aversion to death is the built-in mechanism by which God ensures that we shall reach the term of years He has set for us. It is, in short, the instinct of self-preservation.

Nevertheless, in spite of our understandable reluctance to die, it does seem that Heaven should exert more of an attraction upon us than it does. It will not, unless and until we force our minds to bypass the ugly specter of death and to meditate often on the ecstatic future that shall be ours.

We cannot, of course, reach a true understanding of Heaven in this life. The intensity of Heaven's happiness is so far beyond our wildest imaginings that even God cannot get across to our limited minds the nature of the bliss He has in store for us. If an advertiser were to invent a slogan for Heaven, it well might be, "It must be experienced to be appreciated." A mother could more easily explain to a five-year-old child the nature of conjugal happiness than God could explain to us the happiness of Heaven.

We are not so naive as to think of Heaven as a beautiful, placid park where we sit around at our ease and chat with relatives and friends, while God walks by occasionally to give us a benign nod of recognition. But do we ever try to grasp, even faintly, what it will be like to be caught up in the wild, raging torrent of God's love for us, as this barrier of human flesh is dissolved? Do we ever try to apprehend what it will mean to find ourselves fairly exploding with love as our unscaled eyes perceive Him who is infinitely good and infinitely lovable?

In this life, we find our greatest happiness in the company of the people whom we love and who love us. But we never have known such love, and therefore such happiness, as will all but tear us asunder when we possess God, and God us. Yes, we shall know our family and our friends in Heaven and rejoice (in an absentminded sort of way) that they are with us. But we and they shall be so absorbed in the piercing joy of loving God and being loved by Him as to have little time or thought for one another.

Best of all, the happiness of Heaven can never pall or lessen. It can only grow and grow and grow through all eternity. And eternity, let us remember, is not a long-drawn-out time. Eternity is just one single moment of exquisite rapture—a moment that never ends. In Heaven there is no sense of going on and on. After we have been in Heaven a billion earth-years, if a recent arrival were to ask, "How long have you been here?" our answer would be, "Why, I just came!"

Yes, it is to be feared that we do not get from our faith in Heaven the spiritual mileage that we should. Temptations would lose much of their power and life's troubles would lose much of their weight if we could realize, even dimly, what things God has prepared for those who love Him.

Which of God's attributes looms largest in your mind? The answer to that question will reveal much concerning the habitual tone of your spiritual life.

One person, in thinking about God, may emphasize the attribute of infinite justice. He visualizes God in His role of man's judge. This person's image of God is likely to be that of a stern and exacting Father. As a result, his religious life very well may have an undercurrent of anxiety, even of excessive fear. He worries, not only about present imperfections, but also about past sins. Can he be sure, he wonders, whether those past sins really are forgiven? Can he be sure that God's anger really has been appeased? Paradoxically, this worrier may be a very virtuous person. The ones who have the least to fear from God's justice sometimes are the ones who worry about it the most.

In contrast, there is the person who thinks of God always in terms of infinite mercy. To him, God is the God of compassion, God of the tender heart. Here we encounter another paradox. Often the person who focuses exclusively on God's mercy is a person who is lax in his religious life, perhaps even addicted to habitual sin. He pictures God as an indulgent, tut-tut-my-child kind of Father. He ascribes to God a boundless tolerance, not merely for human weakness but for human sloth and perversity. This image engenders peace of conscience, but it is a false peace; like the relaxation of a person who, unknowingly, is inhaling carbon monoxide gas.

Still another type, not quite so common, is the person who is obsessed with God's attribute of omniscience. To this person, the all-knowing God is not so much a loving and protective Presence as He is a critical supervisor, watching every move with a critical eye. As a result, this person is likely to be nervous and indecisive in matters moral and spiritual. Conscious always of God's monitoring and appraising gaze, he is afraid that whatever he does, it will be the wrong thing. In its most aggravated form, this state of mind is called scrupulosity.

Ideally, our image of God should be a balanced image. God is just, unquestionably. Yet, we must not let His justice cause us to forget His mercy. He is merciful, yes. But the thought of His mercy must not blind us to His justice. He is an all-knowing God in whose presence we live and move. But the regard He has for us is not an I-expect-the-worst scrutiny. God watches only to defend us, to support us, to nurture our spiritual growth.

It is not easy to strike always a perfect balance in our thoughts of God. However, there is one attribute of God upon which we can concentrate without danger of exaggeration. This is God's attribute of infinite goodness. God is good not merely in the sense of being holy. He is good, also, in the sense of being good to us. He is the God of limitless generosity, whose zeal for our best interests knows no bounds.

There are few of us who evaluate God's goodness as highly as we ought. This is manifested by the fact that such a small proportion of our prayers is given to thanksgiving. If we spent our whole day doing nothing else but saying, "Thank You, God," we still would not make adequate return to God for all that He has done, is doing, and is going to do for us.

Take a moment or two to look back through your life. As you review the years, is it not true that you can spot many points at which God's hand was plainly visible? Not visible to you then, perhaps, but visible now from this later perspective? There may have been a time of great temptation when you so easily could have brought spiritual ruin to yourself and perhaps great unhappiness to those who loved you. It seems a miracle now that you survived that temptation or that, somehow, you escaped the consequences of your sin. It *was* a miracle, indeed; although at the time it may have seemed due merely to a lucky chance.

Again, in retrospect, you may recall a time of great discouragement in your life: the death of someone very dear to you, the loss of a job, a grievous illness, or the failure of some cherished plan. At the moment, God seemed very far away. You wondered whether He cared about you at all. Now, however, you can see that great good has come to you out of that seeming disaster. God had you in His keeping even when you thought He had forgotten you.

All of us, if we have given God any share at all in our lives, can look back to these periods of great crisis and see in them the seeds of later benefit to ourselves. There may be a reader of this page who is involved in such a crisis right now. He may be tempted to feel that God has abandoned him. He can see no possible good that could result from the agony he is suffering. But God is good. God *does* care. God *is* on the job. In five or ten or fifteen years, the sufferer will look back and say, "Thank You, God. I recognize now that, for my greatest good, the dark night had to be."

It is hard for us to understand how hungrily God loves us and how urgently God wants us eternally with Himself in Heaven. There are no lengths to which He will not go to bring us securely to Himself—if we but give Him the slenderest wedge of an opening, the faintest bit of cooperation. And to His goodness are allied God's infinite wisdom and power. He knows what is most effective for our particular temperament and weaknesses. He has the command over circumstance to accomplish His ends.

For every great grace that we, looking back, can recognize, there are of course a million lesser graces, not one-tenth of which ever reach our awareness. Like a host of gentle, unseen fingers, God's daily graces keep edging us forward. It is only now and again that we can feel a stronger and more obvious push. Barring a positive and stubborn resistance on our part, the outcome cannot be in question.

How little need there is, after all, for prayers of petition. How much greater need—or at least, how much greater reason—there is for prayers of thanksgiving and, above all, for acts of hope.

5

Love Is the Fruit

The whole spiritual life, as we know, can be summed up in the single phrase: "Love God!" It is for this that God made us—that we might love Him. There is no other reason for our existence. It is love for God, too, that equips us for the ecstasy of face-to-face union with Him in Heaven. Without love, a soul could be in the midst of Heaven and still be in Hell. Such a soul could be surrounded by God, by angels and saints, and be totally unaware of their presence. A soul without charity is a soul without spiritual vision—a soul totally blind.

It is fortunate that God, in Baptism, has infused the virtue of charity into our souls and has given us a talent for loving Him. It is not easy to love someone whom we never have seen. It is especially difficult when our love for the unseen God conflicts with our desire for some lesser but visible good. The truth is that, without God's help, we really could not love Him at all.

On the face of it, it seems a great mystery why our love should mean so much to God. In our honest moments, we have to admit that our love, at best, is very imperfect. There is a good bit of self-interest intermixed even with our most disinterested loves: our love for spouse, for parent, for child, for brother or sister. It may illumine the mystery a bit if we examine what we might call the "anatomy" of our love for God.

In Baptism, the greatest thing that happened to us is that we were made one with Christ; *incorporated* with Christ is the theological expression. We were united with Christ in a way that our human mind cannot quite fathom. Christ shared with us His Spirit, the Holy Spirit, the Spirit of Divine Love. There is no example adequate to illustrate the nature of our union with Jesus. The closest that we can come by way of parallel is to imagine the intimacy of union that would exist between two humans who shared one and the same soul between them. In a sense, each would be the other. Similarly, after Baptism, there is a sense in which you are Christ and Christ is you.

Our spiritual merger with Jesus does not destroy our personal freedom. With our cooperation, however, it does make it possible for Jesus to act in and through us. This He does, most especially, in our act of love for God. Our own act of love consists simply in identifying our will with God's. What God wants is what we want. Our love is expressed in our obedience to God's law, an obedience that involves the sacrifice of self.

Our obedience, our act of self-renunciation, creates a clear channel through which Christ's own love can go through us to the Father. Our personal love, at its best, is ridiculously weak. But our own love is transformed by being made the vehicle of Christ's love. It is not we who love God. It is Christ who, through us, loves God. The millions of baptized souls, in the state of sanctifying grace, are like so many prisms. Through them, the infinite love of Jesus is refracted to the Father in limitless variety. The Holy Spirit, the Spirit of Love, flows from Son to Father in a hundred million ways. And, since divine love is an interchange, the Father's love returns to His Son with just as many variations. In loving each of us, God can and does love His Son.

We are, then, God's created instruments of love. We are God's agents in this commerce of infinite love that forever occupies Father, Son, and Holy Spirit. It is plain that, the more we purify ourselves of self, the more effective an agent each of us is. The more we detach ourselves, not only from mortal sin but also from venial sin, the more perfectly do we fulfill our vocation to love.

God made us to love Him—forever. The whole purpose of life is contained in this vocation to love. Compared to it, all lesser human goals fade into insignificance.

At first glance, it might seem that God is being miserably shortchanged. Everyone is hurrying through the day, occupied with a thousand duties and interests. Fathers work at a driving pace to provide for their families. Mothers, harried to distraction, minister to the needs of husband and children. Men and women in schools, offices, and the marketplace have their own pressures and stresses. We are tempted to say, "It seems that very little time is being given to loving God. If that is what God made us for, His idea is not paying off very well."

Then we reflect on the nature of charity, and we realize that it is not a matter of spending our whole day looking at the sky (or at the tabernacle) and saying, over and over, "My God, I love You!" Explicit acts of love must have their place, yes. But principally, God expects us to show our love for Him by fulfilling our nature as human beings.

This means, at a minimum, that we respect God's will and that we live our lives within the framework of His laws. Still better, it means that God is the target of our total life. Whatever intermediate aims we may have, God is the ultimate objective of all that we do.

In practice, this becomes a matter of trying our best to discharge well the obligations that life has placed upon us. Assuming that we are united with Christ by sanctifying grace, love for God then is expressed in our efforts to be a good father, mother, neighbor, citizen, parishioner. We love God by being a good teacher, nurse, secretary, mechanic, merchant, doctor, lawyer, or politician. We love God even in our recreations and social activities.

In short, we love God by trying to use well the talents, great or small, with which He has endowed us. The circumstances of life have settled us into a certain area of existence and action that is uniquely our own. This area, however unimportant it may seem to be, is the particular part of God's total picture on which He wants us to work. Or, to vary the figure, this is our "beat," which we must cover to the best of our ability.

As we progress through our busy days, we are forwarding God's plan for the world. For God, this is the Seventh Day. God is "resting," as He leaves it to us to carry on (under His guidance) His work of creation. We are not consciously thinking of God all the time, no more than a man is explicitly thinking of his family while his mind is on the work that provides their bread and butter. Yet, every new day, with God as our ultimate objective, speaks of our love for Him.

It may seem to us that we are making a ridiculously weak impact upon the world. We may see very little "creativity" or long-range importance in what we are doing. However, this is not a matter that needs to concern us. A man in a rowing shell bends his back to the oar without knowing or worrying about what lies ahead. He leaves the guidance to the coxswain. For us, God is the helmsman—and our contribution to God's own final objective may be far more important than we think.

No, God is not being short-changed on love quite as shamefully as the world's busyness might lead us to believe. True enough, it is sad that there are so many persons whose lives are not oriented to God. But this sharpens our own challenge. It is for us to make up to God, by our own more perfect service, for all the love He seeks and does not receive.

We know that if we love God, we must love all whom He loves. We must love our neighbor. God has made this the proof and the measure of our love for Himself. If anyone says, "I love God," and hates his neighbor, St. John warns us, "he is a liar" (see 1 John 4:20).

Moreover, love for our neighbor must be patterned upon the love we have for ourselves. "Thou shalt love thy neighbor as *thyself*" (Mark 12:31) is God's commandment. There is a specious kind of self-love that is reprehensible. This is the narcissism of the self-centered and self-worshiping person. However, there also is a true and wholesome self-love that God expects all of us to have for ourselves.

Genuine self-love manifests itself, on the natural level, in the intelligent care we have for our physical and mental well-being. We avoid unnecessary dangers to our health and integrity. We seek to provide ourselves with whatever is necessary for the welfare of body and mind: food, clothing, shelter, medicine, knowledge, affection. We avoid unnecessary corporal and mental pain and search for such happiness as this world may afford. We try to extend our natural life to its allotted span.

On the supernatural level, the strivings of self-love are similar but with a higher objective. We seek *eternal* life for ourselves. We avoid all that would endanger our eternal happiness. We try, by means of prayer and the sacraments, to provide our soul with all that is necessary for its growth and health, for its preservation in grace.

Self-love on the *natural* level comes fairly easy to us. It largely is motivated by the inborn instinct of self-preservation. The practice of self-love on the *supernatural* level comes harder to us, for it is not an innate instinct. It springs from the virtue of faith fortified by the virtue of hope. And, since the soul is so superior to the body—and eternal life so superior to physical life—it is our spiritual welfare that always must have primacy. There may be times when it is necessary to suffer corporal pain and deprivation for the sake of spiritual health. It even may be necessary to sacrifice natural life in order to preserve supernatural life, as the martyrs have testified.

It should be plain, now, what God means when He says, "Love thy neighbor as thyself." We must want for our neighbor what we want for ourselves: the necessary means to achieve natural health and happiness insofar as possible and, above all, to achieve eternal life.

Love for neighbor manifests itself, on the first level, in the concern we have for his temporal welfare. That is why we give the name of charity, or love, to our efforts to better the lot of our less-fortunate brothers. Either personally or through our bishops and charitable organizations, we feed the hungry, clothe the naked, provide shelter for the homeless and education for the ignorant, combat racial prejudice, nurse the sick, and seek equal justice and opportunity for all.

On the higher and more vital level, we seek the spiritual welfare of our neighbor. We share our prayers with all mankind as we pray for the conversion of sinners and unbelievers. We cooperate with convert work in our own parish and support the work of missionaries at home and abroad. We are willing, if called upon, to help with religious instruction classes. We are ready, if opportunity offers, to explain the truths of faith to others. By word when possible, and *always* by example, we try to encourage the lax to become better and to win the sinner back from his sin.

Our love for neighbor does not have to be an emotional love, no more than does our love for God. It is not how we *feel* towards our neighbor (he may be a very unlikable person) but what we are willing to *do* for him that proves and expresses our love.

Considering the supreme importance of love for neighbor, it is well to examine ourselves periodically on our fidelity to this duty. Each Sunday morning after Holy Communion, as we tell our Lord of our love for Him, we well might ask ourselves, "Just what did I do, this past week, to show my love for my neighbor?"

It would be much easier to love God if God did not demand that we prove our love by the love we show our neighbor. Sometimes the obligation to love our neighbor is the hardest of all our Christian duties. The reason is that our neighbor is not only that nice person who is so easy to get along with. Our neighbor includes the nastiest, meanest persons we may come up against.

Just listen to Jesus: "You have heard that it hath been said, 'Thou shalt love thy neighbor, and hate thy enemy.' But I say to you, love your enemies: do good to them that hate you: and pray for them that persecute and calumniate you: That you may be the children of your Father who is in heaven" (Matt. 5:43–45).

Our human nature—our *merely* human nature—rebels against this whole idea. If someone has hurt us, everything within us cries out for vengeance. If we can find no way to "get even," we nourish bitter thoughts against the offender. We imagine all kinds of evil things happening to him—and hope that some of them do. At least, this is our first impulse.

Fortunately, God does not ask us to love our enemies with a *natural* love. Natural love is an emotion aroused in us by people who attract us strongly. It is almost impossible to have this natural love for an enemy, to feel an affection for someone who has hurt you deeply.

God asks only for supernatural love, which does not depend upon feeling at all. By supernatural love, we rise above our emotions and look at our enemy through God's eyes rather than through our own. We see this disagreeable person as a soul whom God created out of love, a soul whom God wants with Himself in Heaven, a soul for whom Jesus died. If our enemy is so precious to God, we dare not set ourselves up in opposition to God. We dare not wish evil upon our adversary. We dare not condemn him (or her) to Hell, not even in our thoughts.

On the contrary, we labor bravely to bring our resentment under control. The words come hard, but we say with sincerity, "Yes, God, I do forgive this person who has hurt me so." Then we proceed to pray for the person, that he may receive the graces he needs to change his ways and to become the kind of person God wants him to be.

Prayer is the perfect antidote to hatred. If you can pray for a person, you do not hate him. You still may feel a strong aversion to the person, but your supernatural love is on a higher plane than emotion, like sunlight above the clouds.

You have forgiven your foe. You are praying for him. Is there anything further that Jesus expects of you when He says, "Love your enemies?" Must you accept your adversary into your circle of friends and act as if nothing had happened?

Not necessarily. If you know that this person will hurt you again, given the chance, it is the part of wisdom to avoid him if you can. Moreover, you have a right to seek redress for the damage he has done. You may sue him in court, even while you pray for him.

However, if the one who has offended you offers an apology, you must accept the apology. You already have forgiven him interiorly; you now forgive him exteriorly also. You will treat him civilly and be willing to speak if you pass him on the street or meet him at a social gathering. Indeed, it is the perfection of charity to meet your enemy more than halfway, to make the first move towards reconciliation. A simple "hello" when you meet him will make it plain that you harbor no grudge. If he refuses to answer or answers in unfriendly fashion, you have done your duty. There is no need to speak again unless and until he takes the initiative.

Forgiveness, prayer, reconciliation. For one who has been deeply hurt, none of this is easy. That is why love for our enemies is such infallible proof of our love for God.

There are few proverbs more often misapplied than the axiom, "Charity begins at home." Usually this maxim is invoked to warrant excusing ourselves from some obligation external to the family. "I can't give much to the parish building fund," a man says. "My own house isn't paid for, and charity begins at home." A woman, asked to participate in some outside activity, begs off on the score that her family needs all her attention. "Charity begins at home," she quotes as her clincher. Both of these people may be fully justified in declining the proposed responsibility. However, when they say, "Charity begins at home," they are not using the phrase in its true meaning.

The right sense of the proverb is that, in the home of all places, love should reign. If we do not practice charity towards those who are closest to us, how can we claim to love our neighbor? How can we honestly claim to love God? "Charity begins at home" means that home is the *real* test of our charity.

It is one of life's continuing tragedies that we so often cause the most hurt to those who have the most right to our love. True enough, the home does present many temptations in the area of charity. Within the family, we are so exposed to one another's faults and weaknesses. It is inevitable that we do at times get on each other's nerves. And little things can so annoy us. "Do you always have to suck your teeth that way?" we say. "Can't you ever sit down without drumming your fingers on the table?" "Do you have to clutter up the bathroom with your things?"

Another source of uncharitableness in the home is the fact that we are so defenseless against each other. Having nothing to fear from those who love us, it is easy to unload upon them the hostility and aggression that belong elsewhere. A psychological commonplace is the man who, rebuked by his boss, comes home to give his wife a rough time. She catches the resentment that he dare not vent upon the boss.

Children, too, frequently suffer from misplaced wrath. Johnny commits some minor misdemeanor that calls for no more than a mild admonition. Mother, however, has had a hard day and is filled to the neck with frustration. Johnny's peccadillo brings down upon him a blast of anger all out of proportion to the gravity of his offense. Johnny does not know that he just happens to be a convenient lightning rod for his mother's pent-up ire. He can only brood tearfully on the injustice of the adults in his world.

But Johnny takes his turn at making the family an outlet for his grievances. He made a fool of himself in school today and was humiliated by the laughter of his classmates. He comes home from school in a wilful mood and exacerbates the stress of the family for the remainder of the evening. There is some excuse for Johnny, of course. He does not have an adult's insight into the dynamics of human behavior.

Yes, charity must begin at home. For a family in which there is frequent snipping and snapping, there is a simple remedy. Let the members of the family agree to treat each other as friends rather than as relatives. Let them show toward each other the same consideration and courtesy that they would show not merely to friends, but even to casual acquaintances.

Let them make liberal use of such phrases as, "Please," "Thank you," "Would you mind?" "Excuse me," and "I'm sorry." Let each watch himself carefully for resentments that are brought in from outside and are seeking ventilation upon an innocent head. Let each be especially vigilant when he finds himself unduly fatigued or worried. Above all, let each have enough of a sense of humor to bear with one another's faults.

Such a family will find their efforts richly rewarded by the peace and harmony that descends upon their home. Charity *has* begun at home and will flow out from there to the world. And Christ can dwell there in comfort as one of the family.

6

The Hinges of Holiness

The word "prudence" has fallen into some degree of disrepute in our day. The old admonition, "Let your conscience be your guide," has given way to the modern shibboleth, "Follow that impulse!" If you *feel* that something is right for you to do, go ahead and do it. Don't let yourself be hamstrung by the dictates of reason. So runs the personal philosophy, if it can be called that, of a great number of our contemporaries.

One evidence of this fact is the increasing casualness with which marriages are made and broken. Ignoring all responsibility to God or to children, men and women move on, via the divorce court, from one infatuation to the next. For them, reason has been dethroned in favor of emotion.

The prudent person is not a slave to emotion, but neither is he a timid or excessively cautious individual. The virtue of prudence is simply the habit of acting according to the principles of right reason. Prudent behavior is rational behavior, as distinguished from impulsive behavior. A prudent person weighs the consequences—to himself and others—of his actions before making a decision. He acts not on the basis of what he feels like doing, but in the light of what, all things considered, he ought to do. Prudence is the hallmark of genuine maturity. Invariably, the person who "never grew up" is lacking in prudence.

Prudence may be either a natural or supernatural virtue. Natural prudence is principally concerned with matters temporal. You practice natural prudence when you lock your doors at night to keep out thieves. You are similarly prudent when you keep your credit good by paying your bills promptly.

Natural prudence is an acquired virtue. It is acquired through experience—our own experience and that of others. We learn especially through our mistakes. Having done something foolish, with regrettable results, we are careful (if we are intelligent) not to repeat that same foolish action.

Supernatural prudence, however, cannot be acquired. With the other cardinal virtues of justice, fortitude, and temperance, supernatural prudence was infused into our soul with the grace of Baptism. These four virtues receive the designation of "cardinal" from the Latin word *cardo*, which means *hinge*. All other moral virtues hinge upon prudence, justice, fortitude, and temperance. Without these four, no other moral virtue could be practiced with any degree of perfection.

Supernatural prudence is a God-given facility for distinguishing between what is right and what is wrong in a moral sense and for distinguishing between what is good and what is better. If you pay your bills in order to preserve your credit, you are practicing natural prudence. If you pay your bills because you consider this an obligation in conscience, you are practicing supernatural prudence. If a married man says to himself, "I must stop flirting with that girl or I may hurt my reputation," he is naturally prudent. If he says, "I must stop flirting with that girl or I'll be risking the sin of adultery," he is supernaturally prudent.

It seems obvious that prudence, natural as well as supernatural, is a virtue highly to be prized. Sometimes it will be hard for us to determine, in a particular case, whether our prudence has been natural or supernatural, as it is often hard to know whether our motives have been this-worldly or other-worldly. We need not worry. If we have a natural prudence upon which to build, it will be much easier for supernatural prudence to operate. It is an axiom of theology that grace works most effectively when underpinned by natural goodness.

Probably not many people think to ask God, in their prayers, for an increase in prudence. Yet, it is only from God that an increase in supernatural prudence can come. With our happiness, here and hereafter, hinging so heavily upon prudence, it would seem grossly imprudent to omit this petition from our daily prayers.

Justice is the virtue by which we render to every person that to which he has a right. Conversely, injustice is the vice by which we deprive a person, against his reasonable will, of that to which he has a right. Justice is one of the four cardinal virtues—one of those four "hinge" virtues upon which all other moral virtues depend.

Textbooks of moral theology, which are studied by candidates for the priesthood, give far more space to the consideration of "Justice and Rights" than to the treatment of any other virtue. This is not surprising, since no other virtue gives rise to as many questions as does the virtue of justice.

"Is the theft of $25 a mortal sin or a venial sin?" "Am I obliged to restitution if I have knowingly accepted a stolen article?" "Is it a sin to cheat on my income tax?" "What must I do if a store makes a mistake in my favor on my bill?" These and a thousand similar questions revolve about the virtue of justice. Such questions can best be left to one's confessor or to the Question Box of our diocesan newspaper. It is not our purpose to discuss them here.

Neither shall we dwell here on that aspect of justice that so plagues our contemporary scene: racial justice. The moral evil of denying a person his economic, educational, or social rights because of his color is undeniable. Just as undeniable is the fact that few of us are without blame in this area, either by active discrimination or by passive acquiescence. However, there already is enough being said and written on this subject to stir the conscience of anyone whose conscience still is functioning. It is not my present purpose to add to that body of admonition. I should prefer for the moment to direct attention to the practice of justice in a more limited arena.

Physical belongings are not a person's most precious possessions. There may be individuals who consider money to be the highest good, yet most of us will agree that happiness is far preferable to wealth. Happiness is a compound of many things: a feeling of self-worth, a confidence that one is loved by some and respected by many, contentment with one's lot, and peace of mind are a few of the ingredients.

Now here is an oddity of human behavior. We admit that we gladly would exchange our worldly possessions, if faced with such an alternative, in order to obtain or preserve our happiness. (Many, in fact, do just that by embracing voluntary poverty.) Yet, we who would not dream of stealing so much as a dime from anyone will disturb or destroy the happiness of others with scarcely a twinge of conscience.

There are many ways in which we can rob others of happiness and thereby sin against justice. Gossip is one very common thief of happiness. If, by gossip, we whittle down a person's reputation and diminish the respect in which he is held, we sin against justice as well as against charity. If, by sly digs and insinuations, we set neighbor against neighbor, we are as much a bandit as a man with a gun. If we go into a sulk at home and cast a spirit of gloom and unease over the family, we are filching happiness from our own flesh and blood.

There are many other ways, too, in which we may defraud people of their happiness. Harsh and unfriendly criticism, ridicule, snubs, and sharp answers to well-meant questions are all, in varying degrees, assaults upon the happiness of family, acquaintances, or fellow workers.

Mindful of the infinite compassion of our Lord Jesus towards all who suffer, we have reason to be concerned if we have been an unjust aggressor against the right to happiness of any other person. The thief of money will have an easier time of it, in judgment, than the thief of happiness. We shall do well to pray that no one ever may weep upon his pillow or clench his fists in mental pain because of any act or word of ours.

In the minds of many people, the word "temperance" is linked with the use of alcoholic beverages and thought to be synonymous with complete abstention from intoxicating drink.

This concept of temperance is mistaken on two counts. In the first place, temperance is the moral virtue that guides us in the use of any of God's creatures. The application of temperance is by no means limited to the use of alcohol. In the second place, temperance does not necessarily mean abstinence. A temperate person is one who uses God's gifts with moderation. He avoids both the extreme of excess and the extreme of defect. In other words, temperance is the virtue of the golden mean: not too much, not too little.

There are times, of course, when "not too much" does mean "not at all." For a person with alcoholism, the virtue of temperance must mean total abstention from alcoholic beverages. However, a person free from this affliction can drink in moderation for sociability's sake and still be a temperate person.

Similarly, for an unmarried person or for a person with the vow of chastity, any indulgence of the sexual urge would be intemperate. For a married couple, on the other hand, intemperance in sex would occur only if a spouse were either unreasonably demanding (excess) or were to refuse the reasonable request of the other spouse (defect).

Given the high percentage of overweight people in our society, we might well conclude that intemperance in eating is prevalent. Medical science assures us that obesity is a killer, yet we continue to load ourselves with calories. A person of healthy weight, eating a healthy diet, offers a good example of temperance in action.

There is hardly any phase of life to which the virtue of temperance is not applicable. For example, people who would let their homes become dirty and unattractive would be intemperate in cleanliness by defect, while people who have such a passion for cleanliness as to put neatness ahead of family comfort would be intemperate by excess.

Temperance is one of the four cardinal virtues. Its role in our spiritual life is much like the function of one who operates a piece of machinery. The purpose of the operator is to keep the machine running at its most efficient speed, neither too fast nor too slow.

Usually we think of temperance in connection with things physical, but temperance also is essential to our spiritual practices. A person who hardly ever prays certainly is being intemperate, by defect, in his piety. On the other hand, a parent who spends all his spare time in church, to the neglect of his family, would be intemperate in piety by excess. A parent's vocation is not that of a cloistered monk or nun.

Similarly, one person might refuse to participate in any civic or parish activity, even though he has the time for it. Another person might be so busy with outside interests as to slight his or her duties at home. Each would be in temperate in the practice of fraternal charity—one by defect and the other by excess.

Unsurprisingly, most of us will find, with a little self-examination, some evidence of intemperance in our lives. It is not easy to maintain a perfect balance at all times and in all matters. However, temperance is the ideal for which we must aim. God be thanked, we do have the basic skill for the task—for we have the cardinal virtue of temperance, infused into our soul with the grace of Baptism.

Fortitude, as we learned in our catechism many years ago, is the virtue that enables us to suffer all things, even death, for the sake of Christ. It is one of the four cardinal virtues bestowed upon us at the time of our Baptism.

If ever we give thought to this virtue, we probably hope that, faced with the choice of denying Christ or suffering death, we would be brave enough to choose death. In all likelihood, we do not dwell long on this possibility, since martyrdom seems, for most of us, a remote contingency. Consequently, we may not esteem fortitude as a very important virtue, as one having practical, here-and-now significance for us.

Such downgrading of the virtue of fortitude would be a grave error. The truth is that fortitude is vital to the everyday practice of our faith. We need moral strength to resist temptation. We need spiritual courage to accept God's will cheerfully and to do His will bravely.

Eternal merit is the reward of effort and struggle. A virtuous person, in the ordinary sense of the term, is not a person without temptations. He is a person who has faced strong temptations and has conquered them. A person without temptations may be innocent, but he becomes virtuous only when he has been tested and has proven his fidelity.

Perhaps it is a disregard for the virtue of fortitude that accounts for the sophistries with which sinners sometimes try to excuse themselves. For example, there is a woman who has divorced her husband and has several small children. She lets herself become interested in another man and, by a civil marriage, embarks upon an adulterous union. "I know it's wrong," she says, "but the children do need a father. Surely God won't hold it against me."

Or there is a mother whose health simply will not stand another pregnancy. Yet her cycle is irregular and her husband finds abstinence too difficult. Contraceptives are the easy answer. "God will understand our predicament," the couple assure themselves. "There just isn't anything else we can do."

Then there is the businessman who indulges in unscrupulous practices with the excuse, "I've got to do it to meet the competition," and the holder of public office who defends his shady deals with, "It's a part of the game."

And again there is the long procession of people who lie to escape a moment's embarrassment, who cheat to get out of a financial jam, or who gossip to court popularity.

You will have noticed that in all the examples we have mentioned, the persons involved assume that God expects us to be good only when it is easy to be good. When the practice of virtue becomes difficult, then we are absolved from the necessity of keeping God's commandments. No one puts this fallacy into words, of course; the absurdity would be too evident. Often this dilemma is escaped by pretending to distinguish between God and His Church—by talking about what the Church forbids or commands rather than about what God expects of us. This leads only to another fallacy: that Christ and His Mystical Body are divisible.

The fact is that in all these examples, the individuals concerned are lacking in the virtue of fortitude. Or, more accurately, they are not exercising that virtue which is theirs by reason of their Baptism.

It is not true that martyrdom is a rare privilege enjoyed only by some persons who live in Communist countries. There is a little bit of martyrdom in the life of every person who undertakes to follow Christ—someone who tries, day by day, to live his faith with fidelity. Indeed, it has been observed with some truth that often it is easier to die for Christ than to live for Him.

7

Prayer Gives the Power

"Is there something wrong with me, Father? I just can't seem to feel spiritual, and I don't get any lift from prayer. In fact, I find it awfully hard to pray. I never seem to get any pious or keyed-up feeling in church. For me, religion is pretty much a plodding, unexciting form of drudgery. Am I lacking in faith?"

Every priest is presented with this type of question from time to time. It is a question that indicates a lack of understanding of the basic nature of religion.

Our primary duty in life is to love God. It is for this that God made us—to love Him. It is here that we can fall into error, through judging our love for God by the intensity of our emotional response, like we judge our love for other humans. Emotional response is an integral part of human love. Love for God, however, has its source in the will, quite independently of the emotions.

To love God means simply to esteem Him above all else, to give Him the supreme position in our scale of values. In practice, it means that whatever God wants, we also want. We shall allow nothing or no one to take precedence over God, and we shall make

His will the norm by which we live. In short, our love for God will prove itself by our obedience to God.

If a person has thus fixed his will upon God, then he loves God. Indeed, he has a very high degree of love for God, even though, emotionally, he may feel quite cold toward God.

We all recognize that there is a wide variation in temperaments. Some persons are by nature cold and reserved, while others are warm and ebullient, with all gradations in between. Psychologists still are uncertain as to how much of this variation is due to the differing environments of infancy and childhood and how much is due to differences in the glandular and nervous systems. Whatever the roots of the diversity may be, it is plain that we may take no credit for the temperament that is ours.

Obviously it is not a *bad* thing if our love for God overflows into our emotions. With some people this does happen, and when it happens it can be looked upon as a bonus, a dividend for which we should give due thanks to God. Spiritual delight can make prayer pleasurable and religious observances a joy rather than a penance. However, we must be very sure that underneath the emotion there is the solid substratum of will. Otherwise, there is the danger that when emotion subsides, attachment to God also may weaken or disappear.

All things else being equal, the person who finds it difficult to pray will gain more merit by his prayer than does the person who finds prayer pleasurable. The harder it is to do something for God, the more credit is accrued to us for doing it. Again, this does not mean that spiritual elation is to be contemned. It means only that we may not safely judge the extent of our spiritual progress by our emotional temperature.

One final observation may be useful. A person may be tempted to excuse himself from prayer because he does not feel like praying and is not in the mood for prayer. At such times, he must remind himself that the fundamental purpose of prayer is not to give ourselves an emotional lift. We pray primarily because prayer is an essential duty we owe to God, a duty of creature to Creator. The duty remains, regardless of whether or not we find comfort or inspiration in prayer. In other words, I pray first of all for God's sake, not for mine.

No matter how spiritually arid we may feel, we still have the obligation to acknowledge in prayer God's infinite greatness and goodness. We still have the obligation to thank God for His graces and to beg His forgiveness for our sins.

"How well do you pray?" To that question, the average Catholic probably would answer, "Not as well as I'd like to." The better the Catholic, the more likely it is that such would be his answer. To those of us who are dissatisfied with our efforts at prayer, it is a comfort to remember that God asks of us only that we do our best. It may be that we are not praying as well as we might wish, but if we are praying as well as we can, we are praying well.

However, it is possible that some of us are more imperfect in prayer than we need to be, simply because we understand poorly the nature of prayer. We all learned in childhood that prayer is "the raising of our mind and heart to God." In spite of having learned the definition, a surprising number of people think of prayer as "talking to God," as though words were the important element in prayer.

Some of our best prayer is prayer in which we use no words at all. Silently, we turn our thoughts to God in a spirit of reverence. We think of Him, of His goodness and His mercy perhaps. Our heart moves in an act of gratitude to Him, or we experience a sense of shame and sorrow at not having done more for Him. We think of His lovableness and wish that we could love Him more ardently, and we perhaps resolve to try harder to deserve His love. All this is done—or can be done—without any words at all. This activity of mind and heart is called mental prayer, as distinct from vocal prayer.

To make more graphic the nature of mental prayer, let us imagine a father standing at a window watching his children playing in the yard. Wordlessly he gazes at the children, while his heart goes out to them in an act of love and protectiveness, with a determination, too, to be a good father to them. Similarly, in mental prayer we "look at" God, and our hearts go out to Him in an act of love. Perhaps with our love are mixed sentiments of gratitude, repentance, or renewed and more generous loyalty. This is a moment of prayer at its best.

If we wish to make progress in prayer, we have only to make room for more such moments in our lives. We can do it in church, with prayer book closed as we gaze at the tabernacle. We can do it in the privacy of our own room. We can do it on a solitary walk. We can do it on the bus, with eyes closed to the passing scene. There are many opportunities, if we watch for them.

The great advantage of mental prayer is that it gives God a chance to speak to us, and this is essential to fruitful prayer. I am not saying that vocal prayer is to be abandoned. There are times and places when vocal prayer is the best prayer—at Mass, for example, and in other public services when we pray together. There are times, too, when the mind is too distracted or tired to focus wordlessly upon God, and there are times when we wish to gain the indulgences attached to certain vocal prayers. The point I am making is that prayer is (or ought to be) an interchange with God.

It is an occasion of special and intimate union with God. If it is to be a true interchange, a genuine union, God must have His opportunity. There must be moments of silent contemplation when God can speak (wordlessly, as we have spoken) in His turn to our heart.

These moments will come more easily if we try, habitually, to live our lives in union with God. This means that we begin our day with a whole-hearted offering of our day to God—all our thoughts, words, actions, joys, and sufferings. Following our morning offering, our day becomes one great prayer, with every moment a source of eternal merit. Our mind will not consciously be on God all the time, for we must give attention to our work and other activities. However, the thought of God will never be far below the surface. We shall find it easy to cast Him, now and then, a quick glance of love.

We have to pray. It is an obligation that we cannot escape. It is not only that we as creatures owe obeisance to our Creator. We do. But, even more essentially, it is by prayer that we maintain our union with God and keep our soul open to the flow of His grace. Prayer is as vital to our spiritual life as an air hose is to the physical life of the deep sea diver.

Nobody can say exactly when and how much we ought to pray. Certainly no day should begin without offering the day to God, and no day should end without thanking God for the graces of the day and begging His forgiveness for the sins of the day. Between these fixed points, our own generosity toward God will help to establish our prayer schedule.

It would be utter nonsense for anyone to say, "I haven't time to pray." This is a matter of life or death. Time must be made for prayer, even if the daily paper must be neglected, or TV, or social activities, or recreation. We never say, "I haven't time to eat." We may miss a meal, but we soon make up for it. We know that we have to eat if we wish to continue living—and so we do.

The important thing is to have a fixed and definite time for prayer. The period should be long enough for us to gather our thoughts and to allow for something more than a hasty Our Father and Hail Mary. We may be able to use some of our lunch hour for the purpose. We may be able to set aside some time before or after dinner. If ours is a jam-packed day, we can find time for prayer by rising a little earlier in the morning.

It is important, also, to build a fence around our prayer time to protect it against trespass. We do this for our meal times. The dinner hour is kept as sacred as we possibly can make it. "No, not then," we say; "that's our dinner hour." When schedules grow tight, prayer never should be the first thing jettisoned.

Happily, most Catholics are alert to the importance of prayer. "I have no time to pray," is not heard nearly as often as the complaint, "I just can't keep my mind on my prayers. I have so many distractions!" To voice such a complaint is merely to confess that we are human. The mind is more of a mischief-maker than is a child of four. Sometimes, talking to God in prayer is like trying to talk to a friend on the phone when there are two or three small children in the room.

We have to remind ourselves that unwanted distractions do not destroy the effectiveness of prayer. Once we have settled ourselves to pray and have fixed our gaze upon God with the intention of communing with Him, then no number of distractions can invalidate our prayer. Inevitably there will be times when the mind is especially preoccupied. We may have to peek at God by fits and snatches, as we might watch a TV program when people are walking back and forth in front of the screen. It may be that at the end of ten or fifteen minutes of prayer we can only say, "Dear God, I haven't a thing to offer You except a lot of distractions." Let us say it then. God will accept the offering with as much loving pleasure as if we had had Him in sight all the time. Amid the tornado of our distractions, God still was there in the calm heart of the whirlwind.

Fortunately, we know that prayer is not always such a struggle. If we have prayed regularly and with perseverance, there have been some wonderful moments when we have felt the intimate nearness of God. We have found new courage and strength. We have gained new insights. We have seen ourselves more clearly through God's eyes. We have discerned the direction in which we should walk. It is worth a dozen distracted prayer times to experience one such clear-eyed vision as this.

There are many well-intentioned persons who think of prayer almost entirely in terms of "asking." They come to God always with hand extended: "Give me, give me, give me." They fail to realize that our first duty in prayer is to give something to God: our adoration.

In prayer of petition there is some element of adoration, inasmuch as we do confess our dependence upon God and do admit that all good comes from Him. In real prayer of adoration, however, God is the whole object of our attention. Our eyes are completely upon Him. Adoration includes all those acts of mind and heart that acknowledge God's infinite greatness, wisdom, goodness, justice, mercy, and love. An act of faith is a prayer of adoration; so are acts of hope, contrition, thanksgiving, and praise.

An act of love, above all others, is the prayer of adoration most pleasing to God. It is by giving Him our love that we give Him greatest honor. "My God, I love You!" is so easy to say. Weak though our present love may be, God still is pleased to hear us assert it. We can depend upon Him, too, to strengthen our love—to increase the value of the gift we offer. Like the steady beat of the drum in an orchestra, "My God, I love You!" should reverberate steadily through all our other prayers.

These other prayers necessarily will include some prayers of petition. At a minimum, God expects us to ask for the graces we need in order to reach Heaven. This is the one great responsibility we have in life: to save our soul. It is the one thing above all others that God requires of us. If we fail in this, then we have failed in the only thing that really matters. It is a duty that we must fulfill ourselves. It is not a task that others can do for us.

Ordinarily, selfishness is not an admirable character trait. In the area of prayer, however, it is our obligation to be selfish. In all our prayers of petition, our first intention always must be, "For the graces I need, God, to do Your will and to come safely to Heaven." We pray, in brief, for the grace of final perseverance, for the grace of a happy death. There is no other request that we can make of God that may take precedence over this.

It also is the one request we can make of God to which we do not have to add the qualification, "if it be Your will." All other prayers of petition are conditional. We ask for this favor or that, provided that it is in accordance with God's will. Not, however, when we are praying for our eternal salvation. We *know* that this is according to God's will. We need add no "if."

Our neighbor's salvation is likewise of urgent importance to God. Having discharged the duty of holy selfishness by praying for our eternal union with God, charity demands that we pray for others. There should be no limits here to our love. At Mass and in our other prayers, our list of intentions should be a long one.

"For my parents, family, friends, and relatives, living and dead. For all for whom I ought, or have been asked, or have wished or have promised to pray. For all for whom I am in any way responsible, especially for all who may have suffered because of my bad example or my neglect of charity. For my enemies. For our Holy Father, for all bishops, priests, and religious, especially our own bishop, our own parish priests, and the Sisters in our school. For missionaries and for the people among whom they labor. For the sick and the dying. For the souls in Purgatory."

It is a long list, and our own particular intentions will make it still longer. It may be well to have it written down so that, under pressure, we simply can say, "For all the intentions on my list, Lord." Fortunately God can read—our mind as well as our writing.

8

Saints Are Doers

"Be yourself!" Of all the phrases frequently bandied about, this is one of the most misleading. The truth is that I have no right to be myself unless mine is the kind of self God would want it to be. Or, to put it another way, unless my self is fit to be another self for Christ.

Many people assume that their personality is no one's business but their own. Such an attitude completely ignores Christ's rights in the matter. In Baptism, we became "other Christs," members of His Mystical Body and sharers in His work of redemption. We became the tongue and hands and heart of Jesus in the world. Himself invisible, He must reach others through you and me or not at all. To make Jesus better known and loved: this is at once our highest privilege and our most serious obligation. We make Jesus known and loved when we exhibit those qualities of mind and heart that make Jesus Himself such a lovable Person.

Personal popularity may not be a particularly admirable goal if cultivated for its own sake or to achieve social or business success. However, to court popularity for the sake of Christ is a highly meritorious undertaking. We shall be much more effective instruments in the hands of Christ if we have a pleasing personality. If other people are attracted to us, we can exert a much greater influence for good upon them.

To bring this home to yourself, examine your own circle of acquaintances. Isn't it true that those whose opinions you respect and whose advice you follow are most often those persons whom you like? Isn't the opposite also true—that if you find some person disagreeable, you tend to resist his opinions and reject his suggestions?

It should be obvious then that Jesus does want us to be popular, in the best sense of the word, for His sake. We might say that Jesus has a vested interest in our popularity.

By nature, we may be inclined to be irritable or gloomy or short-tempered or critical or selfish. As Christians, we have no right to say, "Well, that's the way I am and people will just have to take me the way I am." On the contrary, we have the duty to identify our shortcomings and make a determined effort to eliminate those qualities that are offensive to others.

Christ respects the free will with which, as God, He has endowed me. He will not force His own pattern upon me. However, if Jesus could make me the person He would like me to be, without encroaching on my freedom, what would be the result? I then would be an exceptionally friendly person, with a smile and a cheery word for the bus driver, the girl at the checkout counter, and the neighbor next door. I would be a thoughtful person, quick to notice the needs of others and quick to give a helping hand. I would be a kind person, with genuine sympathy for the troubles of others, never taking refuge in the alibi that "I've got enough troubles of my own." I would be a charitable person, not given to gossip or unkind criticism. Everyone's reputation would be safe in my hands.

I would be a very patient person, tolerant of the ignorance and stupidity of others, even when I suffered from their mistakes. If in a position of responsibility, I might at times have to impose discipline or administer a rebuke. Even then, however, my own pain at having to voice the correction would be evident.

Friendly, cheerful, thoughtful, helpful, kind, sympathetic, charitable, patient, and tolerant: this is the kind of person that Jesus would like me to be. And how others would love me! It may seem a formidable task to undertake, but with God's grace all things are possible. At least I can make a beginning—and make it now.

Most of us, in our better moments, are ashamed that we do not do more for God. We read of missionaries who, in steaming African jungles or in drab Korean villages, consume their lives for God. We read of men and women—physicians, nurses, teachers, farmers, and mechanics—who have packed themselves and their families off to an underdeveloped country to labor as lay missionaries at subsistence pay. Right around us, we see men and women who have little time for recreation or pleasure because they give so much time to causes of parish, neighborhood, and civic betterment. We think of such people, and we are ashamed.

It is good that we do feel humbled in the knowledge of such heroism and generosity. However, the real tragedy is not that most of us are not doing big things for God. It rather is that so many of us do not do even the little things for God, the little things that are so close at hand and that, in the aggregate, could add up to quite a sum.

If we have any real understanding of how much Jesus loves each one of us, then we must realize the depth of compassion that He has towards all who suffer. We live in a world in which there is much physical and mental pain, much trouble, and much anxiety. Anything that we can do to ease our neighbor's burden, ever so little, will be immensely pleasing to our Lord.

From your own experience, you know that it does not take much to brighten your day. If you are a parent, you know what a pleasant glow you feel if someone says, "You do have the *nicest* children." If you work hard to keep up your home and show others hospitality, you walk a little lighter when someone remarks, "Your home always looks so attractive and welcoming." If you are an office worker, you feel an inch taller if a friend or your boss says, "That was a great piece of work you did." Even a remark such as, "I like your necktie," or, "That's a very pretty outfit," can give a lift quite out of proportion to the importance of the comment.

There is also a tremendous lifting force in a smile, with or without words. The power of a smile has been lauded so often in song and verse that the truth of it has been dulled by triteness. Yet there still is magic in the smile you give to the fellow shopper whose eye catches yours in the supermarket, the fellow parishioner whose name you do not know, the policeman on the corner, the clerk behind the counter, and the postman at your door. Perhaps it is because an action as simple as a smile can seem so ridiculously small that we underestimate its value from the viewpoint of charity, from the viewpoint of Christ.

Recently I attended the funeral of a friend, a man who had had a small business of his own. His business could have been larger and more prosperous if he had not spent so much time in performing little acts of kindness. The priest who preached his funeral sermon said, truthfully, "If an epitaph were to be carved on this man's tombstone, it should read, 'He always had time to be friendly.' He will be remembered for a longer time by more people than many a wealthier and more prominent citizen. If all his little kindnesses were added together, they would reach pretty high in the eyes of God. They would weigh more, on Christ's scales, than some deeds of international importance of which we read."

Each one of us who claims the title of Christian could and should be deserving of such a tribute. To earn such a reputation requires no heroic qualities. It requires only that we be conscious of the fact that we are instruments of Christ—that Christ urgently wishes to speak and act through us, to make us channels of His compassion.

For a starter, we might ask ourselves, "How many times have I smiled today? How many times today have I spoken an encouraging or cheerful word to another?" We can go on from there to examine ourselves as to our performance in wider fields of apostolic activity.

When examining your conscience, does it ever occur to you to ask yourself, "Have I failed in the practice of the virtue of zeal?" Unless we do ask ourselves this question from time to time, we easily can fall into a false (and dangerous) complacency in the practice of our faith.

We assist at Mass regularly. We receive the sacraments with reasonable frequency. We pray daily. We contribute to our parish and diocesan collections. Having done all this, we feel comfortably assured that we are good Catholics. Perhaps we are, but only if these practices generate and feed in us the spirit of Christian zeal.

Zeal may be defined briefly as a concern for God's interests. The zealous person lives a life centered on God. Whatever is important to God is important also to him.

Some people, however, are quite egocentric in their spiritual lives. The egocentric Catholic views religion simply as a means of saving his own individual soul. He sees the Church as an agency, external to himself, provided by God to guide him safely to Heaven. He ignores the fact that he himself is the Church—along with so many brothers and sisters around the world for whom he has a responsibility. "God loves me," the egocentric Catholic says confidently. "Jesus died for me. I shall be saved." His first two statements are true. However, his salvation is dubious if he cares nothing for the billions of other people now living for whom Jesus also died.

One good measure of the intensity of our zeal is the amount of prayer time we devote to the honor of God and the works of God. Some of our prayer must necessarily be for ourselves. God expects us to pray for the graces we need in order to get to Heaven. However, petitions for self should not consume the major part of our prayer time. There are too many other duties to be fulfilled in prayer.

Zeal for God's honor will result in much prayer of adoration: acts of faith and hope, especially acts of love and total self-surrender. Mindfulness of God's honor will lead to acts of reparation: prayers and penances by which we offer atonement to God for the countless sins that affront Him daily. We shall find joy in offering the Mass as an act of pure and perfect worship to the infinitely great and holy God.

Concern for God's interests will show itself also in the prayers we offer for Christ's Mystical Body, of which we are a part. We shall pray for the Pope, that he may have the grace and wisdom needed for his awesome task of leadership. We shall pray for our bishops, priests, and religious upon whom the health and growth of Christ's Body so much depends. We shall pray especially for the missionaries, men and women who are so much exposed to loneliness and discouragement. We shall pray for the people among whom they labor, at home and abroad, so that hearts may be opened to God's saving Word. Most especially and always, we shall pray for each other, remembering that, like a human chain, we enter Heaven hand in hand or we enter not at all. If intentions such as these are prominent in our prayers, then we do have some degree of zeal.

However, true zeal is not content with prayer alone. It is our actions that most surely will evidence our zeal. There is so much that we can do for God if we have His interests genuinely at heart.

One primary step we can take is to strive to make ourselves more useful instruments in the hands of God. This will be accomplished to a considerable extent by a program of serious reading. We can read books that enlarge our knowledge of the Catholic faith and make us more capable of explaining our faith to others. We can read Catholic periodicals that make us more cognizant of the problems facing Christ's Church in today's world and that give us an indication of the part we can play in meeting those problems.

We can, if opportunity is offered in our local community, enroll in adult education classes. Courses in speech and public speaking will engender confidence and make us more effective spokesmen for Christ. Courses in sociology will make us aware of the interplay of forces in our society—forces we must deal with if there is to be a change for the better. Courses in psychology will make us more understanding of the roots of behavior in ourselves and others, better equipping us to communicate with our neighbor. Courses in philosophy and theology will enable us more accurately to cut to the heart of a problem and see the problem from God's point of view. Courses in literature and history will broaden our horizons, free us from narrow parochialism, and give greater depth to our thoughts and our words.

God expects us to cultivate the talents, few or many, with which He has endowed us. However, we should not await the full flowering of our self-improvement program before undertaking more active works. Right now and all about us, there are many channels for our zeal. The St. Vincent de Paul Society is dedicated to the corporal works of mercy and the Legion of Mary to the spiritual works of mercy. And these organizations seldom have sufficient members. The Confraternity of Christian Doctrine has a chronic need for more personnel—to teach religion to public-school children, provide transportation for children, and do home visitation. Another challenge to our zeal is the Christian Family Movement, in which couples work together for the upbuilding of Christ's Body in home and neighborhood.

And what of our convert work? If there is an inquiry class conducted in our parish, zeal surely will urge us to recruit members for the class. If the parish is too small for an inquiry class, we still shall have a sharp eye for friends and neighbors who may show a glimmer of interest in the Catholic faith. We shall persuade them, if we can, to accompany us to the rectory to meet one of the priests and enroll for a course of instructions.

It is characteristic of healthy cells in a living body to reproduce themselves. In Christ's Body, there are far too many sterile cells. It truly is a tragedy that there are so many Catholics who never have been responsible, under God, for a single convert to the faith. Our Lord depends upon us to be His instruments of conversion. It requires no great ability on our part, but just needs a little zeal—and God's grace will do the rest. It is true that many of us, by prayer and by sufferings offered, may have made converts of people we do not know. However, we can and ought to *do* as well as pray. What we do may be a simple thing, such as passing a piece of Catholic literature to a non-Catholic friend with the invitation, “Here is a very interesting article I think you might enjoy.”

In considering outlets for our zeal, let us not forget our civic opportunities. Some Catholics mistakenly assume that a “good” work must be Church-sponsored or have an avowedly religious purpose. On the contrary, anything that contributes to the welfare of our fellow man is pleasing to God if done for love of Him. Neighborhood-betterment movements, parent-teacher associations, community chest drives, interracial councils, and a host of other civic undertakings are worthy of the zeal of one who is concerned for God’s interests.

“But where can I find the time?” someone may ask. Well, the virtue of zeal does call for sacrifice. We may have to give up a night of bowling or an afternoon of bridge, miss a favorite TV program or curtail some other pleasure or hobby. True zeal will find the time. No one of us, of course, can take part in *all* good works. Just let each of us be sure that we do at least a little.

In works of zeal, abilities and opportunities vary widely. The extent of our education makes some difference (although not as much as we might think). Where we live makes a difference, too, as do the demands of our family obligations.

9

Know Yourself

The success of American corporations is due in large part to a policy of continual self-evaluation. Boards of directors and management teams concern themselves with such questions as, "Which departments are successful? Which are not? What needs improving? Why? How?" Without frequent self-evaluation, a business, if it did not fail, would at best miss its potential by a wide margin.

The vitality of our spiritual life depends upon regular self-evaluation, too. We as individuals need self-scrutiny even more than business does. We humans have an unfortunate facility for self-deception. We easily persuade ourselves that we are doing very well when in fact we are not. We have a strong tendency, too, to settle into a rut of habitual behavior and to resist any attempt (even by God) to dislodge us from our accustomed groove. It is uncomfortable to change; consequently we close our eyes to any need for change. This is why a regular examination of conscience is so essential to spiritual progress.

Unfortunately, many people think of an examination of conscience only as a prelude to confession, usually a very brief prelude.

Many make the further mistake of conceiving an examination of conscience as a mere "counting up" of sins. It does not occur to such persons to go behind the returns and ask themselves, "Why did I do it? What needs changing?" The spiritual weed continues to grow because the root has not been touched.

An avowal of love for God is meaningless unless we seriously desire to grow in fidelity to God. Yet, there can be no growth in goodness without a frequent examination of conscience. Many Catholics do make such an examination as a part of their night prayers. Here again, however, the examination too often is confined to the question, "What sins did I commit?" If it always is "What?" and never "Why?" then my sins tomorrow almost inevitably will be the same as my sins today. The only change will be on the side of increase. In a good examination of conscience, causes are much more important than numbers.

An examination of conscience should have a positive side, too. Abstaining from sin is only one half of the Christian life, the negative half. Spiritually, we are walking on one leg if our idea of goodness is confined to keeping from sin. God expects us to do things *for* Him, to practice virtue as well as to eschew vice. A good examination of conscience will include such questions as, "How many acts of unselfish kindness did I perform today? How well did I practice patience under pressure? How often did I speak a word of praise or commendation? How often did I think of God today? How often did I make a decision in the light of what would be most pleasing to God?"

In addition to our daily examination of conscience, we shall do well to make a more extensive self-evaluation at least once a week. It may be possible for us, one day a week, to stop at the church on our way home from work or shopping. There, in a front pew of the quiet and empty church, with eyes on the tabernacle, we can hold our personal board of directors meeting. Our opening prayer will be brief: "Dear Lord, help me to know what You want me to do." We can then proceed to a review of our present status. "Honestly, how much of a part does God have in my life? How hard do I try, day by day, to make God's will the norm and measure of my conduct? How much of my activity is really significant, from the viewpoint of eternity? What needs changing? What needs changing most urgently? Where and how shall I begin?"

With daily and weekly self-evaluation, we shall develop our dormant capacity for greater and greater good. Life will become more meaningful as we experience the satisfaction that a sense of achievement brings.

Among other questions, you may wish to ask yourself, "Am I too self-important?" The self-important person is a pitiable figure. He is the person who talks big, brags of his exploits (real or fancied), studs his conversation with the names of prominent people whom he professes to know, and has the answer to every problem.

Somewhat akin to the braggart is the show-off, the person who is ever trying to attract attention to himself. Another familiar type is the chronic objector, who sees no merit in any plan or idea unless he himself has been the first to propose it.

These are pitiable people because they are unhappy people. Their sometimes ridiculous and sometimes annoying speech and behavior are the mechanisms by which they try to defend themselves against an ever-present pain. The truth is that deep within themselves they suffer from acute feelings of inferiority and inadequacy, feelings too painful to be tolerated or faced. Consequently, all their lives they carry on an unremitting campaign to prove to themselves that it isn't so and that really they are important persons.

Their futile efforts should move us to sympathy rather than annoyance. We should be tolerant of their constant questing for praise, attention, and recognition. We should be tolerant if for no other reason than that these types are but an exaggerated, wide-screen projection of ourselves. We all have a deeply rooted desire to feel important, to know that we excel in some area and that we really do amount to something. Psychologists classify this hunger for some measure of recognition as one of man's basic needs. If we do not have a feeling of self-worth, our personality inevitably will be warped.

There are few of us who do not suffer, at times and in some small degree, from feelings of inferiority and inadequacy. Occasionally, these feelings may be more acute; when, for example, we actually have experienced a humiliating failure of some kind, or when someone else has outstripped us by a remarkable success. I think that retirees and aged persons frequently suffer from a feeling of unimportance and from lack of recognition as their unwilling idleness shunts them to the sidelines of a busy, busy world.

Even for the vigorous among us, no previous age has been as humbling as our own. We read of other people who discover new wonder drugs, design interplanetary space ships, and achieve worldwide fame in art, science, or adventure. Meanwhile here we are, going along in our same old rut.

When we feel these twinges of inferiority, our faith is a wonderful antidote. We know that our one overall purpose in life is that we give honor to our Father in Heaven by a whole-souled dedication to the doing of His will. When we have begun our day by offering it without reserve to God—all our thoughts, words, actions, and sufferings—and live that day in the state of grace, then we have achieved the pinnacle of greatness. Even our least actions have a tremendous meaning and an eternal value. Even the act of tying our shoelaces reverberates in Heaven.

Our day may be ever so humdrum and unproductive from the viewpoint of a society that judges only by visible results. Yet, if it has been lived in union with God, it is a million times more important than the day of a man who, indifferent to God, lands a rocket on the moon.

Inferior? Unimportant? Inadequate? Not while there is breath within us to say, "For You, my God; all for You!"

What is your attitude toward God?

"Why, my attitude toward God is like everyone else's, I suppose," you might answer. "I recognize Him as my Creator and Redeemer. I try to love Him with all my heart. I try to prove my love by keeping His commandments."

That would be a very reasonable answer to an unexpected question. With more reflection, however, you would realize that your attitude toward God is *not* like everyone else's. What you believe concerning God is what every other Catholic believes. God is a spirit. He is a trinity of Persons. He is Creator and Redeemer. He is our judge, our final destiny, and our reward. He loves us. He helps us with His grace. He listens to our prayers.

These are the facts. However, as we received these facts in childhood, we processed them in our own minds. In each of us, these truths were given an individual coloration, which varies with our particular background and personality. Insofar as a spirit can be said to have an image, we fashioned our own private image of God. In no two of us is this image quite the same.

Almost our first knowledge of God is of God as a Father. This is our most meaningful concept of Him—and the most lasting.

Let us suppose now that your father was a rigidly strict and serious-minded man. He was just, yes, but also quick to wrath over childish misdemeanors and severe with his punishments. In consequence, your personal image of God may be a somber one, overweighted with thoughts of divine displeasure, judgment, and punishments. Your attitude toward God may be one of anxiety and even of servile fear.

Or, suppose that your father was a reserved, undemonstrative person, not much given to kissing or caressing his children. You will accept on faith the fact that God the Father loves you, but it may be hard for you to make real to yourself the intense, personal, and possessive love that God has for you. Your own attitude toward God may be a somewhat impersonal and austere sense of loyalty.

Your father may have been a man too absorbed in his work to have much time or thought for his children. If so, you may see God as a distant Being, with little interest in you or your troubles.

Your father may have been a foolishly doting parent who ignored your misbehavior or who laughed when he should have rebuked. As a result, you may be tempted to downgrade God's justice. You may feel that you can sin with impunity, or that you can expect forgiveness without reform.

As a final example, let us assume that yours was a father who tempered justice with patience and understanding. He was generous with outward marks of affection and generous, too, in giving time and attention to his children. With such a father, it is to be expected that your attitude toward God will be one of complete confidence, of cheerful service without fear. You should be happy and fairly tranquil in your religious life.

Scarcely ever can the emotional formation of our childhood be completely counteracted. As we grow in maturity, however, our understanding of God does deepen. Spiritual reading and periodic retreats can be especially helpful in correcting early misconceptions and in reshaping our private image of God.

You still may find yourself dissatisfied with the discrepancy between the God in your head and the God in your heart. You may be especially unhappy that you cannot feel closer to God and that your prayer lacks warmth and spontaneity.

Take courage! God *is* a God of love. He knows you, inside out. He knows your emotional handicaps better than you know them yourself. He asks of you no more than you are able to give. When you have done your best for Him, God is content, however inadequate that best may seem to you.

Are you an oversensitive person? I hope not. An oversensitive person creates a vast amount of unnecessary unhappiness for himself (or herself) and is a great trial to family and friends.

Mary Brown, for example, is abnormally sensitive. She passes her friend, Helen Jones, on the street, but Helen does not speak to her. Mary goes home in a miserable state of mind, asking herself, "Whatever did I do to make Helen mad at me?" The truth is that Helen was preoccupied with whether or not she should buy the dress she had been looking at. She had not even seen Mary Brown.

John Smith is another example. Sitting at his office desk, he watches two of his fellow workers at the water cooler, talking and laughing. John is sure they are talking about him. Actually, they are discussing a freak victory of their bowling team the previous night; John is far from their thoughts.

A third instance is Jane Dowd. The president of the Altar Society said, "I do wish you members would do your visiting after the meeting and pay attention to business now." Jane felt personally insulted and quit the Altar Society.

The person who feels that he "always" is being slighted, insulted, deliberately ignored, or talked about definitely is an oversensitive person. All of us do occasionally meet up with offensive people, but these occasions are rare. People who are purposely offensive are a minor element in our population. It just is not possible to encounter them every day.

Another test of our sensitiveness is the degree to which we worry about what other people think of us. It is quite normal to wish to be well thought of by others. Psychologists tell us that "acceptance by our peers" is a pretty basic human need. The person who says, "I don't care what other people think," is likely to be a more abnormal—and certainly a more selfish—person than the oversensitive soul.

We have a need to be accepted, but the oversensitive individual feels this need with a painful urgency. Many of us take it for granted that we are reasonably well liked and respected. It takes a very unmistakable affront or discourtesy to upset us. The reason why we are not easily disturbed is because we have a satisfying feeling of self-worth. As we look at ourselves in the mirror of our mind, we usually like what we see there, and we take it for granted that other people also like us. This does not mean that we are conceited. It means simply that we are content with ourselves as God has made us. We feel that He has been good to us in making us as we are, and we would not want to be anyone else. This is not pride. It is a perfectly normal and desirable emotional state.

It is not pride, either, that causes the oversensitive person to be so easily offended. On the contrary, he suffers from subconscious feelings of inferiority. These feelings may be due to some unfortunate circumstances of his childhood—perhaps an inability to measure up to his parents' exaggerated expectations. Whatever the reason, the oversensitive person is not satisfied with his own image of himself. He has an unrecognized fear that he may not be deserving of respect and acceptance by others. Unconsciously, he *expects* to be belittled. Consequently, he sees offense where there is none.

In its extreme form, oversensitiveness may need the help of a psychiatrist for its cure. In the milder form in which it most often appears, however, it can be controlled with prayer and effort. The underlying insecurity may not be eliminated, but the outward manifestations can be checked. When we recall that our oversensitiveness causes much uncalled-for annoyance and even unhappiness to others, charity will dictate that we labor at the task.

God intends, certainly, that our practice of religion should be a happy experience. This does not mean that the good Christian should go skipping and singing his way through the day. It does mean that we normally should find in our faith a source of quiet content and interior peace. If anxiety or other mental misery is a chronic part of our spiritual life, we may suspect a submerged emotional problem as the culprit. It is very unlikely that God has visited us with this particular kind of cross.

One of the more common destroyers of spiritual peace is the phenomenon known as *scrupulosity*. A scrupulous person is one who has lost the power of judgment in moral matters. He thinks that he is sinning when in fact there is no sin. He is never satisfied with his prayers, and he repeats them interminably. In Confession, he is afraid that he has not told his sins adequately. He wants to repeat his Confession over and over again. In spite of his confessor's reassurance, he leaves the confessional as anxious and worried as when he entered.

Scrupulosity is primarily a psychological problem, not a moral or spiritual problem. It is a form of neurosis, a compulsive neurosis that, in this particular instance, finds outlet in the person's moral life. The neurosis could have found other outlets. For example, a person could be abnormally indecisive in his profession or other occupation, with a compulsion to check and recheck his work without ever being satisfied. Another person could have a compulsion to sweep the home six or a dozen times a day and still not be content that it was clean.

Since scrupulosity is an emotional rather than spiritual problem, it is not an ill that a confessor can cure. The priest will work patiently with a scrupulous penitent to help him to control his compulsion. The real cure, however, must be the work of psychiatry or some other form of psychotherapy.

Alcoholism is another form of compulsion that can create religious conflict. We know that deliberate drunkenness is a grave sin. The compulsive drinker, however, does not deliberately choose to get drunk. He may be a religious person with a very real desire to abstain from sin, yet he is physically incapable of controlling his appetite for alcohol. Sin enters here when the alcoholic, recognizing his own helplessness, neglects to seek the competent help an organization such as Alcoholics Anonymous might give him.

Guilt feelings are another form of psychological problem that can complicate a person's spiritual life and rob him of joy in his religion. Guilt feelings, in the psychological meaning of the term, do not pertain to some recognized sin. Most people feel guilty when they have deliberately sinned, and it is good that they do. This sense of guilt disappears, however, when the sinner has repented and has obtained God's forgiveness. Psychological guilt feelings, on the other hand, are a vague and generalized conviction of personal unworthiness that repentance and absolution seem powerless to alleviate. The services of both a psychiatrist and a confessor might be helpful.

Christ gave us the sacraments for our spiritual health, not for physical or psychological health. The sacrament of Penance will forgive sin, but it will not of itself cure a neurosis any more than it will cure tuberculosis.

However, prayer and the sacraments can and will help us to bear our crosses, physical and mental, until such time as we can find a cure for them. Meanwhile, God is infinitely patient with us and has compassion for our infirmities. No one ever will go to Hell "because he couldn't help it."

When is a sin mortal? That seems an easy question to answer. We still can remember the catechism lesson in which we learned that a sin is mortal if, in a grave matter, we disobey God with a full knowledge of what we are doing and with full consent of our will. The definition seems simple enough. Yet, in applying it, we do meet with difficulties.

The "grave matter" element is the least of our difficulties. The theologians of the Church, reasoning from the principles of natural and divine law, identify for us those acts or negligences that unquestionably are grave from God's point of view. Thus, it is a grave matter to take unjustly the life of another or to do him serious physical harm. It is a grave matter to deny another his rights as a human being. It is a grave matter to ruin another's reputation. It is a grave matter to indulge the sexual urge outside the limits of lawful marriage. These and dozens of other moral failures have been plainly tagged as grave.

No, it is not the "grave matter" that poses the real difficulty in interpreting mortal sin. Neither is it the element of "full knowledge." It is plain enough that we cannot commit a sin through ignorance (unless the ignorance is self-willed), through forgetfulness, or in a semiconscious state. We cannot offend God without knowing that we are offending Him. Even though we may feel vaguely guilty if we inadvertently eat meat on a Friday, good sense assures us that there has been no sin.

It is when we come to the "full consent of the will" requisite for mortal sin that we find ourselves dealing with imponderables. There are so many factors that can interfere with our freedom of choice and diminish our responsibility. Fear, worry, tension, passion, and fatigue are but a few of the variables that can and do influence the will. For example, a person who is tired and tense is not as responsible for an outburst of anger as is a person who is rested and relaxed.

In addition to such common hazards to full freedom of choice, there also are other conditions of mind and emotions that modern psychology has uncovered. Compulsions, phobias, complexes, and subconscious feelings of many kinds can make difficult (and at times impossible) the free exercise of the will. Obvious examples are the gluttony of the compulsive eater or drinker, the thieving of the kleptomaniac, the Mass-missing of the person with a fear of crowds, or the promiscuity of the girl who was deprived of love as a child.

These are some of the more extreme examples of the stresses to which the will may be subjected. But even we who rate ourselves as mentally and emotionally sound may be affected to a lesser extent by biases of which we may be unaware. Our will does not operate in a vacuum.

It is a faculty of the soul, but it must work in and through the complete human organism that is man. Whatever hidden flaws there may be in our personality, our will has to do the best it can within the sometimes unfavorable conditions in which it finds itself.

What is the point of all this? The point is that God, and only God, can know all the pressures—and their strength—that are involved in any particular act of the will. This fact has two corollaries. One is that the person of good will, who honestly is trying his best to do what God asks, never should grow discouraged if his progress is slow or if at times he seems to fail. God, who searches our hearts, knows how hard we are trying. He knows, even if we ourselves do not, every psychological and emotional handicap that our will has to surmount. As long as we keep trying, we never need to doubt our ultimate victory.

The second corollary is that we dare not judge the moral status of our neighbor. He may have perpetrated some act that is, viewed objectively, mortally sinful. Perhaps we may say, "It is a sinful deed which he did," but never can we say, "He committed a mortal sin." For that judgment, only God is competent.

10

Parents as Saint Makers

If you are a parent, particularly a young parent, you may experience some anxiety as to your adequacy in the field of child psychology. Be comforted! The chances are that you are a better psychologist than you think.

Infancy through childhood is the time of greatest vulnerability in the development of human personality. Parents who bring their child safely to the age of puberty without serious psychological damage can then pause and take a breath. Their future parental responsibilities may not be wholly free from concern, but, by the age of twelve or so, the human personality is well established.

From the moment of his birth, a child's one great psychological need is for love. It is love that gives him a feeling of self-worth. He is loved; therefore he is lovable; therefore he is a worthwhile person. It is love, too, that builds in a child a sense of security. He is a stranger to tension since, being loved, he knows that his needs will be cared for.

The child, of course, does not reason this out. In his early years, particularly in infancy, a child operates pretty much on the level of instinct. But his instinct is sharp and perceptive. It is hard for us adults to realize how acute the sensitivity of an infant is to the presence or absence of love in his environment.

Rejection, or denial of love, is the most severe psychological wound that a human being can suffer. A child who feels himself to be unloved will be emotionally handicapped for life. In his mature years, he inevitably will exhibit personality difficulties. He must defend himself, somehow, against the deep-buried feelings of rejection and insecurity that are too painful to admit to his conscious mind.

It is not only a lack of love for himself that will undermine a child's sense of security. The same result, in a less pernicious form, will be effected by chronic discord within the home. The loud and angry voices of quarreling parents will leave their impress upon the infant's brain and nervous system and upon the child's personality pattern. These antagonists are the two people upon whom the child must depend for survival. Their quarreling instills a fear that his home may break up—a fear that he may be forced to choose between the two people he most loves. Such a child lives under continual tension.

As an example, it has been discovered in classroom research that an intelligent child who fails in his studies quite often is the victim of discord at home.

Considering how complex the process of personality development is, we can be grateful that God has made the principles of parenthood so simple. There really are only two basic rules of child psychology that are of surpassing importance. The first is: Parents, love your child. By word and by action, give him frequent assurance of your love. You never can tell your child too often, "I love you." You never can love your child too much. A so-called "spoiled" child is not the victim of too much love. He is the victim of rejecting parents who, feeling guilty, try to make up by lenience for the love they cannot give.

Love is quite consonant with discipline. If love is there, it will be evident even in punishment. "It is because I love you so much and want you to have a happy life that I must punish—not you, but your misbehavior." The parent may not put this into words, but the message of love will come through.

The second basic rule is: Parents, love each other. Let your children *see* that you love each other. There is no greater assurance that you can give to your children than the confidence that theirs is a secure and stable world.

A wider knowledge of child psychology will be helpful in coping with many incidental problems of parenthood. But, if two parents genuinely love each other and both love their children, they already have 90 percent of child psychology solidly at work.

It is quite natural for parents to be ambitious for their children. If we love someone, we necessarily desire that he be happy. Equating happiness with success, parents are eager to see their children successful, in school now and in their life's vocation later. Moreover, parents tend to measure their own success as parents by the success, both material and spiritual, that their children achieve. If their child graduates with honors, gets a high-level job, makes a good marriage, enters the convent, or becomes a priest, mother and father feel that this is an accolade to themselves. It is proof that they have reared their child well.

Such parental pride is understandable. It is one of the rewards for the sacrifices that accompany parenthood. However, parental ambition and pride contain a built-in danger. This is the danger that, in their zeal for a child's future, parents may try to push a child beyond the limits of his capacity. There is no surer way to implant an inferiority complex in a child than by demanding of him more than he is able to give.

Overzealousness exhibits itself especially in parental attitudes towards school performance. By the very nature of averages, fifty percent of all children will be average or below average in their mental ability. However, many parents find it hard to accept the fact that they have an average child. They assume that any child of theirs is bound to be intelligent.

As a consequence, little Johnny, who has to work hard to get C's on his report card, is prodded and pushed to better his grades. His lot is doubly unhappy if he has a brighter brother or sister in school. Then Johnny's average performance is compared often with that of his more clever sibling. "Why can't you get As and Bs as your brother (sister) does?"

Try as he will, Johnny cannot measure up to his parents' expectations. Frustrated in his efforts, he becomes more and more conditioned to failure. With sympathetic understanding and with recognition of the effort he does make, Johnny could grow into a reasonably self-confident adult. But, as it is, he will be permanently marked in his own mind as a second-class individual. He will suffer, throughout life, from feelings of inferiority.

Feelings of inferiority can be generated, too, by parents who are habitual faultfinders. Such parents cannot bear the thought that their child is anything less than a paragon of virtue. They are lavish with criticisms, with such phrases as, "You are a bad boy [girl]"; "You are a clumsy boy"; "You can't do anything right"; and "I never can depend on you."

Eventually, this child comes to accept, in his own mind, that he really is a bad or clumsy or undependable person. It is a conviction he will carry into adulthood. The harm is intensified if his parents rarely speak a word of praise, perhaps fearing (mistakenly) that praise will spoil the child.

On the contrary, parental praise is essential to build up a child's confidence in himself and to give him a feeling of self-worth. Prudent parents do not flatter, but they do watch for occasions when they can honestly commend the child. The more often such occasions occur, the better. There will be times when a child's behavior must be criticized, even punished. However, when rebukes must be administered, it is important to distinguish between the child's behavior and the child himself. It is much better to say, "That was a naughty thing you did" than to say, "You are a bad boy;" much better to say, "You told me a lie" than to say, "You are a deceitful little girl." And, on balance, approbation always should be more frequent than reproof.

Parents who accept their child as he is and ask of him no more than he is able to deliver—and who counterpoint correction with frequent approval—are parents who are giving their child a healthy image of himself.

Parents have the wonderful privilege to be the first persons to introduce a child to God. The introduction is not quite as simple as saying, "Mickey, this is God." A child's acquaintance with God comes gradually, day by day and year by year. It is the parents, however, who have the honor of unveiling God's face to their child.

His first image of God and his first feeling *about* God will remain with the child throughout his life. The image later will be refined and perfected, as knowledge increases, but the child's basic attitude toward God will be permanent. That is why it is so important for a child to see God, from the beginning, as He really is: a God of love.

A child should hear, "God loves you," as often as he hears, "Mommy loves you" or "Daddy loves you." The child should know that God watches over him, lovingly, as he sleeps and that God is with him, helping him, all the day long. The child should hear often of God's goodness, too—both in nature and in supernature. "Isn't God good to give us the grass and the trees and the beautiful flowers?" "Isn't God good to listen to our prayers?" "Wasn't it good of God to give you such a beautiful soul?"

Love and goodness. A child's concept of God should be built around these two ideas. Eventually, a child must know about God's justice, too, but preferably not until the conviction of God's love has been indelibly impressed upon his mind.

When the subject of Hell does come up, a child should know the true nature of Hell. He should not be given a picture taken from Dante's *Inferno.* Hell is the awful state of unhappiness suffered by persons who have cut themselves off, forever, from God. God doesn't want anyone in Hell. God doesn't send anyone to Hell. A soul in Hell is there because he chose Hell for himself. There was something in this life that he loved more than he loved God. Much as He loves us, God cannot *make* us love Him if we do not want to. God cannot *make* us come to Him in Heaven if we refuse. This is the truth about Hell. It is the truth that a child, according to his capacity, should have.

It is a great tragedy if a parent uses God as a disciplinary tool. It is an injustice to God to use Him as a club over a child's head. "God won't love you if you do that." "God will be angry with you." "God punishes naughty boys." Such statements introduce God to the child as a glorified policeman, with lasting harm to the child's concept of God. If God is invoked in a behavior problem, it should be only in a positive way. For example: "If you love God you will do what He wants you to do," or, "When you are good, you are telling God that you love Him."

A child not only must be introduced to God as a God of love; the child also must be helped to form a right conscience. A child should not be told, "Oh, that is a bad, bad sin," when the little tyke is not even old enough to know the difference between moral right and wrong. A child of three or four is simply incapable of committing sin. To tell such a child that he has sinned is to sow in his mind guilt feelings that may torment him for the rest of his life. As an adult, he may suffer from obscure feelings of unworthiness whose source is lost to memory. He does not know why, but he still feels guilty even after a good Confession.

When a child does come to the use of reason, wise parents will be careful not to magnify the gravity of his offenses. If childish acts of disobedience, anger, or deceit are tagged as mortal sins, a badly twisted conscience will result.

Yes, it is an enviable privilege that parents have, to be the first to introduce their child to God. Let them only be sure that the introduction is made on the basis of truth, to God as He really is.

The age of adolescence is a trying time, for the adolescent himself as well as for his parents. Adolescence begins and ends approximately with the teen years. It is the period of life during which a person gradually leaves childhood behind and emerges into maturity.

By its very nature, adolescence is a time of flux and change. The teenager is not exactly the same person today that he was yesterday, and tomorrow he will not be exactly the same as today.

Consequently, adolescence is a time of emotional confusion, as the youth tries to form a new but constantly changing image of himself.

During childhood, life is quite stable. Having a definitely assigned place in society, a child has a definite image of himself. He knows what it means to be a child because he knows what is expected of a child. This is true also of an adult. The adolescent, however, is never quite sure where he stands. He is reluctant to leave the safe dependence of childhood, yet nature is urging him on to achieve the independence of thought and action that maturity demands. Nature also is developing the procreative power and awakening the sexual drive. The youth has to struggle with tensions and feelings that are wholly new to him. He has to build up controls never before needed. He has to learn what it means to be a man (or she, a woman).

It is not surprising if the adolescent lives in a state (usually unrecognized by himself) of emotional confusion. The patience of his parents is strained as he alternates between childlike moods of affection and tractability and adultlike moods of stubborn independence. Sometimes parents add to the teenager's state of confusion. One day they tell him, "You're too old for that sort of thing. You're not a child any more." The next day they say, "You're too young for that. Don't be getting such big ideas." It is little wonder that the adolescent finds it difficult to answer the question, "Who am I?"

Because of his feeling of insecurity, the teenager tries to find stability by identifying himself closely with others in his age group. Membership in the herd gives him a feeling of safety. In his anxiety to be accepted by his peers, the adolescent conforms slavishly to their standards. He (or she) must wear his hair in a certain style, dress in a certain way, wear a certain kind of shoes, and talk the jargon of his peers.

This addiction to teenage fads can be very irritating to parents. "Do you have to wear your hair in that outlandish style?" they ask. "What's wrong with the jacket you've already got?" "I don't care if 'everyone' at school *is* using eye shadow." These are familiar parental reactions.

However, it is the adolescent's search for independence that troubles parents most of all. Their commands are questioned, their directives are resisted, and their instructions are disobeyed. Like a mother hen who has hatched a duck, parents begin to wonder where this changeling son or daughter came from. They begin to wonder whether they have failed in their efforts to raise this child well.

Actually, this is nature at work. It is not a latent meanness coming out in the child. If the teenager has had wise and loving guidance in his earlier years, he will weather the storms and stresses of adolescence without serious harm. He may drive his parents to distraction in the process, but ultimately he will come to anchor in the calm harbor of maturity.

The adolescent does need guidance, firm guidance. He himself, consciously or unconsciously, desires such guidance. In his emotional turbulence and uncertainty, he is grateful for protection against himself. Firm guidance is especially needed when the teenage code clashes with the moral code or with established norms of decency or courtesy. However, an understanding of the adolescent's needs and problems will enable parents to exercise their guidance with patience and sympathy.

Some of the parents who read this book will learn in the future that their unmarried daughter is pregnant. It is to these parents that I address myself now, with a plea that they face their grave problem with intelligence and charity.

When a beloved child informs her parents that she is pregnant, their first reaction is likely to be one of grief. How can such a thing have happened to their child, perhaps still in her teens, whom they have so loved and cherished? She always was such a good girl—and now this! Where have they, the parents, failed in their guidance? These are the kinds of accusations and recriminations that parents, in their first shock, may be tempted to toss at their daughter and at themselves. Their shock is understandable, but this sort of reaction is the worst possible response to the situation.

In the first place, their child has not changed into a bad girl by the fact of her pregnancy. She may have committed a sin in a moment of sudden temptation. That single sin does not mean that her whole character has changed. She may already have repented of the sin, confessed it, and right now is in the state of grace.

The fact that she is going to have a baby does not make her sin worse. In fact, her very pregnancy may indicate her basic goodness. If she had been a promiscuous sort and had gone out "looking for trouble," she may have provided herself with a contraceptive. Moreover, if their daughter were without conscience, she might have procured an abortion and escaped shame by adding the sin of murder to her first dereliction.

Let it be emphasized, then, that having a baby is no sin. The extramarital sexual relations was a sin, but the resultant pregnancy is not. The child this daughter carries within her womb is a child of God. When this child was conceived, God's creative power was brought into play, as He fashioned a spiritual, immortal soul. It is the beginning of another saint for Heaven.

The girl may confess her pregnancy tearfully or (to conceal her inward fear) casually, or even defiantly. However the news is broken to them, it is to be hoped that the parents will rise nobly to the challenge. If ever there was a time when their daughter needed their understanding love, it is now.

The girl may be frightened, worried, shamed, and confused. This is the moment for parental arms to enfold her with the assurance, "We're sorry it happened, but we still love you as much as ever. The world hasn't come to an end. We'll work this out together." There are important decisions to be made—potential marriage considerations, keeping the baby or seeking adoption, etc. But when the crisis is past, good parents can look back to this as their finest hour. Such parents were able to rise above their own shock and fear in the cause of love. They were able to forget themselves in order to be twin towers of strength for their child when her need was greatest.

11

When You Grow Older

What are you doing to prepare for your old age? That may look like the opening sentence of an insurance advertisement, but preparation for old age entails much more than providing financial security. Indeed, financial security probably is the least of the considerations involved.

Many persons, in planning for their later years, make a fetish of "independence." They wish to have enough money laid aside, or assured by pension, so that they will not be a "burden" upon anyone. Yet, as it works out, many persons who in their retirement have ample economic resources still find themselves quite miserable. What could be the reason?

One reason, I think, is that this urge for independence is a self-defeating mirage. By building up in ourselves a mania for independence, we sow the seeds of innumerable frustrations to be harvested in our later years. Because, unless we die young, we inevitably shall become dependent upon others, to some extent, before we speak our *nunc dimittis*.

No amount of money will take from our joints the arthritic stiffness that makes the supporting hand of another so welcome.

Money will not revive the tiring heart that makes it necessary for other legs to run our errands. Money will not restore the dimming eyesight and the dulled hearing that call for consideration on the part of others. Money will not rejuvenate the failing memory that pleads for patience from those around us, the memory that is so sharp for events of long ago and so forgetful of the roast in the oven today.

Whether we like it or not, we shall be to some degree dependent upon others. If we have made a god of independence, we easily may destroy the happiness of what could be some of our most pleasant years. We shall resent the fact that we cannot do everything for ourselves. We shall be grudging, even ungracious, in our acceptance of help from others. We shall be that most pitiable of persons: the querulous, complaining, self-pitying oldster.

What is the point in so exaggerating the value of independence? If every human being were completely independent of everyone else, ours would be a cold and cheerless world. There would be no field at all for the exercise of thoughtfulness, gentleness, kindness, and generosity—no opportunity for the practice of the many-faced virtue of Christian charity. Mankind's noblest qualities would be stultified for lack of the sunlight provided by other people's dependence upon us.

You and I, still vigorous and active, certainly do not grieve that we must, at times, be helpful to others. On the contrary, we find in the practice of charity some compensation for our feelings of unworthiness in God's sight. We have done many things, in the course of the years, of which we are ashamed. We rejoice to have the opportunity to balance the account, ever so little. As we drive Grandma to the doctor's office or do Aunt Maggie's shopping for her, we feel that we are, for the moment, the kind of person we should like to be always.

If this is our own feeling now, why should we be so eager to deprive others of this merit when we in turn shall reach life's evening hour? No, provision for independence is not the essential problem. It is of ever so much more importance that we equip ourselves for a satisfying use of the days of leisure that old age will bring. After a busy life spent in useful work, perhaps raising a family and contributing at least a little to the world's betterment, it can be a most dismaying sensation to find oneself, suddenly, a mere bystander at life's parade. We all have such a hunger to feel that we are doing something that counts.

It is to fill this vacuum of our later years that the experts advise us to develop, now, hobbies and interests that we can carry with us into retirement. Golf, bridge, handicrafts, collecting, and enjoying good books and good music are some of the things that can lighten and enrich our days later in life. And, if we are not enfeebled by sickness or other handicaps, there will be countless opportunities for volunteer service of one kind or another. Our parish and our community will welcome the time that we now can give so generously. Given reasonable good health, there will be little cause for us to feel bored, useless, or unwanted.

However, barring a sudden death, there will come a day when our bodily resources will be too attenuated for any but the most essential physical efforts. We shall reach the point where we are quite content to just sit. Provision for this stage of our progress toward eternity is surely the most important preparatory step that we can take. Those last years can be our most useful years. They will be (or ought to be) our contemplative, prayerful years.

None of us considers that a cloistered nun, spending her day in prayer, is wasting her time. We do not esteem the Carthusian monk, meditating in his cell by day and by night, as a useless person. On the contrary, we know that these "idle" souls are doing the greatest work that can be done, for Christ and for the sinful world. This is the supreme kind of usefulness that the aged person achieves (if he will) in his last years. There is open to him then the very highest of vocations: the vocation to the contemplative life.

As a person prays the Rosary, recites litanies, and talks familiarly with God, he brings from Heaven a steady flow of grace. His prayers are thrice fortified as he offers his own sufferings in union with the sufferings of Christ. By his prayers and sufferings, sinners are turned back to God, unbelievers accept the gift of faith, discouraged souls find new and unexpected hope, rebellious souls resign themselves to God's will, and Purgatory is emptied. He cannot know, until he reaches Heaven, all these fruits of his prayers. But how ridiculous it would be for an aged person to say, "All I can do now is to pray." What greater work is there?

Of course, the ability to pray is not suddenly acquired with the whitening of one's hair and the loss of one's teeth. If our waning years are to be, as they can be, our most productive years, we must lay the foundation now. By all means let us acquire hobbies and cultivate leisure-time interests. But above all let us learn, by frequent practice, how to pray.

"Shall I live with my children or shall I live in a residence for retirees?" This is the decision that confronts many elderly persons who, being widowed, find it impracticable to maintain a home or an apartment of their own. It may be a long time, if ever, before you have to make this decision. However, your eventual choice will be more sound if thought out now, calmly and rationally, while it still is a distant possibility.

To simplify discussion, let us assume that money will not be the primary consideration. Let us assume also that you are a widow or widower. And let us assume, finally, that your alternatives are a room at Golden Years Manor or a room in your married daughter or son's home.

Having made these assumptions, which will be the wiser choice? It is safe to say that you will be happy in your daughter or son's home, and their family will be happy with your presence there, if you can fulfill the following conditions:

1. You are not ashamed or resentful of being old, but can let yourself relax to enjoy your later years.
2. You do not interfere in family arguments or in the disciplining of the children.
3. You are able to see your child as an adult, capable of making decisions and no longer dependent on you.

If you can fulfill these requirements, by all means go and live with your daughter or son, for the family will be a happy one.

If you are a widower, widow, or single person of mature years but still reasonably vigorous, I should like to propose a question. To the men: "Have you ever thought of becoming a priest or a Brother?" To the women: "Have you ever thought of embracing the religious life?" For many older people, it never occurs to them that there may be a place for them around the altar. Yet, what better way could there be to spend the last years of one's life than in working directly and exclusively for God? Can there be a place in the Church for a newly ordained priest of sixty or sixty-five, or for a newly professed Brother or Sister of similar age? Indeed there can be, and there is.

Admittedly, it might be difficult for an older priest to maintain the somewhat hectic pace of a parish assistant. However, as the chaplain of a hospital, school, or other institution, he could count on the younger men to do the more strenuous work. Or, as a religious Brother, he could be of great assistance in the school, office, sacristy, maintenance, or domestic department of the cloister which he serves.

In convents, too, there are many posts that can be filled by "late vocation" Sisters. One who has a background in some profession such as teaching or nursing will be especially valuable. But there are many tasks for the unskilled Sister, too—tasks that require only a spirit of dedicated generosity.

What are the problems that face a person who thinks that he or she may have a belated vocation to the priesthood or to the religious life? The first problem is to find acceptance by a bishop (for the diocesan priesthood) or by a religious community. Bishops and religious superiors have to be realistic in administering the funds of the diocese, monastery, or convent. They may hesitate to accept applications from people in their 50s or 60s because of the risk involved. The elderly priest or religious may become, through ill health, a financial burden and unable to contribute in the way of services. Some communities have age limits for prospective novices, though exceptions can be and have been made for well-qualified applicants.

One final problem, for both men and women, is of course the problem of adjustment to a new kind of life. As we grow older, it becomes harder to adapt to a strange environment. However, this is not an insuperable obstacle for those of good will. Many later vocations, already bearing fruit in the Church, are proof that it can be done.

For the mature person contemplating a religious or priestly vocation, the first step will be to consult his or her confessor or pastor for guidance and more detailed information. Granted the necessary qualifications, no more constructive use could be made of one's later years than to spend them within the sanctuary or cloister. Certainly there could be no better place to answer, at the end, God's final call.

12

To the Future—with Confidence

Are you an optimist or a pessimist? Is your outlook on life habitually a hopeful one, or do you usually expect the worst to happen?

The nature of our temperament, whether cheerful or gloomy, depends to a great extent upon the state of our emotional and physical health. A person who has had an unhappy or insecure childhood is likely to view life somberly and to be apprehensive of the future. Poor physical health also can result in a morbid and easily dejected personality.

However, we need not be the helpless victims of our "natural" self. In the free will with which God has endowed us, we have an immeasurable source of power to counteract the downward drag of emotional or physical handicaps. We can force ourselves to cultivate the habit of looking on the bright side of events and the good side of people. It has been pointed out that even the worst sinner devotes a comparatively small proportion of his time to his evil deeds.

The truth is that our faith demands of us that we be optimists. If God is in control of His world, as we surely do believe, then things have *got* to move forward towards the ultimate fulfillment of God's plan. Neither man nor devil nor circumstance can defeat God's purposes. Any setback that God may seem to suffer will be but a mirage, a seeming defeat only because we cannot see the distant victory. Even out of evil God will bring good. He somehow will weave human sin and error into His ultimate design.

Let me offer an example of the illogic of pessimism. Today we hear much and read much of the problem of juvenile delinquency, of the breakdown of parental responsibility and family morality. We easily might assume that the world really is on the road to Hell. Yet, listen to Thomas of Celano as, more than seven hundred years ago, he wrote the first biography of St. Francis of Assisi:

> There has spread everywhere among those who bear the name of Christians a most depraved practice of striving to raise their children from the very cradle without any training or discipline whatsoever. On all sides this pernicious idea is as established and defined as if it were the law of the land. As soon as newborn babes begin to speak, or even lisp, they are taught by word and gesture the most disgraceful and detestable things.... Well has one of the profane poets said, "Because we have grown up amid the ways of our parents, from childhood all manner of evil pursues us."

Thomas of Celano, remember, was writing in the thirteenth century, the so-called age of faith when all Europe was Catholic. Even allowing for possible rhetorical exaggeration, no modern writer would dare to condemn today's parents and youth so bitterly.

There will be peaks and valleys on the graph as God's world moves forward, but always the trend will be upwards. The invincibility of God must not foster a spirit of complacency in ourselves.

God still expects each of us to do our best for Him and to make ourselves responsive instruments in His hands. Yet, even as we strive, it must be cheerfully and in confidence.

"God writes with crooked lines," but it still is He who writes.

Psychologists have characterized our present era as an age of anxiety. More people worry about more things, they say, than at any other time in man's long history.

They may be quite correct in their diagnosis. Yet, it hardly would be possible for anxiety to so possess us unless we first had surrendered our first-line defense against anxiety: our faith in God and in His providence. This, it seems to me, is the real source of our nagging fears.

When I say "we," I really do mean *we*—we Catholics as well as other fellow citizens. It is not that we have formally renounced our faith. Intellectually, we still believe in God and in all that He teaches us through His Church. Yet, even as our minds give assent to divine truths, emotionally we are on the verge of atheism. Our faith is not an active, operative faith. Our religious belief does not penetrate and pervade our attitudes and feelings; and it is attitudes and feelings, rather than lofty concepts isolated in the mind, that motivate our actions.

We say we believe that God is infinitely powerful, that He has created and controls the entire universe. We also profess to believe that God is infinitely wise and that He knows always what is best for the accomplishing of His ends. Further, we assert our firm belief in the fact that God loves each one of us with an individual, personal love that seeks always what is best for us—best calculated, that is, to bring us to eternal union with Himself.

God can do all things. God knows all things. God loves me. How can I believe these truths and still be a victim to worry? The explanation can be only that I live my life on two levels. On the level of prayer and religious observance, I live by faith. On the level of day-to-day activity, I am a practicing atheist. That is, I feel that the whole weight of the future is on my own shoulders. Success or failure depends entirely upon human cleverness and ability. If my own skill or intelligence (or that of my fellows) is lacking, then disaster is inevitable. If I guess wrong or falter at any point, all is lost.

The secret of a spirit serene and confident is to let our religious belief breech the barrier between head and heart, to let faith dominate feelings and attitudes as well as intellect.

We are human and therefore by definition imperfect. Consequently, we scarcely shall escape *all* worry even when we have brought our faith alive. However, if we have to admit that anxiety is our frequent companion, we shall do well to assess the state of our faith.

To worry is unchristian. Worry dishonors God. It assumes that God does not have things under control. Worry implies that God is not interested in His world; or, more specifically, that God is not interested in *me*.

A mother may answer, "That's all very well, but I'd be a poor sort of mother if I didn't worry about my children." A father may say, "If I didn't worry about my family, I'd never keep my nose to the grindstone as I do."

Such statements confuse the word *worry* with the word *concern*. Webster defines *concern* as "Interest in, or care for, any person or thing; regard; solicitude." *Worry* is defined as "undue solicitude; vexation; anxiety."

It is our duty to be concerned. Parents must have a concern for their children. All of us, as members of Christ's Mystical Body, must be concerned about our fellow man. We must be concerned about our neighbor who is not a Catholic. We must be concerned about the slum-dwellers in our city. We must be concerned about racial injustice. We must be concerned about the people in pagan and Communist countries. We must be concerned about God's honor and glory—and grieved that so many should dishonor Him by sin. Yes, we have ample cause for concern.

However, our concern must be laced generously with the virtue of hope if it is not to degenerate into worry. Our trust in God and in His constant, loving care must never weaken.

To avoid worry, we need, also, to have a sense of perspective. That is, we must cultivate the ability to see life as a whole and not in small pieces. We need to see our present cross—sickness, loss of job, marital strife, the birth of a child with disabilities—as part of a larger picture into which this darkness will fit as a logical and constructive part.

Our worries will lessen, too, if we have a sense of history, an ability to look back and to look ahead from where we stand. For example, parents worry about the unpredictable behavior of their teenage son or daughter. If they could look back to the emotional turmoil of their own adolescent years, and ahead to when the son or daughter will be a devoted father or mother, concern would not so easily grow into worry.

To paint with a larger brush, we might examine the anxiety that many good Christians experience at the prevalence of sin and the disregard for God's rights. It is fitting that we have concern for God's honor and glory. Indeed, this must be our primary and ultimate concern. However, a sense of perspective and history will keep our concern from swelling into disturbing anxiety.

While Catholics are a mere fraction of the world's total population today, Christ's Church remains the leaven that Jesus proclaimed it to be. There is much unbelief and sin, yes; but there is much faith and virtue, too. Every day, from the hands of priests around the world, the holy sacrifice of the Mass goes up to God, with uncounted people kneeling around those altars. God's honor and glory are not on the wane.

We do well to be concerned for family, for neighbor, and for God—but always with courage, confidence, and hope.

One of the most humbling experiences faced by a newly ordained priest is to find himself, suddenly, an object of attention on the part of Catholics. Yesterday, attired in a necktie, no one gave him a second glance. Today, in his roman collar, men tip their hats to him. Ladies who never otherwise would speak to a stranger smile and say, "Good morning, Father." People ask for his blessing.

The young priest is thrilled by such marks of respect, but, unless he is a complete fool, he takes no pride in them. He knows that it is not himself as a person, but rather the priesthood of Christ that the Catholic laity are saluting. The marks of honor are but a reminder of the great grace that, so totally undeserved, has come to him. For the rest of his life he must try, always inadequately, to thank God for the gift of his priesthood.

Yet, an earlier gift came to that priest in his infancy, a gift more precious, more glorious than anything that has happened to him since: *he was baptized*. Since this gift of Baptism is one shared by priest and layman alike, it will be more practical to turn our attention from the young priest and to speak in terms of YOU.

You came to the baptismal font with a nature that was completely human. You had no capacity for supernatural action, no equipment to enjoy the ineffable happiness that is God's. In the sacrament of Baptism, God endowed you with a new kind of life, a sharing in His own divine life. God raised you to His own level of being and fitted you with the power to perform supernatural acts, acts of eternal value and significance. The sudden change of a jungle ape into an Einstein would not be one-hundredth as great a miracle as the change of you into a child of God.

In Baptism, you became not a blood-brother of Jesus Christ but a grace-brother (or grace-sister), which is a far more intimate relationship. From the moment of your Baptism on, whatever you would do would be the same as if Jesus did it, if you willed it so; and whatever Jesus did would be accredited to you, as long as mortal sin would not sever your union with Him.

Through your incorporation in Christ, you share with Him His eternal priesthood. You have the power to offer with Him (as an unbaptized person cannot) adequate worship to God the Father. You have the power to absorb into your soul (as an unbaptized person cannot) the impulses of divine love that we call grace.

The difference between your priesthood and that of the man you call Father is a very narrow difference, even though it is an essential difference. In the sacrament of Holy Orders, he has received the power to consecrate the bread and wine, to perform the specific action by which your priesthood and his, in union with Christ, is made active and effective. His is a sacramental priesthood, while yours is a participating priesthood.

The truth is that you have almost as much to thank God for as does Father Tom or Father Jim, to whom you doff your hat or bow your head. If we were to express your greatness in graphic terms, we could say that the difference between your dignity as a baptized Christian and the dignity of an ordained priest is the distance of one inch. The difference between your dignity and that of an unbaptized person is a hundred miles.

You do not encounter, as does your parish priest, daily reminders of your dignity. But you have as much reason as he to thank God every day for having chosen you, so undeserving, to be His own child. You are a very special object of God's love. You share in His nature. You share in Christ's priesthood. There is so little that could be added to this.

With such equipment, who could fear or hesitate to reach out for sainthood?

About the Author

Fr. Leo J. Trese (1902–1970) poured himself out for Christ's flock and wrote numerous clear, spiritually rich books to inform, inspire, and encourage Christians worldwide. His works have spread throughout the world and have been translated into Spanish, German, French, Italian, and Korean. Suffused with clarity, warm humor, and simple, down-to-earth examples, Fr. Trese's books continue to help today's readers to know and love the Catholic Faith, and to inspire them to live it out in all circumstances.

Sophia Institute

Sophia Institute is a nonprofit institution that seeks to nurture the spiritual, moral, and cultural life of souls and to spread the gospel of Christ in conformity with the authentic teachings of the Roman Catholic Church.

Sophia Institute Press fulfills this mission by offering translations, reprints, and new publications that afford readers a rich source of the enduring wisdom of mankind.

Sophia Institute also operates the popular online resource CatholicExchange.com. *Catholic Exchange* provides world news from a Catholic perspective as well as daily devotionals and articles that will help readers to grow in holiness and live a life consistent with the teachings of the Church.

In 2013, Sophia Institute launched Sophia Institute for Teachers to renew and rebuild Catholic culture through service to Catholic education. With the goal of nurturing the spiritual, moral, and cultural life of souls, and an abiding respect for the role and work of teachers, we strive to provide materials and programs that are at once enlightening to the mind and ennobling to the heart; faithful and complete, as well as useful and practical.

Sophia Institute gratefully recognizes the Solidarity Association for preserving and encouraging the growth of our apostolate over the course of many years. Without their generous and timely support, this book would not be in your hands.

www.SophiaInstitute.com
www.CatholicExchange.com
www.SophiaInstituteforTeachers.org

Sophia Institute Press is a registered trademark of Sophia Institute.
Sophia Institute is a tax-exempt institution as defined by the Internal Revenue Code, Section 501(c)(3). Tax ID 22-2548708.

Make Me

Last Chance Beach

Bonnie Edwards

Published by Bonnie Edwards, 2023.

Table of Contents

This book is dedicated to fathers and stepfathers who give their best, always, even if no one appreciates them.

Maybe especially to men like that.

And for Ted, always.

What readers like you say about Singles Fest at Last Chance Beach...

On Take Me (And My Kids)

Heartwarming. "This is an engaging second chance romance, it is lovingly written about loss, finding love, children and the blending of families and what it entails. This is Eva and Jessie's story how they navigate through all this. It was a great read and I recommend this wonderful story." **5 stars** – Amazon review by Lois

Great family story

Bonnie Edwards has written another heartwarming story featuring well-defined characters that come alive. I enjoyed this story very much and highly recommend it.

5 stars – Bestselling author Caroline Clemmons

Heartwarming ... Touching ... Full of Emotion

"Jesse knows if he is to stand a chance to get through all that 'traffic' in Eva's mind, he needs a plan. And watching that plan unfold will be worth turning the pages."

Quote to remember: Eva sniffed. "I'm pathetic. I'm a mom with no kids. I'm a wife with no husband. And I'm in a battle to save my future with the kids I don't have. No man will want to deal with my huge mess." **5 Stars** – Amazon review by Robbob19

On Fake Me:

This is your sunshiney heroine meets grumpy hero plot and I enjoyed it immensely...Slow burn. Fake relationship. beach romance, summer fling...I enjoyed this book so much.

> **4½ Stars** — The Highland Hussy Blogger/Reviewer at Got Fiction?

The author has crafted a romance with engaging characters who have just the right amount of emotional baggage, conflict, and attraction. You'll keep turning the pages to discover exactly what his fiancée did as well as what molded Farren into the woman she is.

> **5 Stars**—Joan Reeves NYT & USAToday Bestselling Author and Blogger at Slingwords.com

The grumpy boss and fake relationship tropes combine to make a satisfying romance.

4.5 stars! Singles fest was genius[1] – Romance in her Prime

1. https://www.amazon.com/gp/customer-reviews/R1OOLXCK823A6F/ref=cm_cr_dp_d_rvw_ttl?ie=UTF8&ASIN=B097ND7V15

Make Me

The worst thing that could happen to a man who doesn't want children is to inherit two little boys.

The next worst thing would be to have a nanny with a child of her own.

Archie Jones, a wealthy playboy who's never stayed more than two weeks in any one place finds himself saddled with an old friend's four- and six-year-old boys.

When his brother suggests desperate Archie hire his wife's sister, Archie can't say no.

Equally desperate Beth Matthews is appalled that a man who can't remember her name, or show up for family events, is now responsible for the lives of two adorable orphans. When he proposes she join him in a co-parenting partnership, she's torn between her dislike of the man and the obvious needs of the children. Not to mention she's a broke single mom with an explosive secret.

In this forced proximity, enemies-to-lovers romance set in the charming beach town of Last Chance Beach Archie and Beth must find a way to compromise, live together, and always put the needs of their children first.

Archie soon learns he's underestimated mousy Beth while she finds new appreciation for the footloose man who does all he can to build a loving family despite his many failings.

But when Archie suddenly abandons them, will Beth have faith in the changes she's seen in him or will she believe he's returned to his wandering ways?

In Last Chance Beach love always finds a way.

Chapter One

Friday before Memorial Day

"Not to press, Mr. Jones, but the children are with Child Protective Services and need to be dealt with as soon as possible. A group shelter is the best they have with the long weekend upon us. After the holiday, they'll be placed in foster care." The dry-voiced lawyer cleared his throat. "Unless?" The word was pointed. Leading. Hopeful. Damn it.

Archie Jones swiped a hard hand down his face as he stared out the rainswept window. The unseasonably chilly May day blustered. Fitting. Behind him, the lawyer cleared his throat again. The man must have an obstruction, or he wasn't used to dealing in children's lives.

"Only God knows why but Keith entrusted them to me. He didn't want a state-run life for them." Wind buffeted the glass, and a chill went through him. "They deserve better than me, but at least I remember what their father wanted for his family. Which is more than anyone in the foster system will know." Or care about.

Keith Abbott's long-ago vow rang in Archie's head. "One day I'll make a family of my own. And it'll be a happy one." His college buddy—more like a brother, really—had built the family and life he'd wanted. How was he to know it would be cut short at thirty-three? Archie nodded in vague approval at the remembered words and continued to stare out the lawyer's office window at nothing and everything.

His life versus Keith's. His, full of money and excess. Keith's, full of love. Archie wasn't sure real love existed, but apparently, according to Keith, he'd managed to create it. First with Jayda, the only girl to catch his eye and then with their babies.

Unattainable unconditional love. His buddy probably hoarded it, Archie decided with a quiet snort. Keith wasn't a man who let things go. Friends, especially. Over the last ten years, a steady parade of Christmas cards and birthday wishes proved that Keith had wanted to keep their friendship alive. Archie hadn't minded, had enjoyed the periphery of Keith's happy little life.

No matter where he was in the world, Archie could count on hearing from Keith. After college, they'd kept in touch more frequently. He'd even been Keith's best man. But since Archie's life had taken a non-traditional path and he had no similar milestones to celebrate, the contact between them had been reduced to cards and phone calls. Eventually the calls had turned into texts and now those were gone forever.

The last time he'd seen Keith in person was at his wife Jayda's memorial four years ago. A walking ghost, Keith had cried in Archie's arms. Great sobs of grief. No one expected a healthy woman to die in childbirth these days.

Archie had certainly not expected a man in his prime to die while he waited for a heart transplant. He'd have bought Keith a heart if he'd known how dire the need had been. His fingers clenched and he wanted to punch the glass and shatter it, take out the whole window in one wild swing.

But the lawyer shuffled paper again and indulged in more throat clearing. It was a holiday weekend, and the man must have plans.

"Mr. Jones? I know this is a shock."

"You have no idea." His mind reeled at how this disaster would impact his own life. *Bad things happen to good people every day.* Of course, he knew it, intellectually, but enormous responsibility wasn't his thing. Even minor responsibilities were shirked if he wasn't in the mood.

Keith, what were you thinking? You knew how I live, how I am.

"What about Jayda's side of the family?" He vaguely recalled Keith mentioning grandparents.

"They're older and have serious health issues. But they've asked for updates, pictures, that kind of thing."

"Of course."

He wanted to walk out of this office, flip off the lawyer, and leave Keith's boys to the mercies of the state. But he couldn't, of course he couldn't. He closed his eyes, tilted his forehead to the cold glass. The storm inside his head brewed into a tempest.

Could the opposite be true? Could good things happen to bad people? Keith must have believed it because he'd bequeathed the two best things that had happened to him to Archie. His buddy had loved his boys fiercely and had called them the light of his life.

He snorted less quietly this time, convinced this was a cosmic joke and he'd get the punchline soon. *Keith, you want to make me a father? No way.* No one could make him be a father. Not even Keith.

"There are two of them?" He didn't bother to turn because he was sure he hadn't missed the birth of a whole person. Keith would've told him if there were three. The efficient, dry lawyer was simply tidying up the most important details of Keith's life. The small stuff, like money, didn't concern Archie. The children's futures, their *lives,* were now in Archie's hands. "And what are their names?"

He couldn't remember.

Paper shuffling. "Jeremy Archibald Abbott and Duncan Keith Abbott."

Archie closed his eyes. God help them all.

He drew in a breath, held it for a three count.

Then changed his life forever.

"THOSE POOR CHILDREN," Beth Matthews said on a long breath. Her heart twisted for the orphans. "But Archie *Jones*?" She shook her head, but her sister couldn't see it over the phone. She passed her daughter another chunk of apple and watched as Ryley dropped it to the table. She was full and would soon climb down from her booster seat.

"I know," Karly responded in an identical sympathy-laden tone. "Their dad went into hospital and died. He was widowed and had no other family. The boys would've gone into foster care."

"I'm sorry their dad's gone but *Archie*? Who would leave children to a man like him? He's pretty much useless in the responsible behavior department." Surely their father would've realized what a disaster the man was.

"Beth! He isn't as bad as all that. He just hasn't found what he needs yet. I'm sure he'll do fine for these boys. Look at Bret, he's a great husband and father."

Ryley climbed down to the floor and took off at a dead run for her toybox. That would give Beth a few more minutes to chat.

"Archie is nothing like Bret," she stated. "Besides, Bret was smart enough to find you in college. Smart enough to marry you as soon as he could." Her sister always made excuses for Archie, Bret's brother. But Beth recognized a loser when she saw one. Even ridiculously wealthy families produced losers sometimes.

A thirty-three-year-old man who lived off a trust fund and never settled anywhere for more than a week or two was a loser in Beth's books. It wasn't money that he'd earned, after all. Not only had he never worked a day, but he'd wandered the globe since college like a teen having a gap year.

"You're a romantic," she declared. "You probably think that if Archie finds the right woman he'll grow up and be a decent man. Not gonna happen, Karly." But her sister never gave up on him and invited him to their family functions, children's birthdays, and school plays. Beth shook her head again because her sister was in for a rude awakening.

Archie was bound to mess up with these boys and Karly would finally see the truth. With a sniff, Beth decided she'd refrain from saying I told you so.

"What's Archie's plan now?"

"He's taking them to a resort in Last Chance Beach."

A resort. Of course. Another temporary place that, while beautiful and fun, was not a permanent home. Archie Jones had no home, hadn't bothered to get an apartment of his own. She blew a raspberry into the phone.

Karly chuckled. "Give the man a break. He's only had them a couple of hours. He called us right away."

"Potty!" Ryley yelled from across the room.

"Gotta run," she said and disconnected to the sound of her sister's laughter.

One successful potty session later and she put Ryley down for her nap. Time to check in with her employment agency and continue her job search. She settled in front of her laptop at her desk and ignored the past due notices that sat in a small pile on the corner. When they refused to be ignored, she slid them behind the laptop screen out of sight.

Handling the bookkeeping for Karly's video channel and uploading to her sister's social media accounts gave her busywork to do but didn't pay for much more than groceries. Mostly, helping Karly was a labor of love and she was happy to be of help.

But she needed full-time work that paid well. Her condo was perfect, and she loved the cozy two-bedroom space.

She logged onto the agency's site and went to her account. The good news was that she had an interview to prepare for, but the bad news was that two interesting jobs had gone to other people. Apparently, they'd been serious when they said they wanted degrees.

Not for the first time, she regretted her impulsive decision to step into the workforce before she graduated.

She wasn't an impulsive person, but when she took a hard look at her decisions, she saw the lie. Leaving college had been impulsive and she was paying for it now. And her next impulsive choice had given her Ryley. Being a single mother was never part of her life plan, but here she was.

She shook off her doubt and set aside the concern that she wouldn't get a job in time to save her home. She didn't have time to let fear paralyze her. This interview on Monday had to pan out.

It had to.

FOUR HOURS LATER...

Jeremy, who said he was six, and Duncan, four, came with a backpack and a re-usable grocery bag each. Archie had rented a minivan and dragged the rental guy along to help with the car seats. He'd expected a full complement of toys and kid gear. The youngest had a stuffed bunny and a half-shredded baby blanket with him. Jeremy had nothing but his bags. And soulful eyes that mourned.

Too much for a six-year-old to bear. It was hard to look at the kid. But when he held out his hand to shake, Archie obliged.

Duncan's hand was smaller, and his eyes filled with tears when they shook hands. He sniffled and drew in a big breath to try and look brave.

Archie recognized the expression because he'd worn the identical one for weeks when he'd been sent away. He hadn't been much older than Duncan. With awkward wonder, Archie patted his little head. Small comfort, but it was all he had to give.

Their caseworker stood to the side, observing the initial meet. He glanced over at her and got a nod.

"You look alike," he said, attempting a smile. Keith's stamp was all over them, from their dimpled chins to their sturdy bodies to their brown hair. Keith had been solid with a barrel chest and built for wrestling. "You look like your dad. He was one of my best friends."

Jeremy nodded. "He told us you met in college, and you were nice to him." His lip quivered. "He said you'd be nice to us, too."

Now it was his turn to try and look brave. "I'll do my best," he said hollowly. Solemnly.

He wondered what the boys saw when they looked at him. Each one seemed resigned to their fate.

After he'd told the lawyer his decision, he signed a lot of paperwork. The minor details of Keith's life, like the disposition of his belongings and assets hardly made a dent in Archie's mind. The whole thing was a blur. Like much of his life.

The door to the lawyer's office had opened and a woman from the government came in and explained that their father had told them who Archie was. She said the boys were with a caseworker and he hated hearing it. The caseworker had been called and he arranged to have them handed off at the nearest car rental agency.

Keith's boys were coming to him in a place where people paid for short-term cars. Vaguely, he understood that his name and money meant no one would look too closely at the kind of home he'd provide. They all assumed he had a house and could give the boys whatever they'd need. Aside from material things he had no idea what they needed.

He frowned, startling the caseworker. He understood that he'd never been loved as a kid. That he'd denied his need for it as a man. But could he dredge up love from his hollow heart? Was there any left in there to give Keith's boys?

The caseworker sighed and stepped toward him. "I'll leave you to it, Mr. Jones." She patted the boys' shoulders. "Be good boys, please."

She walked to her car and then turned back. “Oh, and the rabbit and blanket should be kept for as long as Duncan needs them.”

“Where are their toys? Their gear?”

She shook her head, and he learned kids weren’t allowed to go into emergency care with their bikes or trikes. All their toys had been lost in the bureaucratic shuffle.

And then she was gone.

Two little boys dumped on him with no more than a hasty goodbye and an apologetic smile. After all, it was Friday afternoon of a holiday weekend, and everyone was in a hurry to finish their workweek.

The lawyer had blathered about selling Keith’s possessions. Archie imagined the kids’ toys were included in those possessions and gone forever.

He vaguely remembered the lawyer mentioning insurance and trusts for the boys. The minutiae of a young father’s life. He’d sort it out later when he could think.

As soon as he found a place to live that suited Jeremy and Duncan, he’d buy them new gear. Whatever they needed for as long as they needed it.

He decided that phrase was a good mantra.

Chapter Two

It was after dark when Archie pulled into a space in the parking lot of the Sands Resort in Last Chance Beach. He shut off the ignition, and he pressed the button to open the back hatch door. He'd never imagined driving a minivan. The rental clerk had steered him toward a large SUV, but when Jeremy told him Keith drove a minivan, he'd chosen this one.

He climbed out and slid open the side door. The action roused the boys from long naps. They both stretched in their seats and looked around sleepily. Sympathy pinched his heart. Whenever these kids looked around; they were somewhere they'd never been before.

Sure, it suited him to change locations regularly, to wander the globe looking for whatever was missing in his life, but these boys deserved better. They deserved the life their dad had planned to give them, and that meant a stable home.

He could give them a house, toys, food, and clothing. But a home? The concept eluded him. Archie Jones had no clue what a stable, loving home looked like.

"I can get out myself," Jeremy said, who sat in a raised seat with little arms. The guy at the rental office called it a booster seat. The clerk had explained that Jeremy was too short to use it in the front seat. He needed to grow taller and be heavier to move to shotgun.

The younger boy sat buckled into a monstrous contraption that looked like a space engineer had designed it. Apparently, this was regulation size for a kid his height and weight. But since it was rented how could he be sure? More research.

No way would he drive these boys around in a vehicle that wasn't safe. He scrubbed his hand through his hair to help perk him up.

There was a reason he wasn't a father and never wanted to be. The strategic thinking felt heavy and made his head hurt. Other men fell into fatherhood smoothly. Men like his brother made it look simple, but there were unforeseen pitfalls that could make a man walk away. He never wanted to be that man, so fatherhood was off the table.

Until now.

Putting the lives of children into his hands was a serious error in judgment. But there was no one to explain this to. He'd been given these children and would keep them safe, no matter what he had to do.

He shuffled to the side to give Jeremy room to bound out of the van. Apparently, he was perfectly capable of unlocking the regular seatbelt that had held him in place. That part seemed easy. Inside, he groaned at having to face the confusing straps and buckles of Duncan's seat.

"We're here to spend a few nights until I find us a permanent house. Okay?"

"Don't you got a house?" The younger one wanted to know. He slid open the door only to see Duncan already standing. He'd unbuckled himself.

The kid was four and he was free in a heartbeat. A cold shiver ran the length of Archie's spine, and his heart moved into his throat.

"Is it okay that you can do that?" He touched one of the straps that lay loose on the seat of the contraption.

Jeremy explained, "Duncan's smart and he knows the straps stay on until the car stops. Dad made sure we followed the rules about cars."

Duncan piped up. "Don't be scared. Daddy told us you might be."

That gave him pause. "He did?" *Keith, why didn't you tell me you had a time bomb in your chest?* He'd had some messages from Keith about the guardianship of his boys, but he'd never explained why except to say that since he was a single parent, it made sense to have a plan.

Keith hadn't lied, exactly, but he'd withheld the truth about his health. Still, a better man would've asked questions, but Archie hadn't bothered. Not once.

Archie gave Jeremy a sharp glance. The boy confirmed his brother's statement with a terse nod, his eyes wide and solemn. He'd told his sons that Archie might be scared. Keith had known him better than he thought.

"Of course, he did." Archie answered his own question. "I'm glad he taught you about car safety and these buckles and straps. Your dad wanted you safe." And well-fed and loved and happy. He ignored the voice in his head that chided Keith for trusting the likes of him with the most important people in his life. Duncan jumped down and scooted to the back of the van, blanket trailing on the ground. Jeremy followed immediately.

He slid the door shut and got on his haunches to face the boys.

"Your dad was a smart man to teach you all this." Odd, but he had a feeling Keith meant to teach him a thing or two as well. "He was right about me. I'm a little scared. I'm not a dad so I'm not smart about kids."

"Don't worry, we'll help," Jeremy said blithely.

When the trio walked into the building, the boys' eyes went wide as they took in the size and opulence of the lobby. Their jaws fell open in childlike wonder. He guessed Keith's budget hadn't stretched to five-star resorts.

He hid a grin to pause and look at the place with fresh eyes. Marble floors and columns, potted palms, and a view through the dining room to the pool and the ocean beyond.

"This is fancy," Jeremy shouted in approval. Duncan stared mutely. A second later he pulled a corner of his blanket to his cheek.

"I guess it is," Archie responded, shuddering inside with Duncan's actions. *Why would he want that filthy rag anywhere near his face?*

When the caseworker had handed them off, she'd mentioned that the blanket was important to the kid. He shrugged. The bunny he understood, having had a stuffed raccoon named Rocky when he was young, but the blanket was a mystery to be solved later.

For now, he just wanted to get them upstairs and into bed.

"Mr. Jones, your suite is ready as you requested. I see you've brought some friends this time." The woman at the desk was at an age that veered toward matronly and the look on her face was kind and interested.

He glanced at her nametag. "Thanks Janise. These are my wards, Jeremy, and Duncan. Could you have dinner sent up?" Wards. The word stopped him cold. "That's not right. These are my boys." He had to start thinking of them as his own.

"We're offering a prime rib dinner tonight, but I have a feeling these two may prefer chicken strips and fries?" The question was directed at the boys, who cheered in reply. "With dipping sauce?"

"Honey mustard, please," Jeremy replied for both of them. His respect and manners shone through, and Archie turned his face away to hide his rapid blinking. Keith had started them on the right path, but could Archie keep them on it?

An hour later, both boys had polished off their meals and were eying the brownies Janise had just had delivered. She must have children this age in her life because she'd picked the perfect food.

Maybe he needed a Janise. A motherly type who knew more about children than he did. "If you have room for those brownies, you may have them now." If they didn't have room, there was always breakfast.

"Are we getting a bath?" Duncan asked, reaching for one of the gooey looking treats. A second later, he took a big bite and smeared chocolate icing across his mouth and half of his cheeks.

Archie bit back a grin. "That brownie looks too big for you to eat by yourself. Maybe I should finish it for you?" As expected, he got an emphatic headshake in answer.

He looked at Jeremy. "Do you need baths?"

Jeremy shrugged because his mouth was full.

He hadn't considered their nighttime routine. "Did you have one last night?"

Jeremy swallowed, his face no cleaner than his brother's. "No."

"But you had a bath the night before?"

"Uh unh."

"Then, yes, Duncan, you're having baths. Finish your brownies and I'll be right back. And stay at the table until I return." He didn't need chocolate smeared around the room from gooey fingers.

He strode from the living room into the bedroom, where he called the front desk. "Janise, the boys need a bath. Is there anything I should know?" He did not care how stupid he sounded. He had a feeling Janise would understand. After all, the woman had sent them brownies without being asked. She knew things he'd never know.

"They can go in together to play a bit. The water shouldn't be near the rim. They'll splash. And normally I'd say bubble bath, but the shower gel may sting their eyes, so no bubbles."

"Okay. Do I need to do anything?" He had no idea if they could wash themselves.

"Soap up a facecloth and run it over their bodies. Make sure their feet and toes are clean too. The older boy may not need your help. But stay in the bathroom to supervise." She chuckled. "You'll be fine. I take it these boys have recently come to you?"

"I'm a freshly minted guardian, as of this afternoon."

Long pause while she digested the information. "Do you need me to come up there?"

The woman was a goddess. A savior.

"I want to say no, but I'm out of my depth." At least he was smart enough to accept his limitations. That should be helpful for the next twenty years or so. The enormity of what he faced staggered him. For a moment, he wanted to curse his old friend. Leaving these two beautiful boys to him was asinine. He'd always believed Keith was smart.

"Give me twenty minutes," Janise said, pulling him out of his useless thoughts.

Another hour later and he accepted the truth. He couldn't bribe, cajole, or beg enough to hire Janise away from The Sands. Her children were high schoolers and while she remembered this younger time in their lives fondly, there was no way she wanted to deal with little children again. Besides, her job at the Sands suited her family life to a tee.

"You need a nanny," she said. "A live-in since the boys are young." They sat at the dining table away from Jeremy and Duncan who were now clean from tip to toe and snuggled together on the pull-out sofa watching a cartoon show. Soft giggles and comments said they were still awake, long after Janise considered a decent bedtime for growing boys.

"Not to mention, they haven't had a woman in their lives in too long. They don't remember their mother." She kept her voice soft. She'd done the hands-on in the bath and had asked them simple questions. "Is she out of the picture?"

Archie had listened and learned how to handle bath time. It wouldn't be long before he could trust Jeremy on his own, but Duncan wasn't interested in using the washcloth for anything but a hat. But Janise had asked a question about Jayda. Pretty Jayda who'd given her life to bring her baby into the world.

"Keith became a widower when Duncan was born."

Her eyes went wide with sympathy and concern. "And their father?"

"Undetected heart problem from childhood apparently. He got on the wait list for a transplant, but he didn't last long enough." Keith had been upbeat about life. He probably decided he'd get a new heart in time and live to see his boys grow up.

But just in case, he'd mentioned the guardianship clause in passing. He'd made it seem like a trivial detail that any widower would put into place.

"For the rest of my life, I'll regret not asking for more info. I should've known Keith was hedging, done something to help, spent time with Keith." He raised his gaze to Janise's. "I should know his boys already. They should know me, but here we are, strangers."

Janise's hand suddenly covered his and her eyes showed deep concern. "You can make that time up now with these wonderful boys."

All he could do was nod.

"I assumed he was diligent about his children, and making arrangements that we'd never need. Keith was like that. Thoughtful about life." He mentally shook himself. "Of course, I agreed." He'd been stupid and wasted time while his buddy needed him. "If I'd been a better man..."

"Clearly, Keith believed you were plenty good enough." Her sigh resonated with compassion. "You may not know them, but they know you. Your friend talked about you a lot and he prepared them for this time. Their dad advised them as best he could." She stifled a yawn. "Sorry, it's been a long day. I suggest you talk with them about what Keith said to help them through this."

He nodded, struck dumb by everything that faced him. He turned and watched the boys for a long moment as Janise said goodnight to them. He walked her to the door.

"I may need another rescue. May I call you for advice?"

"Of course." She paused at the open door. Turned to him again. Her eyes soft with sympathy, she said, "Mostly, children need the adults in their lives to show up. To openly care about them, give them rules to live by, but room to grow and learn, too."

"All that? At the same time?"

She chuckled. "One day at a time, Mr. Jones."

"I'm out of my depth. Don't have a clue what I'm doing."

"All new parents feel that way. But you'll find your path."

They exchanged phone numbers and his lifeline walked out the door, leaving him to his responsibilities. He dropped his head to rest against the door as he considered Janise's recommendations.

He'd need a bedtime routine and to stick to it. Had to learn what food they required for healthy growth, needed to get them bikes and whatever other gear boys their age liked. Overcome, he let his shoulders sag. Keith had had so much to live for.

More than anything, Archie wanted to give them the life and the love Keith wanted them to have.

Janise's final words as they exchanged contact information rang true. "Look for a nanny ASAP, or you'll feel overwhelmed by the day-to-day and that's when mistakes and accidents happen."

Chapter Three

Sunday morning…

"Why have I been summoned?" Archie asked Bret. His brother grinned and opened the door to them. A three-hour drive was a big deal with two kids. He considered it quite an accomplishment this early on a Sunday.

"You need help, and we've got the answer."

Curious, he guided the boys into the house. Inside, he kept his hands on their shoulders in case they bolted back outdoors. Not that they'd done anything like that, but now would be a bad time to be introduced to the tactic.

He'd figured out in the two days he'd had them, that Jeremy and Duncan were cautious around strangers. He thanked Keith again for having the foresight to tell them about Archie.

"Of course, I need help," he muttered as he ushered the boys ahead of him into the living room on the left of the entry. "That's why I've set up nanny interviews."

Janise had dug up some employment agencies and he'd set a plan into motion. He wanted a woman like Janise. Nothing else would do. She'd bake cookies, know what to feed them, when to hug them, and be ready to retire with a nice pension when the boys left for college.

"Problem solved, Bro. We've got the perfect woman for you."

Archie snorted and looked into the living room to greet Karly. He slammed to a halt when he saw the other woman on the sofa. She stood and looked somewhere over his left shoulder, unable to meet his eyes.

It was—damn—her name escaped him. He'd forgotten Karly's mousy sister whose name started with a B. The one who hated him for no reason he could discern. He'd never done anything to earn her low opinion. At least nothing she'd know about.

Beth—yes, he was certain now—Beth was the quiet, studious one, while Karly was outgoing and friendly. Two sisters; sunlight and shadow.

Karly invited him to every birthday party, special event, and every sport her boys attempted. He'd been invited despite how rarely he accepted. He loved Karly, his sister by marriage, for every kindness she extended.

But Beth? Boring and dull, the proof was in her long, shapeless beige dress that covered her in blah. He couldn't recall even a glimpse of her curves. Maybe she didn't have any.

A girl child peeked out from behind her legs. Golden hair, two fingers stuck in her mouth and wide brown eyes.

An image of Janise flashed before his eyes. *She* was the perfect woman to nanny his children and Beth was...Beth. Boring, judgmental Beth.

And Beth came with a kid of her own. A vague recollection passed through his mind and inside he nodded. She'd chosen to have a child alone some time back. Probably because no man was good enough to partner with.

Everything stilled while Archie and Beth took each other's measure.

As usual, he didn't measure up.

THESE WERE THE BOYS left to the care of Archie Jones, Beth thought on sight. *Poor kids.* They'd lost both parents and were locked into life with a man who'd never be around. They'd be lonely, unloved, unwanted. She shuddered inside as she wondered what that would do to a child.

She didn't have far to look to see the effects. Archie and his brother came from just such a background. The wealth of the Jones family was legendary, but too was the lack of care given to their children.

Archie flitted from place to place, never landed, never stayed, never engaged in the day-to-day of life.

The marvel was that Bret, her brother-in-law, was nothing like Archie. Bret was a good family man who made an effort to be wherever he was needed. Karly was a lucky woman to love and be loved by a man like Bret Jones.

But she wasn't sure why they'd gathered here. Normally, she'd only see Archie at holiday dinners. Seeing him with the boys he'd been saddled with surprised her. She'd expected them to be shipped off by now.

"Hello," the bigger of the two boys said. He looked about six or seven while his younger brother's face was changing from toddler cute to sturdy boy. They looked shy and interested at the same time.

"Hello," Beth responded in a friendly tone. Ryley, half hidden in her skirt, giggled.

Archie, tall and heartbreakingly handsome, strode into the room. The boys followed a couple of paces behind, but they still looked interested.

"Beth, hello. Nice to see you again." His deep voice radiated warmth she'd never heard before. In fact, she couldn't recall ever being directly addressed by the man. But Archie Jones was a charmer and she'd always been leery of charmers. They rarely had what she thought of as substance.

She tossed him a glance that called him a liar—he'd never considered it nice to see her— and then focused on removing Ryley's sticky hand from her skirt. At two and a half, her daughter felt in awe of older children and turned shy. She jammed her face into Beth's leg. The damp from her mouth soaked through the material. Great, a blob of slobber, snot, and cookie crumbs now decorated her long skirt. At least the blob would match the one on her shoulder.

For a flash, Archie looked appalled at the mess. Inside, maybe outside, too, she smirked at his expression. If he thought this was messy wait until he cleaned up around a toilet bowl. Boys their age had lousy aim.

Except he'd have staff for the messy bits of life with children. Assuming he kept them, of course.

Last time she'd seen Archie he'd blown into a family birthday dinner late smelling of expensive perfume from a woman he'd probably left asleep. He'd clearly just remembered it was his mother's sixty-fifth birthday. Not that Celeste Jones deserved to be celebrated, but still.

He'd arrived without a gift and had obviously forgotten Beth's name. His gaze had skipped over her, as if she didn't register as a person, let alone a woman. Since his mother called her Elizabeth, despite having been told her full name was Bethany, he'd finally twigged to her name. They were a pair, his mother and him.

And this man was responsible for the care, feeding, and nurturing of these two gorgeous children.

But she couldn't think of them. Couldn't let their situation get in the way of her goal, because all she wanted was to learn why her sister had called her here and then leave for home.

She needed to prepare for her job interview on Monday. That was her only focus. Without that job, her life would fall apart. Her mortgage payment loomed. She'd been late with her payment last month, and she had to find a way to catch up or she'd be forced to sell the condo. There wasn't enough equity in it to give her a stake for a rental.

Moving home with her parents was impossible. They were ready to retire and downsize and she couldn't interfere with their plans. Her heart rate picked up just thinking of what that job meant to her. She patted Ryley's head, running her fingers through her child's soft curls.

"I need to get home," she blurted into the round of greetings that floated to the ceiling. At Karly's urging the boys had disappeared into the playroom off the entry. The former den had once been her sister's home office, but now it had a more fun function, and the sounds of laughter lifted her spirits. Her niece and nephew were happy, friendly and the perfect ages to play with Archie's poor charges.

"You can stay for half an hour," Karly coaxed. "This won't take long, I promise." But Karly's eyes didn't meet hers and Beth went on alert.

Something was up. Her sister avoiding her eyes meant Karly felt guilty. It dawned on her that none of the adults had taken seats or moved around the room. They stood, like her, waiting.

"Bret, what's going on?" Archie demanded. Suspicion dripped like melted tar from each word. She felt the same way.

"Since the kids are out of the room, we'll get right to it." Bret looked at his wife and nodded. "Beth needs a job and Archie needs help with the boys. Live-in help."

When he waved his hands like a maestro, Beth's jaw dropped open in shock. She hadn't taken a live-in position since she'd bought her condo. She shook her head before the words of denial could form in her mouth. Her sister expected her to chain herself to this man.

"How do you mean that Beth needs a job?" Archie frowned. "Isn't she an assistant or something?"

"Or something," Karly muttered, making it clear she'd never told Archie about her career choice. Beth had suspected Karly's support of her impulsive choice was out of loyalty and not because Karly agreed with her leaving school.

"*She* is standing right here." She raised her chin and glared at Archie to shut his mouth. But the man couldn't take a hint. She shifted her glare to Karly, who had thankfully gone quiet.

"Why would she quit a job when she has a child? I heard she'd planned..." The doofus suddenly noticed that three people now glared at him and let his voice trail off.

The jerk was painfully slow to catch on. She was thirty-two years old. Of course, when she found herself pregnant, she let her family believe she'd chosen to have a child on her own. Deliberately and with forethought. That was infinitely better than them knowing the truth.

"Oh," the doofus said, looking contrite. "Things change and the market's volatile and..." he trailed off again. Suddenly, he brightened and clapped his hands. He made for her, lifted his hand as if to offer a handshake.

When she didn't react, he let his hand fall to his side. "This is a good solution to both our problems. I have a place to live for now that's suitable for a family, there's room for you and your little girl." His gaze flashed to Ryley, and he smiled gently. "We'll work out the details between us."

"I have a condo. That's where we live. I'm not moving." The interview on Monday promised to be the answer to her problems. She had to give it a shot.

This was not the time to jump at this ridiculous offer that she wasn't sure had been made. Archie had clapped his hands. Was he a genie? Did he think that whatever idea formed in his head was golden?

"Explain what exactly you mean," she demanded.

"Of course," Archie said with an oily smile. "I need a live-in nanny and since you need a job, you can move in with us. As for your condo, you could rent it out. Between rental income and your salary, you'll probably do better than if you found another job and lived alone." He peered down his nose at Ryley and then did something she never dreamed she'd see.

He crouched in front of her little girl and held out his hand. Ryley held out hers and they shook. He was gentle and smiled warmly. Ryley giggled again, then hid her face.

"This is insane. We don't like each other," Beth snapped. She blew her bangs off her forehead. *Wow. Had that just popped out?*

"No daycare fees. No commute time." Karly now, apparently taking Archie's side. And how had he agreed so quickly? He must be desperate to go along with this.

She understood desperation. It breathed down her neck. But could she bear to be around Archie Jones on a daily basis? Something of her thoughts must show on her face because her sister brightened, and Bret nodded like a bobblehead.

Her sister continued. "We can't see a downside. Can you?" The question was aimed at Beth and pressure built behind her eyes as the other three adults stared at her. Tension strung between her and Archie like a livewire. "And with Beth's experience, this is a no-brainer."

"I guess you didn't hear me say we don't like each other."

"What experience?" Archie said right over her.

Karly blew a raspberry and answered Beth. "That'll change. You two hardly ever see each other. You actually have a lot in common. I'm sure you'll become friends."

They must have worn identical shocked expressions because his response mirrored hers. Consternation and a deep frown, aimed directly at their respective siblings.

Slowly the three of them turned their gazes to hers.

Bret, the traitor, clapped his brother on the shoulder. "Beth isn't an assistant, exactly. She helps Karly with her bookkeeping and other things. She has a head for stats, and numbers and Karly needs the help. So, Beth assists her." He grinned wide. "But her real career is nanny. She's worked for several high-profile couples."

Bret had just nailed her to the floor and Archie's eyes narrowed as he took in this new information. Then his gaze swept back to Ryley, and she watched the gears in his head turn.

Beth hated being the center of attention. Give her a wall covered in a beige flower print wallpaper and she'd wear a beige flower print blouse. Happily.

"I need to think about it," she murmured.

He didn't seem to see that he should stop talking. "I'm desperate for help, Beth. Janise won't change jobs although she'd be perfect. And these boys have never known a mother's love." At that, he eyed her.

She had no idea who Janise was, but she wouldn't ask. She doubted Archie had ever heard the word no in his life. Especially for something he wanted desperately.

Ten minutes later, Beth still vacillated between yes and no with equal ferocity. She didn't speak about her inner battle. Losing her condominium because she had no job. Past due notices piled up and hidden behind her monitor. All those things emphasized the advantages of living and working for Archie, a man she'd rarely see. Once she was hired, he'd be free to make himself scarce.

He could go back to his lifestyle and never give the boys another thought.

Archie was a dog with a bone and repeated his three key points. Desperation. Janise. And no mom.

How could such a lazy wanderer could be this persistent?

On the surface, nannying for him seemed like a good opportunity, but over time she'd come to hate living-in and had vowed she wouldn't do it again. There were too many pitfalls living with a family. She'd fallen into the largest one imaginable and would do anything to avoid that kind of danger.

But there was Ryley. More than anything else she couldn't fail Ryley. She eased her hold on her daughter's shoulder and contemplated the boys losing first their mom and now, their father.

Karly dragged Bret off to the kitchen to 'help' her get coffee for the adults and snacks for the children.

She and Archie faced off, he with a smooth smile, she maintaining her cool detachment. At least on the surface.

Archie claimed to want the children he'd inherited. But it wouldn't last, and what kind of example would he be for the boys? And for how long? Sooner or later, he'd ship them off. That was just who he was.

She shouldn't look at this as a long-term commitment, but a bridge to a better situation and a way to keep her home and her credit score in decent shape. Six months. A year at most.

"Jeremy and Duncan need more than I can give them," he was saying. She couldn't resist a light snort. "You can help me round out their lives."

Clearly, in the days since he got them, he'd learned something about his failings as a human being. Archie understood his limitations and was thinking of Jeremy and Duncan instead of his dissolute, selfish lifestyle.

"If I had a wife, it would be easier," he explained. "But I'm on my own and lost." He cleared his throat. "Look, right now we're in a suite at a resort. Just until I can move to a house I'm borrowing. The boys sleep on a pull-out sofa in the living room. The first night was fine. They slept like the dead."

"But?" There had to be a but. His eyes told her there was more. And already he had plans to move them around, keeping them rootless.

"Last night, I felt them climb into bed with me. Nearly made me jump out of my skin. Why would they do that? Then they sniffled and sobbed. Both of them, one on each side. Two kids crying in surround sound."

Not what she needed to hear. *Poor babies*. Her heart cracked. "What did you do?"

"Patted them both on the back until they toned it down to a dull white noise. When they finally conked out, I went to sleep on the sofa."

"Were they okay this morning?"

"By three a.m. they were with me again."

She ducked her head and blinked. "They miss their father. I'm sure when they were scared, they climbed in with him."

Archie frowned. "Kids do that?"

"Didn't you?"

"When I was that young, I don't think I knew where my father's room was. He stayed in another wing until he was gone one day."

"So, your mom's bed?" But she already knew the answer. Karly had told her the loneliest, saddest stories she'd ever heard about Bret's family home. She put up her hand to stop his reply. "Don't bother, I get it."

He hadn't just offered her a well-paid job and place to live, he was giving her the opportunity to make a real difference for these boys who'd already lost more than was bearable.

"Look, if I hire a stranger, they'll expect to move on. But with you..."

She gasped at the implied insult. "You don't think I'll want a life of my own?"

He ran a hand down his face. "That came out wrong. With you, there will be more than a contract, there will be real affection, honest caring. At least, that's the impression of you I've had over the years. We're already extended family."

Which could be the biggest problem. If things didn't work out, they had Karly and Bret to consider. This could be an unholy mess.

Chapter Four

Archie watched the play of emotions cross Beth's face. He saw sympathy, interest, doubt, and concern. When he'd told her about the way the boys had climbed into bed with him, her features had crumpled into some emotion he couldn't read.

Everything Bret had told him about Beth made her the least-interesting woman Archie knew. Most of the time, he'd tuned out his brother whenever her name came up. Some nuggets rose out of the depths of memory. Beth was motherly. Sweet. Kind.

He had no experience of women like her. No idea what to expect from them except boredom.

All he knew was that he wanted her in his life for the boys' sakes. They were the ones who needed a woman like her. He didn't and he never had.

"Well? What do you say?"

"I need more time. You're asking a lot."

"Yes, I am. But if it helps, I believe their father would've picked a woman like you if he'd had more time. The boys should know what a mother's love feels like. Can you give them that?" He'd expected the hunt to take a while, maybe months, but Beth had wanted a baby enough to go it alone by choice. That made her mommy material in his eyes. If Keith met her, he'd say the same.

She bowed her head. "I need a day to consider. Tomorrow I'll know my answer."

"I can give you a day." He'd get her contact information and stay in touch. She needed to know more, to understand how committed he was. He needed her to see the boys needing her, too. "Here's my number. Call anytime." He held out his phone and raised a brow in question.

She took it and put her number in, then fished hers out of a pocket in her skirt. Now he was armed and ready. When he finished, she'd have no resistance left.

Bret and Karly returned, laden with trays of coffee and cookies. They set them on the coffee table. After that, he explained about the island called Last Chance Beach where he planned to live with the boys and their nanny and her little girl Ryley.

"It's still sleepy but on the verge of big changes."

Karly broke in when he took a breath. "We've been there. It's lovely. Remember when you told me about Singles Fest, and I posted about what a great idea it is? The owner, Farren gave us a weekend with the group, and we had a wonderful time. We stayed at that motel, The Landseer, where most of the families stay." Her smile was full of fond remembrance of the '60s era motel, where he planned to stay with the boys. There was a house attached to the motel that he could use until he found a permanent home.

Karly's happy expression eased Archie's mind. Surely, Beth would listen to her sister.

"With tourism kicking up and new resorts being built, it's a good time to buy land, and build a home where we can all live." Selling her on Last Chance Beach should be the easiest part.

"You and me, together. Co-parenting." She seemed to need clarification. "In a house you have custom built?" She sounded skeptical.

He nodded. "Co-parents. I hadn't thought of it in those terms, but yes. I like the idea of co-parenting. A nanny is a caregiver, but Jeremy and Duncan need a woman who cares." If Keith had found a woman like Beth, he'd have given the boys a stepmom. But when his wife died, Keith had had his hands full with a newborn and a toddler. He decided to wait until the boys were older, but time ran out.

Beth snorted lightly. *Again.* She needed more convincing.

"It's not called Last Chance Beach for nothing. People find their lives changed. My buddy Jesse, did. The same for Grady O'Hara. Heard of him?" He didn't think that falling in love and marrying would impress her as a life change. She was the least romance-oriented woman he'd met. Not that he'd ever given her much thought. Her choosing to have her child alone showed she hadn't wanted to wait for romance to find her. She didn't want the traditional kind of life. He could relate. Tying himself to one place held no appeal.

But a home with kids in it who needed him? That was another thing entirely. Maybe he hadn't chosen that kind of life, but that didn't mean he was immune to the charm. He'd do whatever was best for Keith's kids. No question. With any luck, they'd be in college before they figured out what a terrible choice he was for guardian.

Beth tilted her head. "You're talking about the business tycoon who lost his fiancée the night before their wedding." Her expression opened, looked interested. "Everyone heard about that. It was tragic."

He nodded. What happened to Grady should never happen to anyone. "What few people know is that he holed up in The Landseer for months. When he emerged, he married Farren, owner of Singles Fest and his future righted itself."

She looked doubtful, but still interested. "These two told me about Last Chance Beach and Karly's subscribers increase dramatically whenever she posts about Singles Fest."

"Let me tell you about the house at the motel." He gave her the pertinent details. "Three bedrooms upstairs and a main floor study that has a closet. That could be your room." Jesse and Eva had stayed there while her cottage underwent renovations.

"I'm sure the house is fine," she muttered. "Why do you think Last Chance Beach is a good place to raise kids?"

"Because Jesse and Eva say it is. They met when he and I bumped into Farren and Eva during a planning session and we helped them out. That's when I suggested Karly might mention the dating app on her channel and social media." He'd visited the island a few times, but naturally, hadn't bothered to check out the family-friendly places. His focus had been on bars, women, and fishing. Not always in that order.

"I'll get back to you tomorrow. I promise."

He was already thinking of ways to sway her between now and then.

"Tomorrow, I'm taking them to a petting zoo. Care to come along?"

"No, thanks. I want a quiet day to ponder my future without you interrupting me."

Not a chance, woman. Not a chance.

MONDAY, NOON

Beth closed the lid of her laptop. Her shoulders sagged. The interview had ended two hours ago. Too soon to have a response. She'd stretched her qualifications, but her desperation had made her hold onto hope. The exclusive private pre-school expected a degree in early childhood education, and she was lacking. Her years as a nanny counted for little.

Still, she felt the interview had gone well and hope still burned.

But thoughts of co-parenting with Archie were top of mind, even during the video interview. Had she seemed distracted? Disinterested? She hoped not. But there was nothing more to be done except wait. Which gave her more time to mull over Archie's offer.

Sure, it might be unconventional to have unmarried platonic co-parents, but there were millions of other unconventional people making loving homes for their children and creating non-traditional families. If they could do it, then she and Archie, with some work and dedication, might grow into a functional partnership.

And if Archie reverted to his self-indulgent lifestyle she'd be there as a steady influence for his boys. If she chose to join him. That was still an *if.* She gave her head a shake and tried to order her mind, but this was a pivotal moment and she'd often blundered at moments like this.

Ryley was busy with her toy kitchen and her soft babble brought home a stark truth. They may not be living here for much longer. Beth turned to look into the play area next to the sofa. Ryley talked softly to herself in a voice deeper than normal.

"Are you pretending, sweetie?" She asked.

"Tea!" Ryley announced.

"Mommy will be right there." She made to rise.

"No! Suzy has tea."

She sat back down with a thump. "Who's Suzy?"

Ryley giggled and poured invisible tea into an invisible cup for an invisible Suzy.

Beth closed her eyes. Her daughter needed friends. As much as she loved her little girl, she couldn't be her everything.

Long ago advice came to mind. She'd been spoiled one summer in college when she'd taken a mother's helper position and enjoyed a whirlwind of travel to exotic places shepherding toddler twins. The mother had been grateful for Beth's extra pair of hands and confessed that she hadn't wanted to hire a helper. But having Beth made her realize she'd been too exhausted to handle the twins alone. *She couldn't be their everything.* Beth had soaked up the woman's appreciation, had loved feeling needed.

Beth had changed her life plans on the strength of one fun summer. That had been the first time she'd been lured by what she hoped was a viable future. She'd been warned by her parents and her sister to stay the course for her business degree, but she hadn't listened. Instead, she impulsively pivoted away from school and followed a different path.

Impulsive decisions had consequences and she was living with them now. She opened her laptop and checked with her agency as the clock moved toward twelve twenty. A notation on her file gave her the bad news. The interview, while great, couldn't make up for her lack of education. She logged off and powered down.

Time to face facts. To think strategically. To take control and have a plan. There would be no more interviews before her mortgage payment was due. She'd run out of time.

Her phone rang. Archie. She put a smile in her voice and answered. "Hi! How's it going now?" This was the fifth call of the day, but each one had been kind of fun. He was much easier to talk to than she'd have imagined. Also, he'd kept his conversations about the children rather than pressuring her for her decision. Clever of him.

Instead, she'd pressured herself.

"A goat just butted the food out of Jeremy's hand, but at least he's still standing."

"The goat?" She couldn't help it.

"Working on your stand-up routine? Got a couple of gigs?"

"Amateur night's just around the corner."

She felt his chuckle to her toes.

"I don't hear any tears in the background. That's a good sign." She'd suggested that the petting zoo could be a bit much for an inexperienced man with two curious boys, but he'd wanted to take them somewhere fun. Somewhere to take their minds off the many changes they faced. Jeremy and Duncan were such lovely boys. Sturdy and trusting that Archie was the right guardian.

She wished she were as convinced. While they enjoyed a chuckle here and there, he was far from ready to deal with the daily grind. The question was, was she?

There was only one way to find out.

"I'll do it," she said. "I'll try co-parenting with you. Because of the boys." He'd been in constant touch and struggled with the smallest things. A part of her had cheered his never-give-up attitude, while another part understood he was badgering her. She'd wanted a quiet day, but he hadn't quit calling.

Her lack of options aside, Archie had worn her down like water on a stone.

"Good," he said. "Start packing. We move into the motel house tomorrow morning."

Inwardly she admitted to riding a thrill of excitement as she threw clothes into luggage and toys into boxes. The impulsiveness invigorated her in a way she hadn't felt in a long time.

But this decision felt nothing like her two earlier rash choices. They'd been fueled by emotion. The first was the thrill of travel to exotic, interesting places. She'd been excited to toss off the constraints of college and forge a different path. The next time, she'd believed she was in love. Believed her future lay with a lying charmer who abused her desire to help. Her kindness had worked against her.

This time, she had her eyes wide open about Archie Jones. She knew exactly what to expect from the man and it wasn't his support or steadfastness. No, Archie would be around to see his new family settled into a house, then he'd move on.

The next time they'd see him would be at a Jones family function. He'd arrive late as usual. Ignore her, as usual, and maybe spend an extra day pretending to be interested in his friend's children.

But they'd have her, and she'd be as steady an influence as she could be.

Meanwhile, she'd be saving what she could while building equity in her condo. When Jeremy and Duncan went to college she and Ryley could move back home and the boys would know they always had her love.

Love.

Was she giving up the dream of a relationship by moving into a platonic partnership? Maybe. But Singles Fest would supply lots of opportunity for connection. She'd get settled into her new situation and then keep her mind and heart open to possibilities.

This decision was fuelled by logic and financial necessity and was the best pivot she could make. Confident this was the best way forward for her and Ryley, she swept through her closet with razorlike efficiency. Flowing dresses and skirts and sturdy sandals filled her luggage.

If Archie Jones assumed he could charm her, he'd have to go through her armor first.

Chapter Five

Tuesday, Eleven a.m.

The Landseer Motel stood silent but for several gulls calling overhead and the flap of a flag in the breeze. Beth took stock. The place looked just as it had on the internet, but better.

Sun shone on the blue roof and danced off the gentle ripples in the pool water. She stood with her arms around Jeremy and Duncan while Archie got Ryley's stroller out of the back of the minivan. According to the boys he'd bought it after they'd met on Sunday.

Archie's decisiveness seemed out of character. But clearly, the man got what he wanted when he wanted it. Look at her, here less than forty-eight hours after he proposed this scheme. He made a snap decision that he wanted her, and she caved after a few phone calls, a poor job interview and a pile of overdue bills taunted her. The bills would be paid with her first pay deposit. She'd already set up automatic bill payments.

No going back now.

The man had gone full-bore dad with the minivan that had every option she could think of. It had more room than she'd seen in an SUV, cupholders everywhere, heated seats, screens that dropped from the ceiling and more. He seemed proud of his choice and his goofy man-grin made her hide a smile. Clear memories of her parents being delighted with their first minivan ambushed her and she let loose with a smile that Archie intercepted.

"It's a great vehicle for a family," she said. Her first comment on it made his smile broaden.

She turned away. "I half expected the motel to look decrepit or decaying. But it looks just as you described it."

"Not rundown, but retro. Cool like 1960s cool," he reminded her. Archie set her luggage on the pavement.

She squeezed the boys' shoulders and they both looked up at her. They were sweet and trusting and she'd fallen for them on first sight. Yesterday, she thought about them when they were apart. Hard not to, considering how often Archie had called to tell her about the petting zoo adventure.

Apparently, Janise, a front desk supervisor at the Sands Resort had suggested the outing and Archie had jumped at it. His regular calls through the day had the earmarks of a planned military maneuver. She wondered if Janise had suggested that, too. She'd have to ask the woman if they ever met.

Still, hearing from him had become a bright spot in an otherwise disastrous morning. She idly wondered how she'd be feeling now if she'd been successful with the job interview. Would she have forgotten Jeremy and Duncan, or would she have regretted her decision? No way to know.

The speed of events was dizzying, but the immediacy of their need had goaded her to be quick.

The crazy scheme still had her shell-shocked, but Ryley needed a stable home and Archie promised to give them a reasonable facsimile. With Beth making her best effort, a fragile hope had grown that they might pull this off.

The boys had continued to climb into bed with Archie, but she hoped once they got settled, and the worst of their grief had passed, they'd stay in their own room. Here at the motel, they'd share their room while Ryley had a room of her own. Maybe it had been the instability of being in a hotel room that had made the boys need to be close to Archie overnight.

Jeremy and then Duncan tore away from her to explore.

"Stay where we can see you!" She called after them.

First stop was the gate to the pool. They groaned when they found it locked, but she puffed out a relieved breath.

"I hope being in the house and in their own room means they'll be content to sleep there."

"Me, too." Archie's fervent tone made her smile as he lifted out more bags and boxes from under the floor. "I haven't had a decent night's sleep since I got them."

"Is it just their company that keeps you awake? Or is there more going on in your diabolical mind?"

He shook his head. "They wake me, but once my mind starts churning, I lose hours. For the record, I may be many things, but diabolical isn't one of them." He chuckled. "Determined, persistent, and relentless, absolutely."

"Yes, I have firsthand experience of your relentlessness." She grimaced in mock severity. "You didn't have to continue your petitions after I said yes."

"I was afraid you'd have second or third thoughts. I couldn't risk a change of heart."

"I figured." He must be running on empty, given his lack of sleep, so she relented. "Look, parenthood is a lot. At least with pregnancy I had months to get used to the idea." He'd had no warning and stepped up at once. That said more about Archie Jones than she'd ever considered.

"If I'd known ahead of time, I might have weaseled out of it. Keith understood me better than anyone in the world. He downplayed his health situation with good reason. He played the odds, hoped he'd get the transplant he needed, while having me as back up." Reluctant respect underscored his words.

He shrugged and changed the subject. "What do you think of the place? Aside from the cool factor. Not exactly a five-star resort, but it grows on you."

The Landseer had two wings, a right and left. The center court held the pool and farther down, a large playground full of brightly painted equipment. Wooden loungers ringed the pool. Off to the side she saw a large portable barbecue with a cover on it. The office was on their left and apparently, attached to it was the two-story house that faced away from the center court for privacy.

The real jewel though, was the beach beyond the property. Sand dunes and an unbroken view. From here she could see a wooden walkway to the beach. She could just make out a viewing deck on the right side of the walk.

The salt air was exquisite and made her feel, vaguely, that she'd landed in the middle of someone else's vacation. This place would be good for the children. The boys could forget their sadness for brief moments of play and their hearts may begin to heal. At the moment, they were in a footrace around the pool enclosure.

"A pool and playground. A barbecue. A beach. What's not to love?"

His smile lit his eyes and she saw why so many women had fallen for his charm. Good thing her shields were up.

"The back door to the house is down that breezeway," he explained. "It opens to the kitchen. The front door is on the far side. The house is surprisingly quiet when the kitchen window's closed."

"I'm sure it's fine," she murmured. "When is the next Singles Fest?" He'd told her it was soon, but the date had drifted away from her frazzled mind. Too many details to keep track of.

"We have a week and a half of relative privacy. This is the quiet before the storm of single parent families descending." He rolled his shoulders and looked out toward the beach. "I wanted to find a routine that works before it's broken by partying adults and children. This was Janise's suggestion and it's a good one."

She nodded. "I'll have to meet this Janise. She's made quite an impression on all of you."

"The boys took to her on sight, and she has experience with kids of her own. Common sense advice, too. Her kids are older and do well in school. A daughter's off to college in September."

He sounded impressed. At least now she understood why her name had come up at Karly and Bret's house.

"Settling in before Singles Fest is smart. The family events will be fun for the kids and will give them structured time with other children. They'll have a chance to just be kids." Singles Fest provided daytime family activities where parents and children could mingle while having fun. The evenings were set aside for the adults. If connections were made Farren's clients went home happy. "Karly tells me there have already been a few weddings since Singles Fest started."

"I didn't know. I've only been back to town to visit Jesse and Eva. Since I'm not a single parent, I didn't pay it much attention." He had unbuckled Ryley from her seat and set her on the ground. Beth took her hand.

"I guess, in a way, we're single parents together."

He gave her a long glance. "You're right."

"Let's give the boys a few minutes to burn off some energy then we can check the house."

"Sure thing. I'll unload the van." They'd packed the essentials while Karly and Bret followed with another load of personal items from her condominium. She'd decided to leave it furnished while she took time to feel out the living arrangement here. Archie had made the rental suggestion and she needed to give it more consideration. The money would come in handy, but having strangers living in her home would take getting used to.

"Jesse and Eva will be over later, too. I'm sure you'll like Eva, she's great."

Ryley chattered about the pretty pool while Archie slung her diaper bag over his shoulder and began the push past the office.

The boys zoomed by them in a race to nowhere.

"Is this pool ours now?" One of them asked on the wind as they tore by as fast as their legs could carry them. She noticed that Jeremy had allowed his little brother to take the lead.

"No. But we can use the pool and the playground." Archie answered the breathless question.

"Can we play in the playground whenever we want?" Jeremy asked as he slowed to a stop a few feet away.

"Unless it's dark, yes. But not alone or when we're in the house and can't see you."

Archie's rules were reasonable, and it was clear he had safety in mind as he made them up. She slanted him a look of approval. "These are good rules. I'm sure they'll follow them." She considered her response. "Most of the time. But temptation is hard to ignore."

"Where is the people?" Duncan wondered as he took in the view. Archie reported that he'd cried leaving the resort this morning.

Being four meant he probably liked a routine, and this day was nothing like anything else he'd experienced. The boy had suffered too much upheaval; her heart had cracked at his frustrated wails in the van.

"What's that thing with the clothes and stuff on it?" Jeremy again. He was observant and liked to get his information immediately.

"That's a housekeeping cart with towels and sheets and little bottles of shampoo," she responded, while wondering why this motel didn't have parking in front of each unit. Instead, there was a lot that stretched across the front of the property. Today, there were only three vehicles parked, and one of them was theirs.

"You saw one or two of those carts in the hall at the resort." Archie veered left as they passed the office. He turned down the breezeway that separated the house from the left wing of rooms. "The key for the house should be under a rock by the door."

"Really? Who does that anymore?"

"The people who live here. Last Chance Beach is that kind of town." He bent and picked up a rock from the ground. A key waited for anyone who knew it was there. He slid the key into the door that opened into the kitchen. "Apparently there's another key beside the front entrance."

She turned and looked at the view behind them. "But from here you can see the pool and some of the center court. People can see the hiding place."

By now he was inside and turning on lights. She doubted he heard her, so she allowed her observation to hang without response. And there was no one here to see anyway. She heard the rumble of the cart and wondered if they should introduce themselves, but Archie, being a Jones, would likely never talk to the cleaners.

The kitchen held some surprises. Duncan discovered the dishwasher disguised behind a cabinet door. He took delight in finding a hidden appliance, so he made his way down the counter opening each door on the way. He soon learned these cabinets had soft close and slamming them didn't work as he expected. He frowned while she pinched her lips together to keep from smiling.

The fridge made her heart leap. She ran her fingers over the cool highly polished stainless steel.

"I wanted water in my fridge door," she commented to no one in particular, "but I couldn't afford the higher price." She opened the French doors wide to see the interior and sighed. This counter-depth refrigerator was all that was right in major appliances, and she wondered giddily if the water was piped in from a natural spring somewhere. Fanciful thoughts for a strange day.

She spied the dishwasher and opened it next. A top rack just for cutlery. Perfect for a family of five.

Archie watched her face with interest. "I'm glad you like what you see. Grady upgraded the kitchen when he moved in."

"For me these are dream appliances. My budget couldn't stretch past basic models."

"This was his aunt's motel, and he has fond memories of the place when he was a kid. When his life took that bad turn, he figured no one would find him or bother him here."

"You said Farren did, though."

"The story is, she refused to take no for an answer when she wanted him to open the motel to her clients. She was sailing on a wing and a prayer, with everything at stake. Once he opened the door to her, he didn't stand a chance."

She nodded, amused. Archie had mentioned that Last Chance Beach could be life changing. She frowned. Grady and Farren's story felt weirdly familiar. Archie had also been determined to convince her, relentless in his pursuit of her agreement. And it had all happened quickly. And here they were, at The Landseer Motel house.

When she met Farren, she'd ask her about how she and Grady had met.

Jeremy wandered into the living room. "Wow! This is a big TV."

Curious, she followed him into the spotlessly clean area. What she saw made her look harder. Her eyes swept the room slowly, taking it in. "When did your friends move out?"

"A couple of months ago. Why?" Archie had his head in the pantry.

"Is this new furniture?" The room was gorgeous. Fresh soft white paint, an accent wall in sea blue and comfortable looking overstuffed furniture a body could rest in. Not sleek. Not cold. The room looked "family cozy" with a large toybox with extra deep shelves hanging over it on the wall just waiting to be filled. "I love it," she admitted on a soft breath.

He pulled his head out of the pantry and let the door close. "I figured I wouldn't have time to deal with an empty house once we moved in. I spent a few hours online and ordered what I thought would work. A designer friend made some suggestions, but they sounded too cold and too New York skyscraper for kids. But she proved useful by getting painters in here immediately. Farren sent in her cleaning crew."

"You chose all this *yourself*?" She bit her lower lip to keep from spewing more condescension. She hadn't meant to be rude. Perhaps he hadn't noticed.

Archie stalked toward her with a man's grace. Smooth, sure footsteps, head up, eyes on hers. A niggle of something she refused to name expanded in her chest.

He stopped and stood three feet away.

"You don't like it? I wanted comfortable and easy. But we can change it if you're not happy." He frowned. "I should've sent you pictures, got your opinion. But you had enough on your plate. I started this the day after the boys came to me. By Sunday, when we met at Bret's, most of the choices had been made."

"I love it, Archie. It's perfect." She turned a circle as she took it all in. The television was a decent size without dominating the space. The colorful rug echoed the blue on the wall and warmed the light gray tone of the engineered hardwood flooring. "It's warm and current but great for children. Where did you find the time?"

"Online shopping is twenty-four seven and I make fast decisions."

"No kidding. You decided on this co-parenting idea in a hot minute." As soon as he saw her, in fact.

"In the grand scheme of life, you've made some interesting choices too." He gave her a half smile while his eyes glowed with humor. "Maybe we're both rebels."

She chuckled. "Maybe we are. Except I spend way too much time fretting about nonsense."

He nodded as if he understood. But he couldn't. Archie Jones hadn't fretted over a decision in his life. She'd swear to it.

Chapter Six

Archie looked pleased with her reaction to his decor choices. With his wandering lifestyle, he'd never decorated a home before, which impressed her even more. The man had great taste.

"On second thought," she said, "rebels are warriors, not worriers. They don't wring their hands in indecision. They decide on a course of action and follow through. That's what you did with this place. You didn't hesitate or doubt yourself." She would have second guessed everything.

"I doubt myself plenty. It's a new thing I do. It started the minute I heard about the boys coming to me. I'm waiting for it to stop, but I'm not sure it will."

He tilted his head while she processed his confession. Archie Jones doubting his abilities seemed ludicrous. But parenting could humble the most arrogant people.

"That's what you did when you wanted a child," he added. "You decided to have a child and had Ryley."

"I guess," she muttered. She didn't want to think about how he believed her lies. "I've spent a lot of time staring at the ceiling instead of sleeping. You hit on something by making those dark hours productive." She hoped he wouldn't notice her deflection.

He shrugged off the compliment while Ryley ran off to follow the boys. She'd already claimed them as playmates, and they didn't mind a bit. They seemed to enjoy have a younger child dog their every move.

"I did my share of staring into black holes as well. The only thing I found there was regret," Archie admitted in a gentle tone. "At three a.m. there's nothing anyone can do with regret." He considered her. "Maybe being at the Landseer will help us, the way it helped Grady."

A brief smile made him look vulnerable, but she brushed off the idea. "Maybe we should join in some of the Singles Fest outings for adults," he concluded vaguely.

"Maybe," she said, overwhelmed. She recalled thinking much the same thing, but the idea of putting herself out there gave her hives. "Being a live-in nanny made dating difficult. I felt isolated."

"But the travel must've been great."

"It was at first. But in my early twenties I missed out on after work drinks with colleagues or girls' nights. My vacations were spent with my family." Life had passed her by during those years.

As she mulled, it came to her that there were a lot of reasons she'd been vulnerable to the attentions of a smooth-talking liar. She'd never wanted to be single with a child. The truth made her close her eyes so he wouldn't see the tears. "I don't want to repeat those choices now. We should talk about our private lives. How we'll manage dating and that kind of thing."

"I understand. My life was very different. So, for now, I've got enough on my plate without adding dating to the mix. When I mentioned the adult outings, I meant that we could go together." He raised his hands to forestall her reply. "Not as dates, but as co-parents who need to be around other adults. Jesse tells me that's important. They have regular nights out together."

"They're married. Date nights are important."

"To keep the spark alive?"

"Exactly."

"Since we have no spark, we'll stick to the family stuff. The kids take priority."

"Right. I'm in no rush to reboot my dating life." She'd gladly put the whole thing on hold until Ryley was old enough to have a dating life of her own. "Unless someone irresistible shows up," she quipped.

He brightened. "Irresistible sounds great. And you should feel free to enjoy the adult stuff. I wouldn't want to hold you back."

"Good. I'll keep that in mind." Although she'd have enough new acquaintances with Farren, Grady, Jesse, and Eva. Maybe it would've been better to accept his invitation to enjoy the adult events, but changing her mind could be misconstrued.

"We need time to settle in with each other," he said she followed him into the kitchen. His brows knit as his fingers wrapped around the doorknob. Then he huffed. "I've never settled in with any woman. I may be a challenge on the domestic front."

"I have no doubt."

He gave her a measured glance. "There's more to get from the van."

"We'll unpack quickly and put their favorite toys on the shelves you had installed."

As he opened the door, he said, "There's a bike rack at the other door. Jesse installed it. Tomorrow I'll take the boys to buy bikes. Does Ryley need one?"

"She has a trike. Karly and Bret will bring it later."

While he was gone, the three children scooted around the house checking behind each door and in every closet. She heard a suggestion for Hide and Seek. Ryley was too young to understand the concept, but the boys would figure that out on their own.

Two minutes later Jeremy called a halt on account of girls who giggled too much and gave away their hiding places.

Archie appeared again with bags of Ryley's toys.

"We can help Ryley put her stuff up here," Jeremy stated, patting a deep shelf. The children busied themselves while she and Archie retreated to the kitchen to talk.

"By the time Bret and Karly arrive with the other boxes and gear, we'll be hungry." She'd brought whatever had been in her fridge and the basics like coffee, milk, and cereal. "I don't have enough food to feed the horde without doing a major grocery run."

"There's enough to do to settle in. I'll run down to the Jolly R and pick up food when everyone is here."

"The Jolly R?"

"A beachside joint with the best fish and chips I've ever had. We'll walk there on the beach sometime. It's not too far for the kids."

"Sounds like fun." And that wasn't a lie because while she loved condo living for herself, this home and easy beach access appealed to her on many levels. Jumping to conclusions wasn't smart, but the more she saw of Archie, the more her old opinions wavered. For a man who'd been thrust headlong into this new life, he seemed to have his act together.

"Have you told your local friends about us moving in today?" Trepidation niggled at her as she wondered what they'd think of her. Beth hoped to develop long and warm friendships while she walked this new path ahead of her. True friends had been another casualty of living in.

"Yes, they'll be here later. They've been great to talk to. Eva, especially, has helped me figure out some things because she was widowed, and she's helped her daughters with their grief."

"And Janise?" She'd learned from the boys about the warm, friendly woman who'd helped them at the resort.

"She's great. Motherly, kind. And incorruptible. I tried my best to get her to leave her job, but she has great reasons to stay where she is." He winked at her. "But now? I'm glad she stuck to her guns. I'm sure we'll see plenty of her. The boys are fond of her, and she likes them, too." There was a part of her that was happy Janise had chosen to stay employed at the Sands, too.

The tour of the house continued, and she followed Archie into the study which was situated past the kitchen in a quiet corner near the main floor bath.

Archie touched her back to guide her into the room. Odd, but his touch felt comfortable. She'd never liked the gesture of a man's hand on her back, especially on short acquaintance. The old-fashioned gesture was out of step with today's etiquette and being guided had always felt invasive. But his fingers were light, his touch gone almost before she felt it.

"Beth, I think this would be a good fit for you." He waved a hand toward the far wall. "There's room for a desk and a full-size bed if you put it against that wall."

She spied a bump out in the wall that would accommodate a desk. On the wall were desk height power receptacles. "I assume that's where Grady had his computer station. If it worked for him, it'll work for me." Not that she needed a desk, but she liked to keep her laptop in one place. She still helped Karly with her blog and social media bookkeeping, so she needed regular hours online.

Archie headed out of the room and took the stairs to the second story two at a time, impressing the boys into trying themselves. Jeremy managed slowly, while Duncan's legs were too short to stretch that far. She carried Ryley on her hip.

"I wanna do it," Duncan announced, with the sole of his foot on the edge of the second stair.

"I predict your legs will be long enough by the time Christmas comes."

She turned her head so Duncan wouldn't see her doubt. She caught a wink from Archie and stifled a grin. By Christmas, Duncan should have forgotten the prediction.

The primary bedroom had a balcony that faced north with an uninterrupted view of sand dunes and grasses. Distant rooftops were low and sparse and didn't hinder the view of the horizon. Ryley would take the smallest room because she'd be alone while the boys would share a room the way they had at home, leaving Archie to occupy the primary.

"This is the safest way," Archie said in a low voice. "I'll have the balcony door locked when I'm not in the room. I hope the boys know not to climb the rail, but we don't want the risk."

"My balcony door was locked at all times. You don't know this, but Ryley is a climber. The higher the better for her."

"That itty bitty girl?"

"I swear she's half mountain goat." After that parting remark, she found her way back down to her room.

Her closet was small, but she'd only brought her beachwear and a couple of light jackets. Her sister could send her warmer clothes as the seasons changed.

Jeremy and Duncan appeared in the hall and asked to check out the playground. "We want to go out," Jeremy announced.

Archie had followed them and stood behind them. "First you need to finish putting away your clothes. I'll help. Then we'll go to the playground."

"Aww," came the chorus from the pair. But rather than argue, the boys turned and thudded upstairs again.

Archie raised both brows. "I'm surprised that worked."

"They had a great dad and they're testing you to see how you measure up. It's natural."

"I guess, but sometimes stuff comes out of my mouth, and I have no clue if it's the right stuff."

She walked over, set both hands at the top of his arms and squeezed. Not that he'd feel it, his arms were steel hard. "You're doing fine. Believe me. I've lived with plenty of other dads and your instincts are great."

Red slashes of color appeared across his cheekbones, and he turned and fled upstairs while Beth grinned at his retreating back.

"Here," she said at the kitchen door ten minutes later. "Sunscreen." And she sprayed some on both boys while Archie stood by. He gave her a mysterious smile as he observed the children raising their arms and closing their eyes while she sprayed.

"Thanks. I wouldn't have thought of sunscreen. But it's obvious you've done this many times."

"Of course." He had a lot to learn about caring for children, but he seemed happy to observe and learn from her. "You can spray them next time."

"Deal. You tell me when." He checked his watch. "I'll set a reminder."

She chuckled. "I'll unpack Ryley's stuff and we'll follow you out. They need playtime." She felt her lips turn up at the corners. "Maybe we do, too."

"Fake it until you make it," he responded as he ushered the boys out the kitchen door.

"Sounds like as good a plan as any." Her comment was true, she realized twenty minutes later. She and Archie were feeling their way into a future together, and they'd have some misses and disagreements, she was sure. But they had to fake things around the children and be cheerful and cooperative. Given time, the boys' grief would mellow, and their smiles would become reasonable facsimiles of the real thing.

With Ryley's clothes neatly away in drawers, and her Teddy bears lined up on her toddler bed, Beth had no more excuses to hide in the house. Besides, she heard childish laughter and happy shouts from outside. Time to see what mischief Archie had allowed the boys to get up to. She hoped it wasn't dangerous or stupid.

She'd gently quizzed both boys about their trip to the petting zoo, but they'd assured her they'd been safe and held Archie's hand when he asked them.

With that thought, she clasped Ryley's little hand in hers. "Thank you for helping with your clothes. Do you want to go play?"

"Play!"

She couldn't help but grin at Ryley's excitement. The girl was a natural climber. Beth couldn't take her eyes off her daughter for a second at a playground. Beth feared that Ryley's adventurous nature would make her fall.

The moment they stepped out from the breezeway into the center court Ryley saw Jeremy and Duncan in the playground. She took off as fast as she could run, which was fast enough to have Beth jog behind her. She squealed in delight as if she'd missed them. Twenty minutes could feel like a lifetime if you were under three.

But it was soon obvious that it wasn't the children she was happy to see. It was the climbing equipment. *Of course.*

Archie, caught between pushes on Duncan's swing, laughed as Ryley bolted for the child-size climbing wall on the side of the equipment. Tiny hand holds and footholds allowed for a six-foot climb. Ryley was halfway up before Beth got there to supervise. She stood at the ready in case the little girl slipped. But, as usual, Ryley took the wall like a spider monkey in a tree.

"I don't know how I'll get through these next years without heart attacks when she does this." Ryley was agile but cautious. Careful when she climbed, Ryley never let go of one bar before grabbing another. On the climbing wall, she tested her handholds and footholds like a pro.

Archie stepped over to Beth, but kept his gaze trained on Ryley. "She's fine. You were right. They need this."

"The pool makes me nervous," she confessed. "I can't swim. I'd be useless if one of them got into trouble."

He looked surprised. "I'll do pool duty with them."

"You grew up with a pool in your yard. Or should I say on the estate?"

He shrugged and then eyed her closely. "No public pools nearby or swim lessons available in your neighborhood?"

"Two working parents meant less time for leisure pursuits. We joined softball teams in the summer and played volleyball in school. My parents carpooled to softball games, and we traveled on a school bus for volleyball." Saturdays had been set aside for errands and chores, Sundays were family day, when they'd all hung out together, until she and her sister had preferred the company of their friends.

"But you saw your parents every day?" His surprise made her blink.

What an odd question. "Breakfast was a sit together meal because dinner was often scattered over the evening. We'd wait for dessert and eat it when our last parent got home. So, yes, we saw them every day and..." she trailed off because he'd told her he and Bret had been shipped off to boarding school as early as possible.

Archie stared at her. "This is why you're important to them. You'll bring those memories into your mothering and round out their lives and experiences."

"I'm not their mother, but I hear what you're saying. I'm the next best thing." She hoped she'd be enough.

"As long as they feel loved, that's what matters most. Janise told me that and I believe her."

Chapter Seven

The Landseer Motel – Five p.m.

"How are you holding up?" Eva asked Archie with concern as she swept into the kitchen with Jesse right behind her. Their kids had joined forces and run to the playground. Seven children in a thunderous herd. The laughter and excited squeals told them all was well.

Ryley had woken from her nap and Beth had rushed upstairs at the first thud of little feet. She'd be back downstairs in no time. For a few moments, the three friends could talk without interruption.

"I'm not sure how I am at any given moment. But I'm scared spitless about the kids." They'd combined his new family with Beth's, and he had doubts. Not about Beth, she was great, but he wasn't sure he could pull this happy family stuff together. It wasn't like pulling a rabbit out of a hat. He couldn't reach in and produce what everyone expected. What everyone hoped to see.

He was no magician.

Eva drew him into a hug. Her next words were against his ear, softly. "Everyone is scared with children. That's normal and healthy. You have Jesse and me. And you have Beth. You'll do fine. All they need is love and you have lots of that in your heart. Just keep showing up."

It sounded simple when she said it. She expected some kind of response. He nodded, drew in a deep breath, and let her go, this woman who'd reassured him in the best way. The woman who'd given his best friend his life back.

Jesse chuffed a disgusted breath. "Hey, get your own girl. Eva's with me," he teased. "And I had to work hard to catch her."

Eva rolled her eyes. "Why do men think they do the chasing?"

“Ho ho!” Jesse laughed.

From upstairs came the sound of Ryley’s voice in querulous demand. She wanted the boys, and she wanted them now.

“Beth will be right down with her daughter. They’ll be happy to meet you. Apparently, Ryley’s nap was later than usual. Beth expects a late night.” He supposed naps followed a routine, too. “Today, everybody’s routine is off.”

“I look forward to meeting them both.” Eva moved farther into the kitchen to give Jesse room to pass. He carried a large green plant in a pot into the living room.

“It’s time to replace the plant Grady killed while he was here,” he said with a smile.

“Thanks, I think.”

“Relax, there’s a tag right here with instructions on how to care for it.”

“So, we get instructions for plants but not for children?”

Jesse and Eva burst into laughter and from behind him, Beth joined in. He turned to see her with Ryley on her hip.

“Who do we have here?” Beth asked with a welcoming smile. Ryley looked sleep tousled but alert as she took in the new strangers. In the next second, she slammed her face into her mother’s shoulder.

Archie made the introductions and Eva gave special attention to Ryley, after a warm one-armed hug with Beth.

“Welcome to Last Chance Beach. We’re happy you’re here,” Eva said with a light pat for Ryley. She stepped back, giving Ryley room to decide between shyness or friendliness.

Archie had seen the girl vacillate with strangers.

“You’ll have to fill me in on Last Chance Beach,” Beth responded. “I’ve only ever seen it online when I checked out Singles Fest for my sister Karly.”

“You’re Karly’s sister,” Eva blurted. “Of course. Farren and I were thrilled to hear about her that first day we met Archie and Jesse. Her support was instrumental in the early days.”

“I’ll tell her you said that.” Beth’s wide smile was genuine and happy, and Archie felt good about the women meeting for the first time.

“Last Chance Beach is a small town, but growing, quiet, but lively sometimes and full of retirees with a young vibe. Traffic is light away from town and kids can ride their bikes safely.”

“Sounds perfect.”

After that, it was easy. Beth and Eva warmed to each other as the women chatted about raising daughters. The women were similar in age and seemed to have a lot in common.

Eva had Jesse put the plant in a sunlit corner of the living room and Beth seemed happy to have a healthy plant to care for.

After a few moments, Jesse raised his eyebrows suggestively and gave him a look that said he thought Beth was pretty. She wore her usual loose flowing skirt that ended just above her ankles. But for the move she wore a short-sleeved tee with a picture of a sleeping kitten on the front. She was lush and lovely, and he hoped that soon she’d pull out her beachwear. Not that he wanted to ogle her, but a man was allowed to be curious about the woman he lived with.

Her heart belonged to Ryley, but Archie had to admit Beth brought light into every room she entered. He frowned as he remembered how often he’d dismissed her in the past. He’d been a fool.

And what was worse, he suspected she knew how dismissive he’d been. He’d dug himself a hole without knowing it.

ONE WEEK LATER

"I didn't know you'd move this quickly. This is a shock. We don't even know how living together will work." Archie had bought a property without consulting her. His breezy tone while he'd announced the purchase had her stunned.

"We've done okay this past week." He walked beside her, his flip flops in one hand while he carried Ryley on his shoulders. He walked at the water's edge while Beth preferred to stay clear. They'd already formed unspoken rituals. If they were married, they'd have chosen which side of the bed to sleep on by now. She was glad she didn't have to give up her nightly sprawl.

In the past week, Ryley had come to expect a ride from Archie whenever she tired of chasing the boys. Beth tried not to be rankled by how much her little girl enjoyed his attention. Tendrils of a bond had formed between man and girl in the last few days.

"And okay is good enough?" She prodded for no reason at all except that a decision this big should've been discussed considering it affected her and her child. "Have you taken the children's needs into account? Considered the proximity to schools?"

"Okay is better than I hoped for, to be honest." His tone was cautious and his glance wary. "Beth, I know I have a long way to go and a lot to learn, but I'm willing to do whatever it takes for us to give the children what they need." He reached up and booped Ryley's nose with a gentle finger. She giggled like she always did when he paid her attention.

Beth shifted in discomfort because she hadn't expected him to move the family again this soon. The children were just becoming comfortable, not to mention she and Archie were still antsy around each other. "You *bought* this property. You're committed, then? Financially, I mean." Her belly twisted at the expense even though Archie was a Jones of *the* Joneses of New York.

The boys poked at buried clams at the shore. Everyone moved at a snail's pace so the buried clams could be given due attention.

Archie accepted her steady regard and shrugged. "No point waiting," he said.

"When will we move?"

"When the house is built. It'll be a long time in kid years, but I'm guessing a year for us."

She broke into a relieved laugh. "You had me going there. I worried you were moving us immediately."

Archie's handsome jaw, lightly dusted with bristles, fell open. "No, not at all."

"Down now!" Ryley kicked her legs in impatience. Archie lifted her safely to the ground and she scampered to where the boys squatted.

He bumped his shoulder against Beth's in a friendly gesture. "No wonder you looked horrified. No, I'd never move the kids again right away. Or you either. We're doing well together, but we need more time to get to know each other."

"So, we're doing better than okay?"

"Poor choice of words." He looked contrite. "Every day we get more used to each other. I know how you like your coffee, eggs, toast. You know I'm a bear before coffee and I'm slow to move before nine a.m."

"I put your slow mornings down to jet lag."

"I've been with these boys for almost two weeks. Jet lag's long gone."

"Two weeks in one place must be a record." She hoped he saw the tease in her face and her words.

"Funny." He stopped walking and his expression turned serious. "I opened a letter from Keith. I forgot about it until now. The lawyer passed it to me in a file with other instructions for the boys' trusts." He nodded and continued. "I need to run this by you. And Eva and Jesse, too. They've had experience with this problem."

She checked where the children were. With the breeze whipping sound away, and surf at their feet, they wouldn't hear the conversation.

"This could be the most privacy we get today. What did the letter contain?"

"His final wishes." Archie looked off to the horizon. "Keith requested no service because he didn't want the boys to go through one. Keith was raised in the foster system and had no family to handle the details anyway. Apparently, he explained to the boys that they'd be able to visit their parents' graves when they were ready, but there would be no formal gathering."

She nodded, unable to speak while she digested the loneliness of Keith's request. Then, she stepped in front of Archie and wrapped her arms around him. "I'm sorry for your loss, Archie. And for theirs."

His arms, warm and surprisingly firm came up around her and he held her close for three breaths before releasing her. But she held on. To comfort him or herself, she wasn't sure. He set his head back and looked into her eyes. She hoped he saw her compassion because it filled her up.

"Thank you. Do you think this is wrong of Keith? Should the boys have something more?"

"I think that if he told them his plan, they'll expect it to happen just that way. Talking to Jeremy about it would be smart, though. He may want to visit right away or wait until he's ready."

He nodded. "I believe you're the best woman these boys will ever have in their lives."

It was her turn to well up. "Thank you."

A shout from Duncan made them look toward the children. He wailed while Jeremy and Ryley laughed hysterically.

"What's that about?" Archie called to them.

"Duncan got sprayed by a clam!"

The younger boy wailed again and walloped his brother in the shoulder for laughing.

Archie stepped over to the child and crouched in front of Duncan. He smoothed his large palm down Duncan's face. "Better? Clams spit out water when they're eating. I guess you disturbed him while he was having his supper."

"Yuck!" Duncan stomped the pea-sized hole in the sand.

Crisis over, the children ran ahead together but decided the clams should eat in peace. They chose to search for seashells away from the shore, instead.

"I'll tell them in the morning about the move."

"Seems too soon. Like you said, a year is a long time to kids."

"Agreed, but I may have a way to make the whole process fun and get them involved."

The warm moment between them passed, as it should. She set the feel of his strong arms around her to the back of her mind, never to be thought of again.

By the time they'd been bathed and dried, the children were tired and although they protested that they were wide awake, they went to bed happily enough. The nightly routine worked well. A walk on the beach to say goodbye to the day, whether they were on the way home after dining out or running full tilt into the sand after using the playground. The five of them enjoyed the walks and the feel of another day coming to a close.

After he tucked them in, Archie read to the boys while she read to Ryley.

She set aside her concerns about Keith's letter to Archie, but her instincts told her there was more in the letter than he was willing to share. He'd had a haunted look in his eyes after he told her about Keith's final plans.

A haunted man needed a hug and since it was a public place, she'd had no qualms about offering one. But tonight, on the sofa, she'd keep her distance and not mention the letter.

They met on the upper landing and soft treads took them to the living room where they had a movie queued and ready.

“Since it’s my turn to pick I chose this action flick. The hero must rescue his children from a kidnapper in Europe,” she explained. “Funny how Joe Average has these amazing skills to take down the bad guys.”

He snorted and handed her a soft drink. “While we watch, let’s see how many of the places we’ve been. You traveled as a nanny, and I saw lots of Europe.”

“It’s fun to see the locations in the background,” she told him. But in truth, she loved the suspense and the chase scenes. She suspected Archie had already caught onto her secret pleasure.

ARCHIE WOKE THE NEXT morning with a hangover, an emotional hangover from reading Keith’s letter again. After the paragraphs about his final plans, his friend explained the why of his decision. He’d wanted the boys with Archie for reasons that had brought him to his knees.

Keith had seen things in Archie that he’d never live up to. Steadfastness, calm reasoning, gentleness. Kindness for pity’s sake. Him? Kind? When had Keith seen the broken, rowdy college kid be kind? The description made no sense. The way Keith remembered him *made no sense.* Still made him shake his head and he’d had a full day and night to mull it over.

And where did Keith get off telling him he was steadfast. He’d almost had to look up the definition of the word, because it surely didn’t apply to him. He’d wandered for years, lost and uncaring.

All of the descriptors Keith had used for Archie, applied to Keith, not him.

He’d never live up to steadfast, calm, and kind. Never.

The smell of bacon and coffee wafted under his bedroom door, and he rose, thick-headed, to stumble into the bathroom.

At the table, and sipping the ambrosia that was Beth's coffee, he cleared his throat. Archie gave her a nod and began. "I need to tell you kids that after a long time we'll be moving to a house of our own. It will be when Jeremy's seven and Duncan will be five by then. That's a long time, right?"

"Yeah," Jeremy agreed. "Is there a pool? Because I like the pool here." He could now swim three laps without stopping. The boy was smart and athletic.

"And swings?" His brother chimed in about his favorite feature of the playground.

Beth hid a smile by ducking her head. Ryley looked wide-eyed between the boys and Archie.

"NONE OF THOSE THINGS are there yet," Archie explained as Beth wiped Ryley's chin. "In fact, there's not even a house there right now. It's still vacant land with some trees and grass beside the ocean."

His eyes screamed 'help me' so she took pity on him. "You said you have a plan to fill in the time between now and when we move again. Tell us what your plan is."

"Yeah, what's going on?" Jeremy demanded.

Duncan glared at Archie. "I don't wanna go!"

"You will when you hear my plan. I want all of us"—he waved a pointed finger around the table— "to have a say in what we want to have in the house and on the grounds. Beth?"

His gaze searched hers and she watched him struggle to hold his smile in place. But she had nothing to add at this point. Maybe she should have talked to him last night, but she hadn't wanted to mention Keith again.

If Archie wanted to pretend this was an adventure in house design instead of an earthquake of change, then so be it. "Let's listen to the plan since we're all involved." She cocked an eyebrow.

"I'll take you to my meetings with the architect if you want," he finished lamely.

Life with Archie Jones had turned into life at warp speed. She needed to talk to him about slowing down or at the least discussing decisions with her before making them and expecting her to go along. She made a mental note to discuss it when they could talk without interruption.

"What's a arca tek?" Jeremy took Archie's attention off her.

"Architect," Archie replied clearly so Jeremy could hear the pronunciation. "It's a profession or a job where a person draws how your house will look. Where all the rooms will be, what size, how many windows and things like that. It's an important job."

Jeremy nodded, clearly impressed. "I draw our house sometimes. And dad, me, and Duncan."

Archie's gaze flicked back to hers. She blinked along with him. This was hard. So very hard. "I've seen those pictures, kiddo. They're great. You'll have to ask the architect questions when you come with us to meetings." He swilled coffee then stood with his empty mug in hand, looking lost.

"Okay. I will."

Duncan's eyes lit up. "I want my room to have a great big window."

"Why?" she asked.

"Daddy can watch me grow up."

Archie tilted into a turn and yanked the carafe off the coffeemaker. Held up the pot to offer her more. Her heart in a full stutter, she shook her head no.

"We'll tell the architect." She made the promise hoarsely, with a glance at Archie, who looked beyond speech. She directed her next words to him. "Thank you for including me and the children in the plans for the house." She smiled as a thought took her.

"I'd like separate quarters. I enjoy having an office away from the rest of the household." The study/cum/bedroom worked well. She closed the door when Archie had the children in the living area. But for the rest of her years living with Archie she wanted her privacy.

The man was dangerous to her peace of mind. Seeing his kindness toward Ryley and the boys, laughing with him, even giving him a sympathetic hug were red flags. She'd been down this path with an employer before and it led to disaster. To keep her gaze firmly on her daughter, she ruffled Ryley's hair and then watched her jump down from her booster seat.

Archie spoke in a contrite tone. "I get it, you know. I'm not a complete idiot. I *should* have spoken to you before this. We could've looked at the property together."

"You're decisive and you saw something you wanted."

"And I get what I want." His eyes glowed with male interest and another red flag appeared. Archie Jones wanted her, and his desire fueled hers. Oh, mama, this was bad. Really bad. As if she needed more to worry about, now she had to fight her own impulses.

Chapter Eight

T*hree nights later...*

A scream woke him. Archie bounded out of bed, used to the sound, immediately aware of what had happened. *Jeremy, for the third night in a row.*

Because he was on the top floor, he reached the boy before Beth did. But she arrived at the top of the stairs seconds behind him and checked on Ryley before coming into the boys' room.

Archie no longer bothered to search for and put on his robe, just hit the floor running in his boxer briefs. Jeremy would scream until he heard Archie's voice. Fighting with a robe took too much time. Jeremy's screams might wake Duncan, then they'd have hell to pay.

Last night, Beth had arrived in a T-shirt and cotton shorts, after having seen the wisdom of speed over modesty. Raising kids together could blow modesty to the winds. It had for them, anyway. The upside to these nightly disruptions was that he got to see her long, beautifully shaped legs, bare.

He no longer wondered if Beth had curves and shape. She was perfectly formed. Round where she should be, long and lean where he liked. Down, boy.

"Hey, kiddo, I'm here," he whispered to Jeremy. He knelt at the side of the bed and cupped the boy's shoulders. "You're okay. It was a bad dream. A scary one, right?"

Jeremy nodded.

"Can you tell me what it was?"

"No," he said the word through a sniff, as he did every night. "I don't wanna." But that didn't mean he couldn't recall the dream, just that he didn't want to explain what he saw. Poor kid.

"Okay." A rustle behind him said that Beth wanted to take a turn with Jeremy. He felt her hand on his back as she leaned over to check on the boy. Cool fingers rapidly warmed on the skin near his shoulder. She had beautiful hands, long fingered and capable looking. Gentle, like the looks she gave the children, even when exasperated.

The gentle looks she never gave him anymore. The last one had been on the beach when he'd told her about Keith's letter. She'd hugged him tightly. Kept him from embarrassing himself with tears. He'd decided then and there that he couldn't share the rest of Keith's letter with her. She'd think his doubts were foolish, or a phony plea for attention.

He'd taken a bad misstep by not discussing the land purchase. Maybe she'd prefer a house that was already built. But there weren't many for sale on the ocean. And those that were had tiny lots. The children would need a large yard. Still, he understood her reasons for her disappointment with him.

"Hi, you're at home with us, baby," she cooed softly to Jeremy. "Go back to sleep. Nothing bad will happen with us here."

A brief nod and the boy closed his eyes, tears still damp on his cheeks.

Archie turned his head to look at her, so close he could feel her heat, hear her steady breaths as she watched their boy fall back into sleep. "You're good with him. With all of them. Us."

She pursed her lips. "I'm glad to hear you say that." With that, she left the room. He listened to her bare feet on the hardwood floors until she got to the carpeted stairs and the sound disappeared as she descended.

Yes. He definitely should have included her in his search for the perfect place to live.

"I'D LIKE TO KNOW WHAT his dreams are about. He was fine before." Beth worried at the problem as she did each morning since the nightmares had begun. She slid a mug of coffee under Archie's nose. "Here, you need this."

He accepted the mug with appreciation in his smile. "Just the way I take it. Thanks."

Irritating guilt rose. It was the first time she'd poured him a mug. She'd known for years how he took his coffee, a splash of cream with no sugar. And since they'd moved in together, he'd noted the same thing about her.

It was a simple gesture, to pour someone a mug they way they liked it, but one she'd withheld for no good reason. Spite? Likely, although she couldn't say why. Archie had never done or said anything against her.

Maybe because until recently she'd been a non-person? A wraith that hovered in the corners of his mind. She was not beautiful, not accomplished, not interested in being the life of the party. She was different from the women he'd been with. Archie had seen her truth, and, in one dismissive glance, she'd been dismissed as a woman.

It had been a few years ago at a family barbecue to introduce Beth and Karly's family to the Joneses. She'd been overwhelmed by the opulence of the estate and felt awkward and a little intimidated. Archie had blown in from somewhere, long after the meal had been served.

He'd breezed in, discordant, completely unaware of how the conversation had turned to the mundane. Celeste had bulldozed over Karly and their parents' requests in regard to the wedding arrangements and the conversation had fallen to the weather, of all things. Her mother and Karly had slipped into silent communication that consisted of stricken looks and shooting daggers with their eyes. Celeste should have keeled over at the table, but no such luck appeared.

Instead, Archie expected to be lauded just for showing up. He'd been oblivious to the undercurrents of stress around the wedding arrangements.

At first, she'd hoped he'd be a welcome breath of fresh air, but no. When his gaze had landed on her, he'd flicked down her body and moved on. A slight downturn of his lips had expressed his disapproval.

Archie Jones was as judgmental as his mother. He just didn't know it.

He'd dismissed her many times over the years, but now, things had changed. They were in a lifeboat together and had to row in the same direction. They were a team, and it was time she set aside her pique at being ignored.

"Maybe something happened recently?" Archie wondered aloud, startling her back into the conversation about Jeremy's nightmares.

"The family who was here the other day. Remember the large group that took three rooms, and had both sets of grandparents?" They'd been relieved to see the children respond happily to playing with strangers on the equipment and in the pool. "Kids can be cruel. Maybe Jeremy was hurt or got into a disagreement?" She bit her lip but couldn't remember a problem with the other children.

There was a ton they didn't know about the boys. But thus far, they seemed confident, happy, kind, and smart. In short, Jeremy and Duncan were wonderful children.

Ryley zoomed into the room and made for Archie's lap. He picked up her daughter, greeted her with a buss on the cheek and then let her tug his earlobes. "Ow, ow, ow. You're strong. You want to pull off my ears?" He made pincers of his thumb and index finger and growled a phony threat.

Ryley's giggles filled the kitchen with happiness and sunshine. Beth's heart melted at the sight of them. Ryley stretched her chubby hand toward a box of oat cereal, and she supplied her with a bowlful, dry, the way she liked it.

Archie tossed in a few raisins and some almond slivers to round out the easy breakfast. She filled Ryley's sippy cup with milk, while Archie set the toddler on her booster chair so she could eat at the table.

Meals at the table were something Bret and Karly insisted on and she agreed with. No random wandering with snacks in their hands, the children had learned early that food was served in one place. She'd been surprised at her sister's insistence on this one rule, but she had to admit, it kept the crumbs to a minimum in the living area.

She suspected the table routine was what the boys were used to as well. It was one of the reasons they all enjoyed picnics. They got to sit on logs at the beach or cross-legged on the ground to eat.

Archie hadn't questioned the edict, but there were times after the children were in bed that she and Archie ate salty snacks while watching movies. They both feigned guilt and collected any crumbs before they left the room. Leave no evidence had become their unspoken motto.

"Will you take us to the property today?" she asked.

"I look forward to it. Would you like to picnic there? The view is great, and it might make up for my highhandedness in putting in an offer without your input." He looked contrite. "I'll try not to do that again. But this arrangement we have snuck up on us. If we were a normal couple, I'd have grown accustomed to considering your needs. I would definitely share my thoughts more. I mean, I assume that's what people in healthy relationships do. As it is, neither of us knows the other."

Was he sorry or was it lip service to the concept of a partnership between them? There was one way to find out.

"Let me guess, you don't want to provide separate quarters." It was the one thing she'd asked for.

He waved a hand as if the added expense was nothing. "We can talk after you've seen the land. We'll make a list and take it when we meet with the architect."

She gave him a stiff nod. Barely noticeable, she was sure, but he caught it.

He gave Ryley a significant glance as the child stuffed a handful of cereal and raisins into her mouth. The boys were in the living room enjoying their favorite cartoon show. They wanted to eat right after waking, while Ryley preferred to play a bit first.

"I was taken aback by the purchase when you told me yesterday. I'd been left out of a major decision. But I hear what you're saying about needing time to adjust. Because of our cold relationship in the past, I have adjustments to make too. Seeing you over these days with the children, I believe I've misjudged you." And wasn't that a heavy admission. But it was out in the air now and she was glad she'd said it.

He shifted, straightened in his seat. If she had to say what his expression was she'd say guilty. "I see. And I know what you judged me on, and I don't blame you. My life before this was empty, selfish, and I was blind to what I was missing." He rolled his shoulders as if a weight had been lifted. "It's best for all of us if we move forward from here."

"Agreed." She let out a long breath. This showed yet another side to Archie. She'd never peg him as a man into self awareness.

"For what it's worth, I've had my impressions of you blown apart, too," he added with a sly smile.

"Progress then."

"Progress." He finished his coffee and took their empty mugs to the dishwasher. When he saw how full it was, he dug out a gel pack of detergent and set the machine to run.

Pleased that he didn't leave the minor chore to her, she cocked an eyebrow and asked, "Who's making lunch for this picnic you have in mind?" She made a mental list of the sandwich fixings in the fridge. "If you don't like PB and J, we'll need to make a grocery run. We're low on supplies for actual meals. Breakfast for the kids doesn't count."

"We'll pick up from the J Roger." His expression made her grin.

"Chicken!" yelled Ryley, who followed their conversation even if she seemed oblivious.

"Let me guess, you love their fish and chips?" He'd said as much before.

"We started out as friends, but one taste at the J Roger made me fall in love." He waggled his eyebrows, making Ryley giggle. He was good at making her happy.

He leaned against the counter and crossed his ankles. "I hope you like the property as much as I do, but if you hate it, I'll get out of the offer to purchase, and we'll look for a different lot."

"You'd do that?"

"I'm committed to this working for both of us. We need to cooperate to make a happy home for them. Clearly, I have a lot to learn. Much more than you do."

"I'm not sure about that." If he knew the truth about her past, he wouldn't have this much confidence in her.

"As you've probably picked up over time, I'm not a settling down type," he offered. "Never considered fatherhood an option for me."

"And?"

"I understand your need for private quarters whenever you need them. For now, though, I believe being in the same building will be easier on the children. I suggest two primary suites. We're co-parents and that makes sense."

She had no argument with his reasoning, so she nodded her agreement.

"Let's look at the property and envision what we want as separate people who need to raise these kids together."

Something inside her deflated. "Sure. Sounds good." And then she let spite rise again. "That'll work for now, because if I meet someone permanent, he'll be involved as well."

Archie blew out a hard breath. "We'll cross that bridge when we have to. But this lot is large enough for another home to be built. Eventually. Should the need arise."

She nodded but didn't mention all the ways this could go wrong. It was clear he'd looked ahead, too. If *he* married, her position in the pseudo-family would be redundant.

Until now she assumed he'd leave and return to his wandering life, but the longer she saw him with the children, the more she believed he'd stay. And these ideas for the new house seemed perfect.

Maybe it would be fun to be involved in planning an estate. Because that's exactly what Archie was building, even though he called it a house.

But if he married, she wouldn't, couldn't stay to watch another woman with him. Another woman with Jeremy and Duncan. Her rattled heart rebelled.

Chapter Nine

Archie rolled the minivan to a stop at the entrance to a gravel driveway. "The chain's up to prevent parties at night. With no lights up here it would be pitch black and the owner doesn't want to be responsible if kids get injured."

"Kids can get hurt here?" Jeremy asked from the backseat.

"Not little kids who are here with their family," Beth explained as she opened her door to climb out. "But teenagers who drive sometimes like to find places like this to have fun with their friends without grownups around." She closed the door and slid open the side. Her breezy, easy explanation was accepted, and Jeremy unbuckled himself and Ryley, while Duncan undid his own belts and buckles.

Beth handled these simple questions smoothly where he'd have made a mess of it. He'd have gone into way too much detail and likely scared the boy.

Archie unloaded the food and blanket they'd brought for their picnic. Somehow, his simple plan to walk the property and talk about the views had turned into a family adventure. Grinning inwardly, he hauled out Ryley's stroller and opened it.

But the girl had already chased after the boys. He kept them in view and passed the blanket to Beth. Next, he put the cooler and bags of food in the stroller for easy transport.

"It's okay that we're here?" she asked, taking in the surroundings. Trees hid the rest of the lot. "It's secluded."

"I called Grady to let him know. He's the broker for the property. It's no problem. He's told the local police that they may see my vehicle come and go occasionally."

She looked surprised. "I guess two acres of prime oceanfront would be a property he'd want to broker." She tracked the children with her eyes. "And protect from vandals or teens up to mischief."

"They're fine. The ocean is that way." He responded to the way her eyes watched the children, then he tilted his head toward the west. "We're about a mile north of the Landseer. We could walk there if we wanted to. By the way, you handled Jeremy's question perfectly."

"Thank you. Simple is best sometimes." She scanned the area with interest. Her reaction appeared to be as excited as his own had been at first sight. "I'm surprised this land is still available."

Trees bordered the driveway. To the right, they could just make out sand dunes and grasses. Gulls cried overhead and the surf was a steady, low pulse.

"I believe the issue is that town services haven't been installed. That adds time and trouble. Water lines, electricity, sewers all need to be brought in."

"And you think it's worth it?" She stepped over the chain that guarded the entrance from vehicles.

"I'll let you judge for yourself. But yes, I believe this will be money well spent."

"I waited months for my condo to be move-in ready. It was easier on my wallet to buy at pre-construction prices."

"Smart planning goes a long way."

"Archie Jones talking about planning? Be still my heart."

"Funny. You're a riot, Beth." He could fall for a woman like Beth. Smart, intelligent, and with a sense of humor he appreciated. "We'll be living in the motel house for longer than I'd hoped, yes." They had enough room where they were. It just wasn't what he'd imagined for them. But close quarters meant he could reach Jeremy quickly when the boy woke up screaming.

The children had moved ahead, exclaiming at the pink, purple, and yellow wildflowers they picked along the borders of the drive. For the moment he and Beth were on their own. He'd come to enjoy the quiet moments with her, as rare as they were. He thought of a topic for easy conversation. "Until now we've watched movies at night. But what kind of series do you like to binge?"

"Nothing too heavy," she responded. "I like my shows light and fun. Even cop shows need some comedic moments." Her gaze slid away.

He nodded but had already figured out she loved lots of action. "At boarding school, we had extracurricular activities and no time for TV. But as we got older, we had movies on disks, and we swapped them around to watch on our laptops. Back when laptops played DVDs."

"Ah yes, back when the world was in black and white, and dinosaurs roamed."

"I ask again if you have some standup comedy gigs in your future."

She tossed him a throaty chuckle that went from his ears to his low belly. He loved the feeling and hoped he had the same effect on her sometimes. "These days, I'm out with friends or women and if I'm home it means I'm deathly ill, or close to it. Which means I'm not up on bingeworthy series."

"Home? You've spent a lot of time in hotels. They don't count as home."

"You're right. They don't count as home." He couldn't blame her for judging him. He'd wasted years on wanderlust. The only real constants were Bret, Jesse, and Keith. Women came and went, some of them forgotten before they left his room.

He stopped and waited for her to notice and turn to face him. When she did, looking curious, he spoke. "Beth, this time with you and the kids has made me rethink my life."

He shrugged to shift the weight of guilt off his shoulders. "I should have been around Keith and his kids more, especially when Duncan was a newborn and Keith was widowed."

"He needed you, but you didn't realize it. It's not your fault. Your life was completely different from his. You couldn't relate or understand."

"I've been a selfish man my whole life." Keith's death had made him think harder and deeper. "I don't ponder the meaning of life, but for the first time, I feel as if I'm living it, rather than an observer." He blew out a hard breath. "I hope this makes sense."

She gazed at him, her lips turning up at the corner. Gently, she said, "You regret your mistakes. This is growth, Archie, and I'm glad to see it. But don't be too hard on yourself because we all make foolish, selfish decisions sometimes. You're not alone in this."

Her response made him wonder about how she'd come to this understanding. He couldn't see serious, thoughtful, quiet Beth making any poor decisions worthy of regret.

"I wasn't always in hotels. Sometimes I stayed on the family yacht for months at a time," he quipped for levity's sake.

"Because you were moving from place to place." She shook her head. "Karly used to tell me about where you were in the world. How sad it made her that you couldn't settle. She wondered why? And now I wonder, too."

He snapped his head back and then ran his hand down his face to stall. "I suppose I never felt I had a home. Not since Celeste shipped us off. There were holidays spent with her at various hotels. Sometimes my father was there, too, until he wasn't. Maybe the act of moving felt like home to me."

"I guess people can get used to anything. Someone's normal is not everyone else's normal."

They both turned, each of them tracking the children by their happy chatter. They were about twelve feet ahead and completely involved in a search for flowers and pretty rocks. Duncan enjoyed rock hunting and already had a collection on his nightstand.

"And now we're here to look at this property with an eye to turning it into a real home for all of us." The breeze softened against his face and a few strands of her hair caught on her lip. He reached out and swept it loose with a light touch. She didn't flinch in surprise or move away. He counted that as a win. Although, why he thought of winning and losing with Beth escaped him.

Regardless, her eyes thanked him. They walked again in silent agreement until the driveway ended a short distance ahead. The sand underfoot was anchored by grasses and the sound of children's laughter drifted back to them.

Peace.

Something like compassion flashed across her features. "Back to the TV discussion. We'll figure out soon enough what we both enjoy. We can each pick a series and see whether we agree on them or not." She shrugged. "But we have to give each show a reasonable number of episodes before we pull the plug."

"I say one."

"I'd prefer three, but I can compromise with two episodes. That should be enough to base a decision on."

"Done," he agreed through a chuckle. The sand made it impossible to push the stroller. He picked up the cooler and passed the bags of food to Beth.

"Jeremy, Duncan, and Ryley. Please stay in sight. We need to know where you are." They all stopped and turned around. "We will," the boys chorused back. Ryley nodded solemnly.

"I'm not the only person who grew up moving around. Military families move a lot." His voice sounded ever-so-slightly defensive.

"And a lot of those children stay put as soon as they're old enough to decide for themselves. I have friends who never want to move again because they moved too often as children."

"I miss my brother sometimes," he blurted. "Bret was my rock, my real home. Now he's married with kids and living his best life, while I've been existing in exile." He sighed and gave her a side-eye. "Your sister is one of my favorite people. Without Karly, I'd never hear from any of my family. And now, with Keith gone, I don't have much connection to my younger years." He sounded pathetic but he couldn't seem to stop the confessions.

She stopped and looked up at him, her eyes swimming. Her hand was on his arm, squeezing lightly. "It doesn't matter why you're here with these kids. It just matters that you are."

"I'm not leaving. I know you assume that I will. But I'm in this for the long haul. It's time." He stared at her, needing her to believe him. To believe *in* him. He'd never wanted anyone to trust him before and he hoped she understood.

She nodded and moved off, leaving him to stare after her, still wanting.

BETH WASN'T SURE WHAT he meant by "it's time," but she hated feeling sympathy for Archie Jones. Karly was empathetic and cared about people and whenever she'd talked about Archie, her voice had been tinged with sadness.

Her sister was a much kinder person than Beth. Where Beth saw the value in avoiding people she didn't like, Karly allowed for their quirks and gave them the benefit of the doubt.

Archie had been one of those lost people Karly wanted to see happy. And now, Beth grew more confused by what Archie was doing and saying as opposed to what she'd witnessed through the years.

They walked together through a stand of wind-swept pines, until the sound of the surf grew, and they left the trees behind.

"Oh wow!" She blurted at first sight of the ocean view. "This is amazing." He looked pleased as a kid on Christmas with her reaction.

"I think so, too. There aren't many lots left with views like this one."

"Just to confirm. You offered on two one-acre parcels?"

With a brisk nod, he explained. "I considered the future. One or two of them may want to live here and this way, we can subdivide the lots. We'll all have a slice of heaven."

"That's thoughtful and kind." When he said he was in for the long haul, she hadn't expected lifelong commitment. Supporting them through college, certainly. Their father had likely left funds for their education, but this was next level commitment on Archie's part.

She'd grown up in suburbia with great parents and a fun sister. But this level of privilege was beyond anything she'd experienced.

"When someone entrusts their children to you, everything changes. Our kids suffered a total loss of home and family. I include Ryley because she's been moved into this instant family. Her world flipped over when we chose to raise them together. As they grow up, I want them to feel that their home will always be here if it's what they want. This is a better foundation than uncertainty."

"Not to mention you're a stranger to the children. Or you were. You're not now," she assured him.

It went without saying that his childhood had been full of uncertainty. She doubted he understood how much he'd revealed to her this morning.

She looked at him with new eyes. It seemed he'd changed, but she'd rushed to judge him before and didn't want to be caught again.

"The best thing about this property is the parcels are side-by-side. We get double the oceanfront."

"Wow, when you decide to settle down, you're all in."

He nodded. "I guess. Speaking of the kids, you settle on the blanket, and I'll go round them up. They must be hungry by now."

He left and she opened the paper bags of take-out from the J Roger. Archie returned a few minutes later with the children trailing behind him. "We brung you flowers," announced Duncan and held out a handful of bluebells, some purple blooms Beth didn't recognize and dandelions. The others followed suit. A bulge in his pocket spoke of additions to his rock collection.

Ryley's offering was squished and sand-filled but absolutely precious.

"Thank you." She smooched each of them on the cheek. "I'll take them home and put them in water."

"There's an empty jelly jar in the recycle bin," Jeremy said. "I can get it out for you if you want."

"Thank you, sweetie, I'd love that. A jelly jar is perfect."

When she looked up at Archie, he looked thunderstruck and distant, as if he were processing something important. Maybe he had second thoughts about having these monkeys live within shouting distance when they had families of their own.

She bit back a smile at the possible future he'd put inside her heart.

Chapter Ten

Archie stepped into the upstairs hall from the boys' bedroom after their goodnights. The door to Ryley's room was half open and gave him a view of the child with Beth, leaning over her. The toddler bed was low to the floor so Beth could kneel at the bedside. A nightlight cast a soft glow that limned her in a nimbus of golden light. As he watched, she tucked a lock of hair behind her ear, giving him a better view of her profile. Beautiful, she looked like a sleep fairy come to visit.

She leaned in and blessed the girl with a light kiss on her forehead, but it looked like Ryley was already deep asleep. She'd been heavy-lidded when he'd carried her to bed and laid her down. He'd pulled the covers over her and swiped his palm lightly over her curls, but he hadn't kissed her. Maybe he should from now on. He'd ask Eva if little girls preferred kisses or being carried to bed.

He sighed now, in the moment, and somewhere near his heart warmth glowed. He rubbed the spot. Whatever these children needed, whenever they needed it, he'd be there to provide.

He'd found home, finally, in these children. Had he found it with Beth, too? Would she care if he had? She was impossible to read. She ran hot and cold and he never knew which way she'd respond. But there were times he'd swear he saw invitation in her gaze.

Beth rose from her knees and walked to him with a finger to her lips and a smile in her eyes. He stepped back to give her room on the square landing.

Hesitation with a woman was brand new. Normally, he'd make a move, get a response, either welcoming or dismissive. He always accepted the woman's choice. But Beth confused him. Therefore, until and unless she offered more, he vowed to keep his hands to himself. Mostly. His brief touches were cautious, and infrequent; easily mistaken for accidents.

Since their picnic, he'd looked forward to quiet time with her in the living room. It meant a lot to him that she approved of the property. He hoped she understood him better after his confessions while they'd walked together.

The moment felt hushed and gentle with the children tucked in and quiet. This close she smelled of flowers and salt air from the beach. Now was the time for them to get to know each other. To hang out. Laugh together. Share steamy looks and steamier kisses.

All of it.

Archie wanted all of it. For the first time, he wanted it all with a particular woman. It was odd to see Beth every day without having slept with her. His relationships were brief because he always left for somewhere else. He'd never invited a woman along. Hadn't wanted to get that close or send the wrong signal.

While he'd never wanted more time with a woman, he'd also never wanted to give her hope for a future with him. He wasn't cruel, just expedient.

The kind of time he'd spent with Beth was opposite to anything else. Life had turned upside down, in the best way.

His gaze locked with hers and he was certain he wore a goofy, hopeful expression that he feared could become permanent around her.

"Up for some television?" he asked quietly. He sounded like a teenager with his first crush. At her nod, he motioned for her to precede him downstairs while telling himself to settle down and not mess up.

When he strolled into the kitchen behind her, he saw she'd already pulled out the popcorn popper. The empty box sat on the floor, ready to flatten for recycling. He picked it up, glanced at the instructions and crushed the corners one at a time.

"I like to add real butter, so I use this instead of microwave bags."

"Extra butter?" He sounded too hopeful, like Duncan might. "And salt?"

She tossed him an easy smile and opened a bag of kernels. "Of course."

"Thanks. I see what you did there."

"Oh?"

"Yes. You mentioned the butter, so I'd have a voice in the decision." Her face encouraged him to continue. "From now on I promise to ask you before I make a decision that impacts us all. So, with that in mind, I'll let you choose the show tonight." He'd said much the same thing this morning, but he wanted to emphasize that he would actually change ingrained behavior for her.

She flashed him a wide grin. "Thanks, I should pick a sappy dating show, but I won't. There's a documentary on dogs I'd like to see." She quirked an eyebrow in challenge.

"Dogs?" In dim early memory, a big brown dog sat looking at him, tail sweeping the floor. He couldn't recall the name, or even if it was theirs. Surely not theirs, because he'd remember more. "Why? Never mind, don't tell me. We'll watch it."

The woman lived in left field because that's where this had come from. She had not mentioned watching documentaries today when they'd chatted about shows to binge.

"Good." She turned on the air popper and the roar drowned out the chance for more conversation.

He tossed the flattened box into the correct recycle container housed under the counter. Next, he opened the wine fridge and waved his hand in front of their selection of soft drinks, juice boxes, and bubbly flavored water. She picked a cherry flavored water, and then he got out glasses, added ice and poured drinks.

Ten minutes later, they settled on the couch, a giant red plastic bowl full of almost, but not quite, soggy popcorn, well salted, between them. He'd hoped for a shared bowl rather than separate. He felt a sappy, juvenile smile spread across his face. "Life is full of firsts," he muttered.

"What was that?" she asked.

"Nothing important. This is the best popcorn I've ever tasted." He saluted her. "You are the queen of popcorn, Beth and as such you are hereby entrusted with popcorn prep."

Her cheeks went rosy, and she glanced at him while the show loaded. "Thanks. Does this mean I'll always have to make it?"

He relented. "Only if you want to. You could teach me your technique."

"A woman needs her secrets, Archie."

"Ah! Of course."

"Does my new title of queen of popcorn come with a raise?"

He shook his head. "Sorry, just a tiara."

She offered her drink glass to clink, and he obliged. The television screen filled with images of puppies while she sighed in delight. "My condo no longer allows dogs. The ones still there will not be replaced when they're gone." She offered in explanation for her viewing choice. "We have a new board and naturally, there's an uproar, but..." she trailed off with a shrug. "I doubt I'll ever be allowed to have one there."

"Your tenants won't be allowed pets either."

"Right. I'll have to make that clear when I find someone to rent it."

"We didn't have pets," he said. "You don't miss what you don't have, but these little guys look cute." A pile of brown chubby pups nipped each other's ears and yawned, showing small, pointy teeth.

"They're mastiff pups and they'll be huge." As she spoke, a huge head appeared from the side of the screen and a long, wet tongue engulfed the face of one of the pups. The camera pulled back and showed the mother walk onscreen and settle amid the pile of her offspring.

His heart melted as the narrator explained the breed, the temperament, and what kind of family would be best for the dogs. After a few moments he realized he wore the same goofy grin he'd worn earlier. His heart rate had stepped up, too, just the way it had when Beth had walked out of Ryley's bedroom smiling at him.

He was hooked and watched rapt as the show moved through several dog breeds, extolling their virtues, and explaining what they were originally bred to do. He absently reached into the bowl beside him and tangled fingers with Beth. He froze and waited for her to ease her hand away.

When she didn't, he turned his head to find her watching him. "You're enjoying the show. I'm surprised," she said.

"Me, too. This is new to me. Thanks for suggesting it."

She noticed their tangled hands and jerked her fingers away. "Sorry."

"I'm not. Bound to happen. But this bowl is big enough to give us lots of room." A series of yips came from the speakers and drew his attention back to the fascinating world of dogs. "Who'd have thought there could be this much to learn about a common dog," he said.

Next to him, she muttered, "Or a man." She chewed a moment. "And the bowl's big because when I add the butter and salt, I need to get my hands in there and toss everything together."

"That's your secret?"

"One of my many secrets."

"Thanks for sharing it. I look forward to uncovering your other ones."

She snorted, something caught in her throat, and he patted her back for longer than he needed to. She didn't seem to mind.

AS SHE BRUSHED HER teeth for bed, Beth looked at her reflection. The woman in the mirror appeared...content. Not happy, exactly, but settled. Comfortable with herself and her situation.

She hadn't meant for the evening to be cozy, but Archie had surprised her throughout the day, and she'd wanted to repay him with a similar kindness. He'd wanted the TV time and it had been easy to give it to him.

What a day! Unlike any she'd had before. First, he'd surprised her with the picnic, then with the tour of the magnificent property. She appreciated his thoughtful desire to include her and the children in the house design.

Brushing his fingers when they'd collided inside the popcorn bowl had been sweet. Like a normal set of parents who shared their taste in television shows and enjoyed their quiet time together. Or dating teens in a family room with a parent in the kitchen.

Surely, if Archie planned on building this home with them, he'd be around for longer than the months she'd given him. She revised her time estimates for his desertion date, because as much as she wondered about him staying permanently, it was a mistake to forget that he was a wanderer at heart.

Maybe he would be with them for a year. Or two. Something fluttered in her chest. Hope? For what? Something permanent between them?

No. No. No.

The last time her heart had fluttered over a man, she'd ended up an unemployed single mom unable to pay her mortgage. *Never again.*

Ruthlessly, she went over each decision she'd made that had taken her down the darkest path of her life. Her gullibility stung, her humiliation rankled, her shame for believing a married man's lies made her cringe inside. There was no way on Earth she'd let it happen again.

No. Absolutely not.

She'd fallen for her boss once and it couldn't happen again. Especially not with a man who had a habit of disappearing.

If Archie came and went from Last Chance Beach, she could work for months alone if it came to that. When he deigned to visit, she could treat him like a guest. But would that be right for the children? They were the priority.

No more quiet evenings with Archie sharing popcorn and tangling fingers. She'd find other ways to fill her evenings. He'd adjust and take his cue to back off.

She climbed into bed, content with her decision to avoid cozy time with him. As sleep pulled at her, she also decided to let Archie broach the subject of his leaving. She would not ask.

THURSDAY

"Eva's arrived," Beth announced as she picked up her purse and slipped into her sandals. As she walked to the kitchen door to open it, Archie responded.

"Have a good time," he called from the living room. "I'll be fine here. I've got bath time down pat now."

She'd already bathed Ryley and had her ready for bed. As she opened the door, she was surprised to see two women. One had the most unusual almost-purple eyes. "You must be Farren?"

"Hi, and you must be Beth Matthews. It's nice to meet you."

Eva piped up. "We can chit chat at the bar. After all, I don't get out with women friends much and I want to make the most of it. Let's move." She used her sternest mom voice and made Farren and Beth laugh.

Beth shut the door behind her and felt the lure of freedom. "I haven't done this in far too long. Being a single mom doesn't leave room for evenings off like this." They were heading to the Sands lobby bar, The Sandbar, for a drink and some girl talk.

Eva rolled her eyes. "Tell me about it. I love my children, but when Jesse came with three to add to my two, nights off became a thing of the past."

Farren sighed. "I tell you what. I'll be the designated driver tonight. That way you two can party."

"Not even one glass of wine, Farren?" Eva questioned as they walked to Farren's car.

A pink tinge climbed up Farren's neck. "It'll be a few months before I can indulge."

Eva's squeal split the evening air as she grabbed her friend in a bear hug. "Really? A baby? I wondered because last week you mentioned having the flu, but I didn't hear another word about it."

Beth grinned, pleased to be included in this announcement. "How wonderful. Congratulations." She turned the lock on her lips. "I'll keep your secret as long as you need."

"Thanks, Beth, you read my mind."

"Secrets like this are the best kind," Eva offered with a wide grin.

SINGLES FEST – FRIDAY

In the time since they'd picnicked on the beach, Beth had learned much about Archie. The biggest thing was that he was an optimist. Odd for a man with his childhood experiences, but perhaps that was nature rather than nurture, or, in his case, lack of nurture.

Last night, she'd warmed to Farren at once and their time at the Sandbar had been filled with laughter and happy conversation. She'd hit the jackpot with Eva and Farren. With them for friends, her future in Last Chance Beach looked rosy.

She already liked Jesse and looked forward to meeting Grady later this evening when he arrived from Egypt. The man's life was a whirlwind, but she loved that Farren could count on him to be here for Singles Fest events.

Eva and Farren had been busy all day preparing for clients. When they needed a pair of extra hands, Beth had volunteered, leaving the childcare to Archie. He'd done a great job minding all three children on his own last night, but today he'd needed time for a conference call, and she had them in the kitchen helping to bake brownies. Jeremy was tasked with greasing the bottom of the baking pan.

"Great job, Jeremy."

"I helped my dad lots, but he never baked brownies. Sometimes he let me cut a roll of cookie dough, though."

"I'm sure you did a great job on those, too."

"I was gonna learn that, but we didn't have time," Duncan piped up.

Every once in a while, these boys could fell her with one simple phrase, and she ached for their loss. But for Duncan, these comments were the simple truth. She swallowed and hoped that he always remembered his dad's love.

She heard a heavy tread on the stairs, and she turned to see Archie step into the kitchen.

"What's happening here?" he asked, looking excited at the prospect of baked goods.

"Brownies," yelled Ryley from her booster seat at the table. She liked to watch whatever the boys were up to, and the booster seat provided the best view.

"Is your call finished?" She asked as she poured the batter into the pan. She passed a rubber spatula to Duncan so he could scrape the remaining batter out of the bowl. He managed to get most of it into the pan.

"Good job, Duncan," Archie said with a pat for the boy's shoulder.

"Dibs on licking the beaters," Jeremy said.

"There's one for each of you, and Ryley can lick the spatula since you all helped."

Archie looked nonplussed and watched as she released the beaters from the handheld mixer and then scraped most of the batter from the spatula into the pan. Each child licked their treat amid giggles and smiles.

"You look surprised," she commented. "Didn't you get to lick beaters?"

He shook his head, his eyes glowing. "But it sure looks like fun."

She refused to feel sorry for the boy he'd been. That way lay danger. She heard the rumble of the grill being rolled into position in front of the center court.

"Archie, you can manage the children again, right?" She washed her hands in the kitchen sink and when he said he had lots of time for the kids, she collected her baking supplies to put away. "I may be needed for final setup with Farren. There will be hotdogs outside tonight. We won't need to make dinner."

She looked forward to seeing how Singles Fest was run and how much fun it would be.

Maybe she'd meet an interesting single dad. That was the point, after all. More than a dating app, Singles Fest aimed to help single parents with their obligations and responsibilities on full display, find partners. These were mature people who didn't want to go through life alone. Last night Farren explained how often her clients said they were tired of dating games.

As a single woman over thirty she felt the same way. Life for her had changed and Archie was right, they both qualified as single parents now. As usual, the idea gave her pause. When Archie left would she be good enough? How would life be with teenagers? Thoughts that were normally front and center during the darkest hours of night swirled, making her doubt herself and her strength. Most especially, her strength.

"Go, I've got this." Archie brought her back to the conversation. "I'll take them to the playground. Ryley likes that." He clapped his hands to get Ryley's attention. "Little girl, your spatula has been licked clean. Time to wash your hands. Your face is full of batter here, here, and here." He tapped a finger to her forehead and each cheek, causing a loud case of the giggles.

The oven chimed that it had reached the correct temperature, and she placed the pan inside. She set the timer on the stove and also set her alarm on her phone for five minutes earlier, so she'd have plenty of time to get back to the kitchen.

"Noooo!" Ryley wailed when Archie picked her up out of her booster. Washing her hands and face after meals had become a chore she resisted despite how often Archie made her laugh beforehand.

With Ryley's protest ringing through the kitchen and knowing the toddler would drag her heels about her hygiene until the pan of brownies was ready, Beth happily stepped outside and walked the short breezeway to the center court. Full sun greeted her and the breeze from the ocean brought the tang of low tide. *Glorious.*

Eva and Farren were busy with the canvas cover from the grill. Beth held out her hand to take it. "I'll fold this and put it away in the storage box."

"Good afternoon, and thanks. While you're there can you get the grill tools out?" Farren asked.

Eva, dressed in denim shorts over her tank suit gave her a wide smile. "We were just talking about you," she said with invitation in her voice.

"You mean gossiping?" She strolled back to them and handed off the grilling utensils. "I'm an open book."

"Not gossip, but interest. How are things going with your live-in partner now?" Eva asked.

"We share living quarters, but I don't think of it as a true partnership," she fudged. "More like a team of mules hauling coal." She chuckled. "To be fair to Archie, we've settled into some routines that work for us all. He spends an hour or two in his room on his laptop after breakfast, seeing to whatever business he has. I take Jeremy to school during that time and drop Duncan at NanaBanana, then I like to walk the beach with Ryley for a bit. She loves climbing The Rock. I believe I'm raising a mountaineer."

"Duncan fits right in at daycare. He has special buddies, too," Eva reported. She owned NanaBanana, a daycare center that catered to the island's employees. Having daycare near their jobs kept all the spots full.

"Duncan talks about his friends when Archie picks him up. Thank you for finding space for him."

Eva softened her glance. "It was nothing. One of the parents changed jobs and found daycare on the mainland. No biggie."

Beth shook her head. "It meant a lot and I believe you let us jump the waitlist."

"Sh. Our secret."

She surveyed the still-quiet motel rooms and pool. "How soon will people arrive?" She was excited to see Singles Fest take the place over. It had been quiet, but for the occasional couple looking for a night or two at the beach. She looked forward to the busy holiday energy of the weekend.

"Check-in for the motel is three p.m. and it's just past that now, so anytime," Farren said, with an excited gleam in her eye. "I think this is my favorite time of the whole weekend. Everyone is excited and hopeful when they arrive. And now that we've got marriages shared on the website, business has picked up. I'm adding weekends through the summer to handle the uptick in demand."

Eva searched Beth's face. "The house is private, and the noise sounds distant from the kitchen. You shouldn't be disturbed. Grady never complained and if anyone was going to be sour about the noise it would be him when he was still grumpy. He's a new man, now," she said with a tip of her head aimed at Farren.

Farren laughed hard, but a pretty blush infused her cheeks. "He took some convincing to allow me to use the motel, but I won him over when I agreed to pretend we were dating."

"No way! I agreed to move in with Archie to co-parent, and that was odd enough, but fake dating? I've only heard that happens in romance novels."

"I can understand co-parenting," Eva said. "I agreed to let Jesse help me with a plan he concocted. He schemed brilliantly to get my stepchildren back in my life, just so we could be together."

"Because he loves you madly," Farren added.

She'd had hints from Archie that Last Chance Beach was a place to regroup and find a happy future. "To be honest, I wonder if I'll find a spark with a dad this weekend. Archie and I plan to join some of the group activities. He's a single dad now and I'm a single mom. We have to move ahead with our respective lives, aside from our agreement."

"While still providing the children with the care they need."

"That will be the easy part. I already love Jeremy and Duncan. They're the sweetest boys. Active but willing to include Ryley. Jeremy is a great big brother and Duncan's funny and sweet."

A man with a twin stroller approached the table where Farren was busy setting out brochures for local attractions. As he moved closer, her friend picked up a clipboard and greeted her first guest.

"Welcome to Singles Fest, I'm Farren, your host." She raised her hand to indicate Eva. "And this is Eva, our lifeguard and childcare co-ordinator."

Eva smiled and waved at the twins but stepped toward Beth. "This will be a great weekend, just wait and see." She raised her eyebrows and flashed a quick glance toward the handsome guest.

He stood close to six feet tall, with sandy brown hair that would lighten in the sun. His twins wore little pink sneakers that showed smudged soles. Toddlers, then.

"You'll have lots of possibilities arise," Eva said in a quiet husky voice meant for Beth's ears only. The guest's gaze roved over the three women and landed with interest on Beth.

"I guess I will," Beth responded faintly.

Chapter Eleven

"Why did you call?" Archie asked Celeste. He hadn't heard from his mother since he'd told her about Keith's passing and the guardianship. She'd been dismissive when he'd said he meant to keep the children and had not asked for details. Her asking for details might mean he'd ask for support and that was too much to expect of Celeste Jones.

"I don't understand your hostility, but then you've always held me in contempt. I'm certain you and Elizabeth are handling things with some level of competence."

"Competence," he parroted back. "And her name is Beth, short for Bethany."

Celeste sniffed in the contemptuous way she had. "Elizabeth is more refined." She sighed heavily, a sign of her pique. Soon, she'd give up and leave the conversation. "Since you've invested an unconscionable amount of money in real estate on that barren little island, I assume you have a plan for the children."

"And there it is. Your reason for calling. Since when do you care what I do with my money?" She had zero interest in plans for the children. With Celeste it always came down to money.

"Since you've taken on these children that have no connection to us. This is a total waste and I'll not have you entertain the notion that you can simply bequeath your fortune to strangers. I'll remind you that it's family money you play with. Whatever you have will belong to Bret's children some day."

"Bret can take care of his own children. Which is more than you did."

Ryley and Duncan made motions that they wanted to go outside. With Beth in the center court, he knew they'd be fine. He waved them out the door while Celeste gave him a long pause meant to give him time to consider his faux pas.

One should never tell Celeste the truth, it interfered with her self image. She sniffed. "I gave your father exactly what he wanted, heirs. You blame me because he left. He never told me why."

He let that one slide. He'd heard it his whole life. Maybe it was true. He hadn't bothered to find out.

"What kind of mother would I be if I ignored this insane idea you have to live with a woman solely for her nannying skills? You never should have burdened yourself with those children."

"Jeremy and Duncan are not a burden. They're a joy and Beth's more mother than you ever were. She's not their nanny." He ground out in exasperation. "She's my co-parent."

"Ridiculous. I strongly suggest you don't sleep with her. You've never shown the least interest in the woman and an in-house affair may give her a common-law claim on you."

"You're right, I have no hold on Beth. She has no interest in me. It's the children she cares about." And the truth of that statement hit him in the chest as he disconnected.

Family money. He knew the day would come and now that it was here, he was glad. He'd spent the last decade tripling his net worth. And now he would happily return the entire amount of his trust fund to the family coffers. He'd love to see Celeste's face when the accountant called to let her know.

He glanced out the kitchen window to see Beth with Eva. She faced the playground to keep an eye on the boys. The breeze caught at her hair and her skirt was plastered to her long, shapely legs. Far be it from him to mention that she'd look great in shorts. He'd seen her in her nightwear and if he mentioned how appealing she looked, she might switch to floor-length flannel nightgowns.

Beyond the women, guests lined up to check in with Farren who stood behind a table, happy and welcoming. She chatted and handed out brochures while she greeted her clients.

The scene was organized chaos punctuated with happy faces and cheerful voices. It was good here. *They* were good here. He and Beth, Jeremy, Duncan, and Ryley. All good.

Curious about the check-in process and because he felt like standing in the sunshine with Beth at his side, he picked up Ryley, and let her cling to his hip. She pointed to the kitchen door. "Out."

"Yes, boss," he said with a chuckle. "Your wish is my command."

Outside, he watched a guest with a set of twin girls stop to talk with Eva and Beth. Archie approached Beth from behind and stood, as he wanted, beside her. The sun kissed them all, warm and bright while the burble of happy adults and children washed over him, cleansing his soul after his tense conversation with the woman who'd birthed him.

"Hi." Beth welcomed him and reached for Ryley. She set her down and Ryley made for the girls in the double stroller. "Isn't that adorable," she said to the father who looked from Beth to Archie and back again. "Your girls already have a friend."

The guy smiled, showing a full set of perfect teeth. Implants, he decided. *No one had teeth like that for free.*

Archie resisted the urge to sling his arm over Beth's shoulders, but she wouldn't appreciate him claiming her. He chose instead to glare at the guest in a man-to-man stare he hoped the women didn't notice.

"My room's on this side," the guy said and named the number.

Archie let a rumble loose from his throat.

"Enjoy the weekend," he said in clear dismissal.

The guy had the *cojones* to glance at Beth one more time before he moved off. Ryley toddled after the stroller, and Archie tagged after her. Once the guy got his kids into the room and out of Ryley's sight, he'd take her to the play equipment. She'd forget about the twins in a blink.

BETH WAGGLED HER FINGERS at Ryley in goodbye.

"Did you see that?" Eva said sotto voce, leaning in for privacy.

Of course, she'd noticed Archie's glare at the single dad, but she wasn't about to admit that she'd been relieved when he'd appeared at the right moment with Ryley. "What? I must have missed what you saw."

Eva feigned shock. "A lesser man would've dropped like a stone if those daggers Archie sent through his eyes had hit their target."

Beth rolled her eyes. "Daggers? Maybe. But if I want to strike up a conversation with that dad or any other, I will. I didn't want him to assume I'm single."

"You must've seen something wrong that I missed. He's good-looking and despite Archie's glower, he looked interested."

Beth patted her shoulder in mock condescension. "It wasn't the dad I had a problem with. Ryley's an active child at her age. Now that she chases after Jeremy and Duncan it literally takes both of us to keep tabs on her through the day. Do I want to encourage a man who has two more the same age as Ryley? Not a chance."

Eva nodded and crossed her arms. "You're talking to a woman with two children who fell for a man with three. I had my misgivings but look how it worked out."

"Jesse pursued you with grim determination after you had time with him without the children around. I doubt a sixty-second interaction with Brand would produce the same result."

"Brand? You caught his name in this hot minute?"

"It was on his name tag. You didn't see it?" Brand Thorsen.

"I was too busy watching Archie size up the threat."

"Hmph. Archie's as free as I am to make connections this weekend."

"Maybe on paper. But connections are made with the heart," her friend said through a chuckle.

Beth watched Archie follow Ryley to the playground. Her daughter moved faster the closer she got to her favorite place. By the time she reached the climbing wall, Archie quickened his stride. She grinned and followed.

"Hi," she said when she joined her family.

"Hi, yourself. Looks like it'll be a busy weekend. We'll mingle a lot if Ryley makes friends."

"You may find yourself with lots of women to choose from." She kept her voice light and teasing.

He barked a laugh. "I've made my choice. And single moms looking for connection is not the choice I made."

"No? None of the women you've dated until now had children?" She ignored the difficult-to-swallow fact that she was a single mother so therefore not his choice. Not her business. It would never be her business.

He shook his head. "When I said I never saw myself as a dad, that included being a stepfather."

She waved her hand to present him with the obvious. "And yet, you're determined to be here for them. For life."

"That's different. I already love them," he said simply and cupped Ryley's bottom to steady her as she reached the top of the climb and wanted to pull her body up to sit on the platform. His forearms looked strong and capable, and his big hands held her little girl securely. She'd never fall as long as Archie had hold of her. When the slight danger passed, he released his hold and applauded her. "The boys are mine. I'm not sharing them with their biological father, in the way a stepdad would."

It was a fine line, but it was good to hear how he loved them, because she did, too. Wholeheartedly.

"Good job," he said to her child. Ryley giggled and scooted on her bottom to the top of the slide. She perched and waited to decide whether to go down. Climbing was one thing, sliding was another. She bit her tongue to keep from rushing her.

"The family activities will keep us hopping anyway," she said to Archie. "Should be fun for all of us."

"Eva's the lifeguard when the pool's open. You can relax while I'm in the pool with the boys. Maybe you could join us with Ryley?"

"I will. With you in the water and Eva on guard it should be a piece of cake."

She tamped back anticipation of seeing him in swim trunks, water glistening on his hair and shoulders as he splashed around with the boys. She already considered the view perfect. Perfect, indeed.

"Also, my parents have decided to visit the island to check it out for their retirement. We'll have a full weekend with my parents here and all the family events Farren has planned."

"Your parents are moving here?" The question was strangled by his obvious disappointment.

"They'll check around with retirement in mind," she repeated coldly. "Is that a problem?"

"No?" he hedged.

"No? Then why the disappointment?"

"It's not your parents, I'm sure they're great. It's another adjustment, more people in the boys' lives."

"In yours too." She hadn't understood all the changes he'd been forced to accept. "You're used to having no family around." And now, he was swamped with children, a co-parent, new friends and even extended family, namely hers.

He nodded and shoved his hands to his hips. "I've been alone for a lot of years."

"I don't know what to say except that you've met my parents before and they're not the kind who need to be with their kids all the time.

They have their own lives to lead and look forward to more freedom now that they're retiring."

"THIS IS LOADS OF FUN for the children," her mom said from her lounger next to Beth's. Her dad had worn Ryley out in the playground and had the napping toddler on his chest. "It's very busy and with so many other children, the boys won't have time to think about anything but their new friends."

Her parents had been delighted to meet Jeremy and Duncan. They were acquainted with Archie, of course, but had already noticed changes in him.

"Archie got it right bringing you here," her father said in his deep rumble. Beth patted his hand, remembering how she'd curled up on him as a child. The sound of his deep voice and steady thump of his heart had lulled her. She was pleased Ryley would have the same experience and memories of him.

He'd been the best dad a girl could have. And now he was the world's best Pops.

"You don't think our living arrangement is odd?"

"It's unconventional, but it's clear Archie wants what's best for the children. In the long term, they'll understand you both love them, and they'll appreciate you."

"Jeremy's had nightmares."

Her mom nodded. "I'm not surprised. He's old enough to let his imagination enter his dreams. Everyone I've loved and lost has visited me in dreams. As an adult I find it a comfort, but for a little boy, it could frighten him as his mind deals with his loss."

She pondered the comment. "I'm glad it's comforting, Mom." She sighed. "We hoped bringing them here would make them feel safe and loved and help with their grief. I guess you're right about the dreams. They're still processing their loss."

"The nightmares will pass with time."

"I hope so. Jeremy's a sensitive, caring boy and I hate the idea that he's suffering." Duncan hadn't had nightmares. Maybe he was too young. She hoped he bypassed these symptoms of grief.

A whistle blew, loud enough to catch everyone's attention. Eva called to three boys roughhousing on the pool deck. She pointed to the lawn on the far side of the chain link pool enclosure. The boys grinned and headed to the lawn where it was safer to show off their imaginary Ninja skills.

Beth searched the water for her boys and saw them with Archie on the edge of the pool. Water droplets hung like diamond pendants from his sprinkling of chest hair. While his sandy-colored hair was plastered to his head and dark with water, his body hair glinted with reddish highlights in the sun. He checked Duncan's water wings and when he looked up, he caught her watching.

He nodded and his face split into a broad grin.

"For a wanderer, Archie Jones looks like a happily settled man." Her mom's observation mirrored her own.

"We'll see," Beth said. Her chest tightened as she watched Archie point her out to the boys. Jeremy and Duncan waved furiously, their smiles as big as the sky. They were happy here. She wanted them to never feel anything but her love and commitment ever again.

"Yes, Archie did right by them. And by you and Ryley. Your mom and I have checked out condominiums in Summerville and cottages on the island. This may not be the hottest climate in the country, but it's near perfect for us."

Perfect. She agreed. "I could ask Archie for a suite for you in the home he's building." She'd give up her separate quarters if he balked.

"Absolutely not," her mom said firmly. "We want our privacy, and you need yours." She tossed her head in a gesture that reminded Beth of when she was a teen and had acted out.

"Thanks for the offer, honey, but your mom's right. And we'll find something that suits us."

Jeremy and Duncan walked through the gate and veered to where the other boys practiced their fighting skills. With various hand chops and kicks, the boys looked serious and focused. They welcomed her boys with smiles. Other boys had taken note and were moving toward the group.

"What do you call a group of boys gathering together to show off their punches and kicks?" She asked idly.

Her father answered. "A mob." He chuckled. "Archie's waving at you. Why not join him while we keep an eye on Jeremy and Duncan?"

She looked over at Archie and he coaxed her to join him. He *had* promised to show her how to swim. *Never too late to try.* She stood and dropped her cover up to the lounge chair.

As she walked to him, Archie's gaze roved over her body from feet to head and back again. The light in his eyes, and the attraction she saw there, gave her a bounce in her step and put a swing in her hips.

She wore a simple tank suit, one she'd had for years, but with Archie looking, she felt decadent and alluring. This man brought out her inner woman and she loved it.

She walked slowly down the steps into the shallow end and Archie walked to meet her. "Come for a lesson?"

"Do you think I'm silly for trying to learn at this age?"

"You don't need to be an Olympic caliber swimmer, Beth, but I'd like to know you'd be okay if you fell overboard. I plan to get a boat when the children can swim." He tugged on her hand and drew her close.

"We'll wear life jackets," she asserted.

"Yes, we will. But panic can interfere with rescues. Let me get you comfortable in the water."

"Yes, please. I'd like that." They walked together to the deep end, but being a motel pool, it wasn't over her head. Once there, Archie bent and lifted her into his arms. One arm slipped under her shoulders and the other under her knees. The sensation was odd, but she felt safe.

"I'll dunk you now," he said next to her ear. "It's no different from holding your breath in the shower."

"Okay, I'm ready." She held her breath, closed her eyes and felt water close over her.

Fifteen minutes later, she was floating on her back on her own and had rolled over several times to float on her front. She rose to her feet with a smile for her teacher. "Thank you," she said to the man who sat poolside watching her.

"Not nervous?"

She shook her head and smoothed water off her face and head. "I'm fine. Next time I'll try swimming."

The scent of grilled hotdogs wafted through the center court. He mimed eating a hot dog and she chuckled at his antics. No one would know by looking at him with his wide smile and his caring ways with the boys, and now her, that he'd been dealt a life-altering blow.

Her life had taken an unforeseen turn, but his had been upended. Archie was still awake for much of the night, probably grappling with the loss of his freedom.

Most nights she found herself in the living room, alone in the dark, waiting to hear if Jeremy would wake from a nightmare. There were times she heard footsteps overhead as Archie padded out to the balcony. Next, she'd hear the gentle scrape of one of the heavy ornate wrought iron chairs as he pulled it out from the café table Grady's aunt had used for years.

One of these nights, she might head up to that balcony and join him in his vigil.

She wondered what would happen if she did.

Chapter Twelve

Archie settled on the blanket next to Beth and across from her parents, Dee and Tom. The blanket next to theirs was taken up with Jesse, Eva, and next to them, their five children. Ryley sat with Eva's daughters, safely entertained.

He offered up a plateful of hot dogs while Beth passed a bowl of potato salad she'd made. He couldn't recall a meal outdoors on a blanket as a child. And because of these children, and Beth, he was already on his second picnic. His family hadn't run to homey, fun meals on the actual ground. It would be nice to have memories of times like this.

"Growing up, meals al fresco were served on the patio under an awning at a table set with linen, silverware, and flower centerpieces," he commented. "Those meals weren't nearly as much fun as this." By the time the bowl of potato salad got to him, there was only one good scoop left. Clearly, potato salad was popular at picnics. He should have thought of that when he picked up food that day they'd gone to beach. The J Roger offered potato salad and coleslaw. He'd remember for next time.

Beth peered into the bowl. "For our next picnic, I'll make more to be sure you get seconds if you like it." She peered into his face as if it mattered whether he liked her salad or not.

He took a forkful and tasted it. His tastebuds danced and he smiled into her eyes. She blinked. "This is the best potato salad I've ever had. Yes, next time please make a bigger batch."

"If I have time, I'll make more later. It improves if it sits in the fridge overnight."

"Hard to believe it could be better than this." He lifted another forkful to his mouth.

She kept her gaze on his and flushed a pretty pink at his compliment. "I took my mom's recipe and gave it a twist. Now, she makes it this way, too." She cleared her throat and looked at her smiling mother, who raised her can of flavored bubbly water in a silent salute.

He returned to his meal, oddly complimented by her mother's apparent approval. He'd wondered about adding Beth's side of her family to his life and worried that more new people would be hard to handle. If this was how easygoing things would be with Tom and Dee, then he was up for it. They were Ryley's grandparents, but also seemed taken with the boys. And they were Karly's parents too and from Bret, he'd heard great things.

That could only be counted as a win.

Keith and Bret had found the families they'd deserved as children. Hope glowed behind his heart that maybe he could find one, too.

His hot dog was smoky, greasy, and smothered in fried onions with a squirt of mustard. "More compliments to the chef," he said with a thumbs up sent to Grady O'Hara, the relaxed man behind the grill. The former grump wore an apron that demanded people kiss the cook. The man looked more like a stevedore than a globe-trotting real estate broker, but he made it a priority to be here for his wife on Singles Fest weekends.

The Singles Fest guests had begun to mingle around the pool, in front of their rooms, and on a few picnic tables around the lawn. Farren's hosting duties took her from group to group to encourage friendly chatter while she answered questions.

Yes, Last Chance Beach seemed to have a magic to it. The laidback lifestyle, coupled with good weather, and its proximity to the mainland and coastal highways, made the island a wonderful place for families and retirees.

"I hear you plan to build a home," Beth's father said as he held a ketchup-soaked hot dog an inch from his mouth. He took a bite and chewed.

"We have a meeting on Monday with the architect. Beth and the children will have a say in the design. I'd like the family to feel at home. Invested in the place." No fancy al fresco dining. Instead, he wanted room for picnics on the lawn. He'd handle the grilling and they'd enjoy Beth's potato salad.

Jeremy spoke up. "Pops, we want a big pool and a playground like we have here." Tom had suggested the name his grandchildren used for him, and Archie saw no harm in it.

"I see," Pops responded. "Then why not just stay here?" he asked the boy.

"Because the windows aren't big," Duncan blurted as if anyone should know that large windows were a must-have.

Beth nodded. "That's right." She patted Duncan's shoulder and gave her parents a look to squelch more questions.

Both grandparents smiled kindly at the boys and let the subject drop by asking about Duncan's training wheels on his two-wheeler.

LATER THAT NIGHT

"Can't sleep?" Beth asked softly from the open slider that led to Archie's balcony. "I heard the door slide, and you move your chair around."

Archie looked up from his phone, surprise lighting his face. "Hi. Here I thought you got a good night's sleep every night." The half moon was bright, and the light gilded his bare shoulders. He had an impressive pair of shoulders. He set the phone down on the tabletop. The screen showed a game of solitaire.

"You're the one who said we should fake it 'til we make it, right?"

He rose and pulled out the other wrought iron chair for her. "Join me. I could use the company." Tonight, he wore his usual nighttime attire of boxer briefs. Nice, snug briefs that skimmed his butt.

Don't notice. Who was she kidding? She always noticed.

"I'll get my robe," he offered.

"Don't bother on my account," she said breezily. "We've seen each other in our nightclothes plenty of times. Family life leaves nothing to the imagination." She cleared her throat and wrapped her short robe tighter around her before taking the seat. The sound of the surf whooshed across the dunes to her as she sat. "Surf sounds better at night. Like infinite comfort."

"That's why we listen to it on white noise machines and in spa massages." He sat down again, his forearms gleaming as the moonlight limned his shape. The table was café sized, and his knee brushed hers. Warmth spread from the contact, but she had no room to move. Truth was, she didn't care to. "Would you like a drink? Water or something?"

"I'm fine, thanks. I just had some. I love having the water in the fridge door." Banal, but maybe that's what they needed at three a.m.

He nodded and looked across the dunes, his face relaxed. "No nightmares for the last two nights. Progress, do you think?"

"Maybe. I hope so." She sighed and followed his gaze to the dunes. The grasses waved lazily along the sides. "Mom said Jeremy was probably processing his grief by seeing Keith in his dreams. That would frighten a young child and he may not be able to explain it."

Archie nodded. "Sounds right."

"My parents stayed until I yawned them out of the house at midnight." They'd missed television time tonight because of the visit. Archie had made himself scarce so her parents could have time with Ryley and Beth alone.

"I like your parents. Getting to know them better today was good. It's all good, Beth." His voice went deep but softer somehow. She felt the honesty in his tone and breathed a little easier. Earlier, she'd been worried that too many people in his life at once might be too much for him.

"I'm glad. If you didn't like them, things could be awkward."

"Bret loves them and that's good enough for me. What is it you want to tell me?"

"Nothing." His question startled her. "I'm not sure why I came up, except that we didn't get our grown-up time on our own. I guess I'm used to ending the day with you on the sofa."

"We've already fallen into a routine?"

She widened her eyes and let her jaw drop in mock surprise. "Are we already old? Next thing we'll be snoring in front of the TV."

He chuckled and his eyes filled with humor. "That's scary, Beth. But I missed our quiet time, too."

She nodded. "I'm looking forward to meeting with the architect."

"I'll be glad when the project's done and we move in." His teeth flashed in the moonlight as he smiled. "Tom and I agree on a lot, it seems. He mentioned to me how you're a natural caregiver, always watching out for people." His eyes shone with interest. "You've been wonderful this whole time."

She felt heat rise at his compliment. "Thank you. I've been pleasantly surprised by you and your commitment to the children." She tilted her head. "The boys listen when you give them instructions or set rules and Ryley's quite smitten."

"Now that we've established that we're not a half-bad team, we need to discuss what to do about the nightmares, because I doubt they're gone for good." He sighed and looked at the table. "It's time for Jeremy and Duncan to talk to a professional. At least for an assessment. They're two years apart and those years make for important differences in their level of understanding."

Surprised at his insight, she chuckled. "Have you been reading child development books?"

"I probably should, but no, not yet. This profound insight comes direct from Dee. And when I checked with Eva, she confirmed." He stood suddenly and she craned her neck to see his face.

"Mom didn't mention your conversation. It's good to know you and she communicate well." He made to step away. "Should I let you get some sleep?" She set her hands to the arm rests to lever herself to stand, but he touched her shoulder to stop her.

He shook his head. "I'm getting my laptop. Since we're up anyway, we can do some research into child psychologists in the area. We can both read the screen."

Now she understood how, in the wee hours, he'd furnished the house in time for them to move in. Archie Jones didn't like to waste time. If he was awake, he was thinking or doing something.

An hour later, they sat with their heads close together as they perused the last of three websites they'd found interesting. They'd combed the area for grief counsellors and child psychologists. They'd bookmarked three as worthy of more research.

"When Jesse's wife passed, he and his children went for help. I'll see what he thinks of these three. The one he used is too distant to be practical for us."

"Good idea." Suddenly aware of how close he was, she turned her face toward his, only to find him looking into her eyes from two inches away. Her heart stuttered at his nearness. "I should probably head to bed," she said, weakly.

He didn't respond except to drop his gaze to her mouth. "I'd like to kiss you goodnight," he said. His warm breath fanned across her lips.

Her eyelids drooped of their own accord, and she moved the millimeters needed to brush his mouth with hers. His lips were warm and softer than she'd thought. They moved in a gentle rhythm she liked without pressing for more. His hands settled on her shoulders, and she wanted him to pull her closer, but instead, he skimmed his palms down her arms to rest near her elbows.

Electric. Of course, it was. Foolish to hope the kiss would be anything but charged. But she couldn't explore what she'd felt. Not now.

Not yet.

Maybe never, because that way lay disaster.

"Good night. Sleep well," she said as she pulled back and rose from her chair.

"Same to you," he replied. She didn't turn to see if he watched her walk away. Because if she did and he was, she might not find the strength to leave.

Chapter Thirteen

Saturday Morning – Barnacle Bill's Mini-Golf

Archie noticed the guy with the twins check out Beth again. He and his party trailed them through the course. This time, he'd also read the guy's name tag. Archie'd accepted long ago that his own name was old-fashioned and never used anymore, but Brand sounded like a character in a graphic novel. He'd be a guy with scars and brand marks with a perpetual scowl who wore a dark hoodie and lived in the shadows, unwanted and unloved.

But the reality was, Brand Thorsen was a light-haired, skinny guy with a disappearing chin and whose eyes were close together. Well, he would be if Archie had his way. In reality, Brand had to be descended from Vikings. Must spend his days off at the gym. And those teeth!

Archie flexed his arms and huffed quietly. "I've got to find a gym." It was more a mutter than a comment for Beth.

"Aren't they lovely little girls?" Beth said, as she gazed at Thorsen leaning over one of his twins to show her how to hold the club. The pint-sized cutie bounced with glee when her father praised her grip.

The Viking also had adorable kids.

"They sure are," Archie agreed, glancing at Jeremy and Duncan with a swell of pride.

Thorsen had been paired with a single mom with a boy a bit older than Jeremy. The woman looked happy enough and engaged with her son and Thorsen's girls.

Her son said something that made the adults laugh out loud. The Viking commented and touched the woman's forearm. She tilted her head and smiled into his eyes.

Archie would love to see that look on Beth's face today. Last night's brush of her lips on his had given him foolish dreams, but he put it down to the quiet swoosh of the surf, the lateness, and their success in creating a plan to help with Jeremy's nightmares. He'd wanted to explore her mouth, but he had zero experience with women like Beth and had floundered with a lame move that ended with his hands on her arms.

He shook his head at his lack of finesse. But the truth was that none of his moves would be welcome. His moves were designed to get what he wanted. He kissed with urgency, he petted with heat, he smoothed his hands down a woman's body while skimming off her clothes. Most of the time, his dates dressed with easy removal in mind. Beth was nothing like them and he struggled with what to say and how to move ahead.

He wanted her so badly that he froze with fear of messing up.

But at night, Beth wore tees and shorts under a robe worn thin with age. He'd noticed her pulling the robe down to cover as much of her thighs as she could. She was no seductress.

She smelled great and while they'd stared at his laptop, she'd leaned close. He'd felt her warmth next to him. At one point, he'd slipped his hand to the back of her chair in a lame attempt to have her move closer, but she hadn't noticed.

Her entire focus had been on the screen as she read it, leaving him to feel like an awkward teenager invisible to the pretty girl.

That particular experience was a first.

"It looks like they've made a connection. Isn't that nice?" Beth commented as the Viking leaned down to whisper in his companion's ear. The woman smiled a flirty response.

"That's the point. Take the pressure off single parents, let them have family fun together and see what happens." He dismissed the other couple, preferring to focus on the woman in front of him.

"Exactly. Farren's beyond happy with how things are going this season."

"So am I," he said on a husky note.

Beth pulled her luscious bottom lip slowly into her mouth. He couldn't look away as he recalled how little he'd tasted of her. He wanted another kiss and this time, he'd go deep.

Tension pulled between them, giving him hope that later, they'd explore each other. An alarm went off in his head as blood rushed through him. She was still a sweet, innocent woman who'd take exception to his usual behavior.

Which brought him back to needing to manage this thing he felt for her. But manage it he must.

Jeremy shouted that he got a hole in five. The boy raised his arms high to an imaginary crowd of fans. "I did it faster than last time," he announced.

"You sure did," Archie said, laughing when Duncan blew a raspberry at his brother. He caught Beth's amused glance and grinned wider. He reached for her hand, and she let him twine their fingers. He tugged her along with one hand while he pushed Ryley's empty stroller toward the next hole.

Being an evolved male meant he did not look back to see if the Viking noticed them holding hands. But he was sure Brand took note.

Beth didn't seem to mind that their hands were entwined. In fact, she initiated several affectionate touches that had Archie in a spin. She swept her fingers down his forearm once and then let him slide his palm to her lower back.

Things were looking up for him. The family groups became boisterous as kids ran from one group to another to check scores, cheer on their new friends, and peer at the various painted undersea creatures that populated the water in the course. A couple of parents attempted to keep order, but it was clearly a lost cause.

"This is mayhem," he said with a chuckle. "But the kids are having a great time. Duncan's run up ahead to see the boys he met on the playground last night. I guess he'll forfeit his turn."

"I'm sure he won't notice." Beth squeezed his fingers and let go of his hand to take her first swing on the ninth hole.

MAYBE SHE SHOULDN'T have held Archie's hand, and she probably shouldn't have kissed him goodnight in the wee hours either. But he'd said he wanted to kiss her, and she knew if she didn't take control, the kiss would get out of hand. The brush of their lips was electric.

It would have been catastrophic if he'd been the one to do the kissing. He'd have pressed close, held her tight, sent her spinning. His eyes had told her as much.

Thank goodness she'd chosen the coward's way out and made the move. She'd had surprise on her side and had kept things breezy. But walking off that balcony had been hard.

Just before she'd fallen asleep, she'd vowed to avoid the balcony from now on. No more late-night visits.

She hoped when night rolled in, and she heard the door slide open she'd resist temptation. A stroll around the center court might help. Yes, she'd do that instead of joining him on that private balcony in the soft dark with the seductive surf sweeping her close to him.

Ryley giggled and clapped her hands, bringing her back to the game, which had quickly deteriorated into a shoving match between the brothers because Duncan had returned and expected to take Jeremy's turn because he'd missed a couple.

"Hey boys," she said, with a raised eyebrow in Archie's direction. "One more shove from either of you and there'll be no ice cream cones when the game's over."

Both boys froze, gave her their best grumpy faces, and shook hands. According to them, Keith had insisted on handshakes at the end of their squabbles. "I'm glad to see you do that," she said. "Your dad would be proud."

"He is proud. He said he'd always be proud of us." Jeremy's declaration made Archie blink and she had to catch a breath.

"You're right," Archie said softly.

They got through the next five holes with Duncan losing interest in anything but his new friends who played up ahead. They allowed him to join the other group as an observer. Jeremy crowed about each swing and how much he improved at every hole. It helped that Archie stopped counting how many swings Jeremy took.

Archie went out of his way to make sure the children had fun everyday and that each experience they shared was good.

Karly must never have witnessed this fun side of Archie, or else her sister would have mentioned it. Maybe Archie hadn't been around enough for anyone to see his innate kindness and generosity.

Archie could be very entertaining. The way he'd kept an eye on Brand had amused her, but she didn't feel a need to explain she'd already decided not to encourage a man with girls the same age as Ryley. She preferred to keep Archie guessing.

Being around him made her feel like a thirteen-year-old with her first crush.

"WHY DON'T YOU TWO SNEAK away and join the others for the beach stroll? We'll stay here and watch the children." Dee's offer hung in the air after they'd enjoyed a simple meal of her Caesar salad, meatloaf, broccoli, and cauliflower. Tom nodded his agreement with the plan while Archie fully embraced the idea. But he took his cue from Beth, who looked hesitant.

"We shouldn't impose after you cooked this entire meal, Dee." Archie said the right words, but he couldn't make them sound sincere. He badly wanted to walk the beach alone with Beth and this offer was a perfect way to get his wish.

"We'll go if you let us clean up," Beth said, with a quick sidelong glance at him. Pink rose in her cheeks as she stood. She gathered dirty plates in a stack and carried them to the counter.

He jumped to his feet and continued where she left off and collected the serving dishes. Opening the dishwasher, he loaded everything while Beth washed Ryley's sticky fingers and smudged face. Ryley had surprised them all with her love of broccoli. Her little hands still held remnants of the tiny green sprouts between her fingers.

The boys had already headed to the bathroom to wash up. "Brush your teeth while you're in there," Archie called.

Muttered agreement floated down the hall.

Tom chuckled. "They like you or they wouldn't agree this fast. I always had to call on Dee for help with my children."

Beth smiled. "You were the softie, and we could delay bedtime with you. Mom, not so much."

"I suspect Keith was a wonderful father. His children have been given a good start, haven't they, Tom?" Dee said quietly. "All you need to do is build on the strong foundation Keith left you."

Archie nodded. "We appreciate you watching them. We've hardly had time to catch our breath today." He grinned. "The fun started at Barnacle Bill's and the pool time finished us off. But the kids have endless energy."

The time in the pool with Beth had energized him in ways he couldn't share out loud. The woman had him in the palm of her hand. A new sensation, but one he welcomed.

He'd had no idea how active the kids could be when other children were around. He didn't just want the beach stroll. He needed it to unwind.

Dee helped Ryley to the floor and the child tore off to see what her older brothers were doing. She didn't like them having fun without her.

"It's been a while since we babysat. It's time for them to get to know us," Dee said. "Small steps."

"So," Tom said slowly, "what is the beach stroll? Sounds formal, but casual, and I'm confused."

"Saturday night is the speed dating dinner at the resort. People change seats between courses to see if they make a connection that way. But if some of the adults have already made a connection, and they don't want to go for dinner, there's a stroll along the beach for family time. Parents can talk with each other while the kids explore the rocks and tide pools together. It's a family alternative to speed dating."

"Some of the teenage sitters entertain the kids by pointing out sea creatures that live in the tidepools. They talk about the rocks, too, and other interesting things, and keep the children from climbing too high. Farren calls it a nature walk. It's a real hit." Archie set the dishwasher to start and turned to face the others. "I didn't realize I'd absorbed so much from Eva. I think there's even a ghost story about the lighthouse."

"It sounds perfect and you two should go along on your own." Tom held out his hand to Dee. When she took it, he pulled her hand to his lips for a kiss. "We'll be fine here. In fact, I look forward to horsey rides with Ryley."

With that, the older couple moved off into the great room, leaving Archie alone with Beth.

"Do you want to walk the beach with me?"

"Yes." The glint in her eyes must mirror the happiness in his. "I'll change my shoes and get my jacket. The breeze will be cool tonight."

"I'll keep you warm," he promised, but she'd already walked down the hall toward her room. The glance she tossed him over her shoulder said she'd heard him. His mouth split into a grin as his heart stuttered.

ARCHIE'S GRIN OF ANTICIPATION lightened her heart. A stroll at sundown on the beach sounded like heaven. They'd be in public, but able to talk privately. The children were safe with her parents.

She freshened up, combed her hair, and put in a barrette at the back of her head. The breeze picked up at night and it would be a rat's nest if she didn't contain at least some of it. A slick of lip color and she was ready to go. Grabbing a windbreaker, she returned to the kitchen to find it empty.

A moment later, she heard heavy footsteps on the stairs. Archie appeared in the kitchen with his navy-blue cable knit sweater in hand. He'd run a comb through his hair and a spicy scent wafted by her nose.

"You clean up well," she commented.

He tugged her hand into his and opened the kitchen door to the breezeway. "Let's go before the kids want to come along."

She chuckled. "Right. Silent escape is our best option." She followed him outside and watched as he quietly pulled the door closed.

"I don't feel guilty, do you?"

"Not at all. Karly tells me she and Bret grab their moments to be alone whenever they can." She felt heat rise in her cheeks because her sister hadn't meant public walks on the beach.

Archie let the comment slide which surprised her. Normally, he'd have quipped a saucy reply.

Instead, he drew her close to his side and she moved in happily. "We'll be all right, Beth."

His reassurance warmed her. "Yes, I believe we will." Vestiges of doubt still lingered about his commitment, but she didn't let them take hold.

Her phone rang as they passed the pool. She should've left it behind, but she wanted to be available if there was a problem with the kids.

"You should take that. I left mine in my room."

She tugged her phone out of her pocket and checked her screen.

Gareth.

After three years of silence. She'd love to answer and give him a piece of her mind, but he wasn't worth the energy. "Oh, it's nothing. Not my parents." She turned her phone off.

"You might want to turn that back on since we're leaving the kids behind." He cocked an eyebrow, obviously curious.

She shook her head. "They'll be fine." She didn't feel like discussing an ex. Not hers and not the multitude of his. But her voice had been curt, and she didn't want their quiet time to start with a snippy comment. "It was an ex," she explained. "No one I want to discuss."

"Fair enough." They walked the boardwalk in comfortable silence. "I want to thank you again for agreeing to this huge change in your life. I don't know of any other woman who would make a shift like this."

Her heart warmed. "I'm grateful, too. This is not the hardship you think it is." She looked up at his strong profile and smiled. "I get to have my daughter with me every day, Ryley has inherited two big brothers who're very sweet boys and even my parents are included. You've provided a home, and I don't have to worry about bills. Even my mortgage will be covered when I rent my place." He had saved her from financial ruin, plain and simple.

But this attraction she felt for him was not rooted in his financial generosity. No. She liked him for who he was at heart. Archie Jones fit her idea of a good man, plain and simple. Was she shocked by the changes she'd seen in him? Absolutely. "Do you see how much you've changed since you got the boys?"

"Any man would do what I've done."

She stopped and he stopped with her. They stood beside the playground slide, and his face was in shadow.

"Some men wouldn't do half of what you've done. Not even for their own children." She cleared her throat and went on, "I haven't thought of things in this way until now. You've made my life much easier, just by sticking around. And you've given yourself over to the needs of Keith's children. He made the right choice in you."

"I'm not sure I agree but thanks for your vote of confidence."

She hated to ask, tried not to, but in the end, she couldn't fight the urge. "Will you really stay for the long haul?"

"I plan to, and I never plan anything." He quipped and stepped out of the shadow. "But having Keith's kids is the best reason on earth to hang around. Last Chance Beach is a good place for them and for me. I hope you feel the same."

"I do." She smiled up into his earnest face and wondered how it would feel to be with Archie; to have the right to touch him, to argue with him and to kiss and make up.

She'd never wondered this way about anyone before. Not even Gareth. She hoped he'd called for a simple reason. There was no way she'd get caught up in the drama of his life again. She'd learned her lesson.

"Maybe I'm the same as I've always been," he said quietly. "Maybe you're seeing the real me for the first time because of the circumstances."

"You've given me something to think about." And she would.

Chapter Fourteen

Beth had gone from a smile to a frown and Archie wondered why. All he'd said was that he'd stay in Last Chance Beach because he loved Keith's kids, and the place was good for everyone. She'd even agreed.

He rested his forearms on her shoulders to pull her back to him. "Where have you gone? Nowhere serious I hope."

"Hm? No, sorry. That call brought up some old stuff I haven't thought of in a long time. His name is Gareth and things didn't end well. I don't know why he'd call me out of the blue. I wish he hadn't."

He nodded. "Still want to join the stroll?" People were coming out of their rooms and the happy sounds of children floated toward them. "We can return to the house if you'd prefer."

"You're not getting out of the beach walk that easily." Her smile wavered, and it was clear she struggled with hearing from the ex.

A couple of teenage girls headed toward them, and he assumed they were the guides for the nature walk. Children called to them by name and a rush toward the playground ensued.

"We need to move, or we'll be swarmed. We can stop on the observation deck and let the crowd move past." Archie led Beth to the deck, and soon the teens were abreast of them, trailed by a line of children chattering and laughing.

Beth reached for his hand and gave it a squeeze, her frown replaced by a shy smile. Sometimes, she took his breath away. "The ex who called."

"Yes?" He used his gentlest voice and gave her hand a light squeeze of encouragement.

"It was Ryley's father."

"Her *father*?" He'd made wild assumptions about how Ryley had come to be. "I was under the impression she was not from a relationship and that you..." he trailed off because it was clear he was an idiot. Nothing new there. "Will he be a problem for you? For custody or...anything?"

They couldn't lose Ryley. Not that sweet child. Just when he thought he had a clear path into the future...

"His wife would never allow him to push for custody." Her eyes were huge, defiant and her chin went up.

This news staggered him. He stood back because it was hard to think while touching her. "Ryley's the result of an affair with a married man?"

She nodded. "This is not exactly how I saw our conversation going this evening," she said with a tremulous smile. "Gareth's call surprised me and I'm tired, Archie. Exhausted by this secret." She sighed and sounded as if the weight of the world came out with the air. "I haven't heard from him in three years."

This guy was Ryley's father and hadn't been in touch with Beth since before Ryley was born? That sweet little girl deserved a real dad, not some guy who could go this long without being in touch.

Stupid to wonder how he could ignore his own child. His parents had been the same.

It was no surprise he'd been a wanderer, unable to connect with any one woman. But sharing his life with Beth each day had changed him. Had made him a better man.

It wasn't just the boys who'd upended his life. He clasped her shoulders, drew her in for a hug. "I need to process this, and we'll finish this conversation on the balcony later. It's too crowded here."

She agreed as more people walked by, voices calling, laughter floating toward the stars. So many happy faces, so much fun to be had.

She cleared her throat. "What do we do now?"

"We stroll the beach, calm down, and think of our options for the morning. I don't care what's going on with his marriage, he's not coming after our girl. I won't let him."

"Oh, Archie." She rested her head on his shoulder, and he murmured comfort words he'd never used in his life.

"We'll be okay. Don't worry. I'm here and I'll never leave." And the one, the big one, he couldn't say out loud. *I love you.*

"Hey, hi! We wondered if you'd come." Eva's voice broke in. "This looks serious. Are you okay, Beth?"

She swept her hands across her cheeks. "Yes, I'm—we're—fine. I just got a call I wasn't prepared for."

"You sure you're okay?"

She nodded. "Yes." She stepped out of Archie's arms, and he felt the loss.

Eva pulled Beth into a hug. "Isn't this great?"

"Yes. Great." She tossed Archie a glance. "Our kids are with my parents. We're here to enjoy the stroll."

Eva gave her a curious look. "And?"

"And that's it. We're here, we're strolling." Her tone left no room for further questions.

Eva's gaze roved from Beth's face to Archie's. "I came so I could see how my new babysitters interact with children. They've taken courses but that doesn't mean they'll be intuitive with the kids. I should move up to see how things are going."

"I'll come with you," Beth offered with a guilty glance for him. He nodded his farewell.

The women moved off. "Great, now I'm stuck with you," he told Jesse.

"But what's worse is I'm stuck with you." His friend shook his head. "We wanted to have a stroll together, maybe hold hands, talk without the kids interrupting, but Eva takes her position seriously and works to keep her standards high with the sitters."

They watched as the women moved briskly along the wooden walkway following the line of children and teens. When they stepped onto the sand, Eva moved close enough to hear the children's questions about the shoreline and tide pools and the teens' responses.

Archie replied automatically to Jesse's conversation until his friend stopped on the sand and poked him hard in the shoulder. "Where are you? I've asked how things are with Beth and you've given me nada."

"Things are fine. Beth and I have come to terms with our arrangement." He couldn't claim a connection with Beth until he knew for certain that she felt the same way he did. She may have given him signals, but this phone call could ruin everything. Beth could have leftover feelings for Ryley's father.

Jesse chuckled. "That sounds like a business merger. You've come to terms? I've heard you say the same thing about investments."

Archie nodded. "And isn't this an investment in the boys' future?"

Jesse narrowed his gaze and Archie saw he'd only created more curiosity, rather than putting his friend off the scent.

"Eva wants the inside info, is that it?" Women seemed inherently more curious than men about other people's relationships.

Jesse had the decency to look guilty as he nodded. "Personally, I think you and Beth would be great together. But since I've never seen you with anyone but short-term women, I know nothing about what you want for long-term." Jesse squared off with him.

Archie took a step back, rolled his shoulders to release tension that had appeared with Jesse's pointed comments. "She just had an ex call her. She didn't talk to him, but I don't know if she's as free as she led me to believe."

"But she mentioned it was an ex. Which means she's not hiding anything. Everyone has exes. Especially you."

Archie snorted. In his mind, Beth was unencumbered by feelings for men in her past. She'd made it seem that way when she ditched the call.

"No one's perfect, Archie, least of all you, but Beth is exactly who you need for those kids. You need to appreciate her and how much she's sacrificed to help you out."

"Good to know." He stomped away with Jesse at his heels. "I hadn't noticed her giving up her home, her private life, her freedom, to come live with me, the ogre who misuses people." Jesse had pricked him in ways he'd never been before. He'd generally taken criticism of his lifestyle in stride because before Jeremy and Duncan, he'd never cared how people saw him. Somehow those boys had made him look deeper into himself.

He didn't like what he saw, what he'd been, but he was a different man now.

Beth turned back to face them, looking uncertain. "Are you two okay?" she called. Did the woman have a sixth sense or eyes in the back of her head?

"Fine," Jesse said. "Just discussing the weather."

She looked doubtful but moved to join Eva.

"Later I'll invite her up to the balcony after the kids are asleep."

"We did that, too. Good place for conversation." Jesse grinned. "And sometimes for other things."

Archie gave him a side-eye. "We have some talking to do."

"Is that what you call it?"

"Yes, because that's what it is." He'd clear the air with her about Gareth and see if he posed a threat. If she allowed it, he'd be by her side when she called her ex in the morning. "You're right, Jesse. Beth is a good woman and I'm lucky to have her in my life."

BETH LOOKED FORWARD to their time on the balcony tonight. If she wanted more from this co-parenting life, and it seemed that Archie did, then sooner or later, she'd have to tell him the truth. The whole truth. She owed him that much. After all, his life was an open book. Everyone knew how Archie had lived.

While no one knew the truth about Beth. She'd let everyone see her as sweet and innocent when she was anything but. What she'd done was unpardonable.

But she wasn't sorry for having Ryley. Never that.

She and Eva walked together beside the crowd of young people. The teens pointed out sea life in the tide pools between the craggy rocks several yards back from the shore. The children sounded fascinated and most of the teens were able to answer whatever questions arose.

Eva appeared pleased overall, but she wandered closer to one group and helped a child to climb down off a rock. She gave the teen some advice on how to keep her charges off the rocks and nearer to the other children. "We can't have them fall behind or wander off on their own as dusk makes the shadows deeper."

The gentle warning made her happy that Ryley was safe with her parents. The boys were of a better age to bring along next time.

She checked over her shoulder and saw Archie and Jesse deep in conversation. Archie caught her look and gave her a wave. He mugged a face. It was clear he was making do with Jesse's company but preferred to be with her.

Drifting toward the shore, Beth walked alone, and mulled over her many blunders. The largest was listening to Gareth in the first place. But three years ago, she'd witnessed the utter breakdown of Gareth and Suzanne's marriage.

No more secrets. She needed to clear the air with Archie and with her family. She hoped they could all survive the truth of what she'd done.

She wasn't the naïve woman she'd been before. Now, she was a mother with a daughter to protect from his lies. Gareth had no clue what to expect from the new Beth and that cheered her, a mother ready to do battle for her daughter's future.

A gentle smile tilted her lips as she turned fully around and waited for Archie to notice she waited for him. He waved immediately as if he'd hoped for a sign from her. He spoke to Jesse who waved, too. Both men jogged to their respective women.

Her heart thudded in synch with every step that brought Archie closer. It was time to give him the full messy story.

Chapter Fifteen

After bath time, tooth brushing, and story time, Archie searched out wine flutes and pulled his favorite sauvignon blanc from the wine fridge. Next, he found some decently aged cheese. The cracker selection consisted of bland white squares with salt on top. He took a sniff, but they smelled like nothing. He wasn't sure if he'd ever had them, but they must be okay.

He heard Beth's shower run but when the water shut off, he trooped upstairs with his treats. He had a couple of dessert plates wedged under his arm. He considered candles, but the table didn't have room. This wasn't a date, anyway, but a time for deep discussion.

Archie told himself tonight wasn't about seduction, but of her comfort should she choose to talk about Ryley's father. A sip or two of wine could help her find the words and ease her fear.

No doubt Beth was nervous about revealing her story, especially when she hadn't yet told her family about Gareth.

He needed to know what had happened to her and how Gareth might be a problem this long after the birth of his daughter. Archie needed to be prepared if Beth's custody of Ryley came under threat. In the morning he'd call his lawyer to give her a heads up. If parental rights were not an area she was familiar with, she'd know where to find the top person in the field.

He set out the plates and food and opened the wine. Then he arranged the chairs side by side so they could see straight out across the dunes. This way, he could hold her hand or pull her in for a hug if required.

A muffled sound alerted him to Beth standing at the opened deck door. "Hi. You're here."

"Hi," Beth said from the door. She looked fresh, clean, and her hair hung in damp ropes that left wet smudges just below her collar bones. Her robe covered her sleep shorts but exposed the smooth length of her legs. Her feet were bare as she stacked one foot on top of the other. Her toenails were painted a sexy pearly pink.

"You look beautiful," he blurted like a teenager who couldn't rein in his thoughts. He blinked. She brought out the most juvenile side of him. A side he hadn't seen in twenty years.

"Since when?" A light in her eyes brought her humor to the surface.

He pulled out her chair for her. "Since I've come to know you." Her scent filled his nose as she sank into the seat. Lavendar and vanilla, a heady combination. They both knew he hadn't always seen the real Beth, the Beth he saw now.

"Oh, thanks," she said lightly. "Is this a formal wine and cheese event? Should I have dressed up?"

"You're perfect." He was in his boxer briefs, a tee, and a robe. "I'm dressed in my usual midnight attire."

"Life with children. By the end of the day, all I want is comfort after chasing Ryley. Today she opened the bottom cupboard in the kitchen and stood on the bottom shelf to try to climb to the counter."

"She's quick. Moves like lightning." He chuckled and picked up the bottle of wine and held it up. "For you?"

She sighed her consent. "A half glass would be great." He poured lightly and gave himself a half as well.

She raised her flute, and he clinked the rims. "The wine's good and the cheese is tasty, but what's up with these crackers? They taste like baked paste."

"Sorry, kids seem to like them with peanut butter or cheese. I'll pick up some with better flavor next time. You don't remember them from childhood?" She grimaced. "You probably never had them, right?"

"My childhood was wasted."

Her laugh made his heart beat faster. She sobered quickly, took a sip of her wine. "About Gareth. I was with Gareth and Suzanne for two years and watched their marriage fall apart in the worst possible ways. After a while, he confided in me. She accused him of affairs he swore he never had. When it came to light that she'd been away for a couple of weekends with a friend of his, the fights became epic. Their children were aware and frightened enough to hide when the screaming started, which became more frequent."

He felt the color drain from his face. This was déjà vu. When he and Bret were still at home, there was a housekeeper, but, while kind enough, she wasn't there for *them*. No one was. "You stayed for the kids."

Beth nodded. "I couldn't leave. Not when I was their anchor. They'd never had another nanny and I wanted to shield them as much as I could."

"And he kept confiding?" A picture formed and he imagined Beth, younger, worried for her charges, witness to the arguments. She'd have been easy pickings.

"He did. Rarely at first but when she moved out, he became relentless in his need for support. I felt beholden and was happy that the children had one involved parent. She left because everything was his before they married. There was a pre-nuptial agreement that said she'd have to leave if they discussed divorce. At least, that's what he said." She sounded doubtful. "He claimed to be relieved that the fights were over for the kids' sake."

"You believed him at the time." She nodded, mute. Suddenly he didn't want to hear about the man that made Beth feel like this. The man that made her so ashamed she lied about the conception of her child. He shook his head. "I'll remind you that my past isn't what anyone would call conventional."

She tilted her head and squished her eyelids together, giving him a nod of acceptance.

"Your opinion of me was correct," he continued. "And I accept your judgment. I never settled anywhere, had way too much fun with way too many women. Some of them were young."

She sucked in a sharp breath.

"Not that young," he blustered. "Old enough, but not of an age where they wanted anything permanent. They were looking for a good time for a short time. I gave them what they wanted."

She gave him a narrow stare. "I know what you're doing." Her hand fell away from the stem of her wine flute to settle on her lap, palm up, fingers curled.

"Please tell me what that is, because I'm at a loss." All he wanted was to forestall whatever confession she was about to make.

"You're reminding me of your past because you want me to feel more comfortable. You don't need to tell me. I remember how you like to live." She smiled and bumped her shoulder to his in what he hoped was affection. "Sorry, how you *used* to live."

"Thanks for clarifying. I'm glad to hear you say it." He shifted and slid his palm to the back of her wrought iron chair. Felt a rope of damp hair at his fingers. "Circumstances change, people change, and here we are in our new normal." It may have been a surprise to get the boys, and maybe he'd never seen this life for himself, but he'd embraced it. The boys had stolen his heart, and no sacrifice was too big to keep them happy and healthy. He understood that, now. He wouldn't have before.

"I'm not the same woman I was when I met Gareth. So, yes, people change. I changed again after he left me. He has no idea who I am now." A lift of her chin, a quirk of her lips showed a woman ready for battle.

"I couldn't be prouder of you."

"Really? I'm surprised. I've spent too much time thinking how stupid I was, how gullible. I never considered someone else would see me differently."

"You didn't trust your family?" This surprised him, but he knew little of families.

"Karly and my parents would've understood, would have made excuses for me. Of course, they would, they love me." She patted her chest. "But I couldn't forgive myself and I couldn't accept their support." She frowned.

"Whatever you need, Beth. If it helps to hear me tell you I've made plenty of mistakes, then I will." He'd changed for the better and never wanted to go back to the man he used to be. "I've never spent time with a woman like you." He dug through his memories. Shrugged. "Maybe one or two of my companions had the capacity to grow into a woman as confident and strong as you are, but I didn't wait around to see it. Never wanted to."

He lifted her hand and kissed her knuckles lightly. "You're the real deal, Beth. A full-grown woman with grace, humor, and strength. I was a fool for not seeing you before, but I see you now. I *see* you and I like what I see. Gareth, and your past with him, won't change that."

COULD IT BE THAT SIMPLE? She confesses all and her poor choices fade into the past, never to infect the present. Fanciful nonsense. Not confessing and lying by omission had isolated her from her loved ones. She didn't like this secret, didn't like how she felt when she remembered her choices in Gareth's house.

Gareth disgusted her and, worse, made her mistrust her judgment. Why hadn't she seen him for the snake he was? Because he'd told her what she wanted to hear, and she'd believed every word.

"I lived in their house, cared for their children. The arguments between Gareth and Suzanne infected the atmosphere in the home. It was terrible."

Archie nodded slowly. "Been there, heard it myself."

Her heart filled with compassion and her eyes felt full. "Of course, you did." She leaned in the mere inches between them and kissed his lips. He closed his eyes and let her lips roam warmly over his. Kissing him had become easy. "Karly's told me some of the things Bret shared over the years." She sighed, pulled back and continued. "Gareth's children suffered and hid to escape the yelling. And I became his sounding board."

"He played on your sympathy, like all bastards do."

"That doesn't excuse the fact that I ignored my sense of right and wrong, my conscience. I ignored every red flag and leapt impulsively into an affair." She'd never been impulsive before Gareth, instead she'd been cautious, cool, and collected.

"His complaints about her weren't all that convinced you. There must've been more. Don't simplify and take all the blame." He lifted her wine flute, and she took it gratefully.

She sipped and mulled some more. "You have a point. I was living there and for months I watched the marriage disintegrate."

"One night I got up to go to the kitchen for a glass of warm milk. On the way back upstairs, I found Suzanne kissing a stranger at the top of the stairs. A kiss goodnight as he was leaving." She accepted Archie's concern, his care. "Turns out that was the last straw."

"What happened? Did you tell Gareth?"

She shook her head. "Suzanne brazened it out in the moment. I remember thinking I had proof that what Gareth said was true." She hadn't slept that night. "The next morning, she claimed Gareth had been having a long-term affair and she'd acted out of anger and a need for revenge. And then she told me she was moving out."

She put her elbow on the table and her face in her hands. "I didn't know what to think. These people were broken, vicious." She'd understood that about both of them, but pulling away from the children was impossible.

"You did what was best at the time."

"Even though Suzanne and Gareth hated each other's guts, they both wanted me to stay to provide the care their kids needed." She snorted. "The children's welfare wasn't the only reason he wanted me to stay."

Archie pulled her into a hug. It was lovely and warm against his chest with his arms across her back. "When Suzanne moved out a week later, she left the children to me."

Gareth had broken down in Beth's arms, had sworn that Suzanne was lying about his infidelity.

"Slowly and steadily, Gareth worked on me. He focused on me. He didn't date, didn't bring any other women home. He played the doting dad to a tee.

"I believed him when he said they were divorcing. He encouraged me to step into place as the woman of the house. I, um, wasn't used to flings. To me, what we had was real." Heat crept into her cheeks. She'd been naïve and inexperienced. Foolish.

"I got pregnant. At first, I was thrilled. I assumed we'd build a family of our own and my child would have siblings that already loved me. I didn't discuss our relationship with my family because he said they may not understand that we were in love, given the bad timing."

"Your family had no idea you were involved with him."

"No. That was a big mistake, not talking things through with Karly. As much as she's an optimist about people, she'd had more experience. I wish I'd gone to her when I saw the marriage crumbling."

"WHAT HAPPENED THEN?" Archie's hands tightened into fists as he imagined smashing Gareth's face in. He forced his fingers to straighten. There were other ways for a man to avenge a wronged woman. Ways where this jerk wouldn't see it coming or know who'd orchestrated his downfall. Celeste would have tips on how to lay financial waste to a life.

"Within a week of sharing my exciting news, Gareth began to disappear for business dinners after work. Then meetings would run long into the night. All the signs of an affair were there. I put my suspicions down to me feeling vulnerable because of hormonal changes." She groaned. "How stupid."

"He's an adulterer who lied to get his own way with you. Not your fault." Archie could be accused of a great many failings, but cheating wasn't one of them. He'd never promised a woman anything but the time they were spending right then. And for a man to be a cheater, he'd have to be committed to one woman.

"Not exactly an adulterer." Her voice was pained, and it killed him to hear her suffer. Her fingers curled so tight that her knuckles went white. "Unbeknownst to me he'd begun counselling with Suzanne and was determined to win her back. She had no idea I'd taken her place in the home or that Gareth would find me attractive. I dressed modestly, didn't care much for the newest styles in clothes or hair. I was no threat to her that way." She studied her lap and her hair fell in a sheet that blocked her profile from view.

He reached over and hooked a finger around her shield of hair and tucked it behind her ear. "Never hang your head in shame, Beth. You're not to blame. You're not the first woman he's manipulated and I'm afraid you won't be the last."

Gareth's wife Suzanne saw Beth the way he'd seen her for years, plain, boring, dull. He didn't know what to say so he said nothing about the wife. "Gareth saw you the way I see you now. Beautiful, loving, and oh-so-sweet."

She gave him a sharp glance and a brisk nod. "You mean like low-hanging fruit? I'm not exactly vivacious and outgoing."

He left his chair and knelt before her. Tilted her chin up with his fingertip. "Look at me," he said. "You have quiet grace and composure. You don't smile easily, but when you do, my heart thuds to see it again.

You are a gem, Beth, and you glow with inner strength. I don't know how I got lucky enough to have you in my life."

"For the boys," she quipped.

"If you think that we haven't moved beyond our beginning, you haven't been paying attention."

"Oh." On the word, her lips puckered slightly so he kissed them. And then she kissed him back. He put his arms around her and gathered her close. "You're the best woman I've ever known."

She sighed against his neck. "My sister's pretty great, as are Eva and Farren."

He leaned back, took in the shine in her eyes. "Well, then, you're the best woman I've ever kissed." And he didn't care if he never kissed another woman in his life. The idea came not from his head, but his heart and it set him back on his heels. He took his seat again, shaken to his core.

"Are you okay?" She asked.

"I'm taking it all in," he waffled. "Tell me what happened next."

"He told me they were reconciling. Naturally, he couldn't tell her about my pregnancy."

"Naturally." The man would suffer for every lie.

"He convinced me that it was better for their children if their mother came home and since no one but he knew my child was his..." She trailed off, to allow him to fill in the blanks.

"He fired you. Still, he pays support for Ryley?" But he knew the answer. She'd been in financial distress when he'd made her the offer to live with him.

"He convinced me to quit. I couldn't have faced Suzanne, anyway." She shook her head. "If I'd had any idea they'd work on their marriage...none of this would've happened.

"Instead of monthly support, he offered to give me the down payment for my condo instead. I felt that a home of our own would be better than paying rent that would go up over time. Also, by then, I understood he'd never be a good father or a decent example of a man. My father and your brother Bret were far and away better men for my child to have in her life."

The jerk had paid her off with a stingy sum and must have convinced her it would be enough.

"No wonder you felt the way you did about me." His voice was hoarse with anger toward the sorry sack of dog leavings.

She quirked up an eyebrow. "Have you ever fathered a child and walked away?"

"No."

"Ever lied to a woman about loving her?"

"No."

"Paid a woman to exit your life?"

"No. Believe me, they've all been happy enough to move on."

"I do believe you." She sipped her wine. "After Ryley was born, I was ecstatic to be free of him. I put the whole mess behind me and focused on being the best mommy I could be."

"And then I pushed you to go back to being a live-in co-parent. I'm surprised you even agreed." And she'd held his hand, let him kiss her, laughed with him, and joined him here tonight. The surf sounded louder than usual and when he glanced up, he saw a full moon.

"This was a mercenary decision. I'd used most of my savings because I was too picky about jobs for six months. I'd fallen behind with my mortgage payments and other bills. Then, there you were, offering me a way to keep my home and save for our future. Mine and Ryley's."

He couldn't find it in himself to be sorry she was dead broke.

"I wonder why he called after all this time? He was free of you, too."

She responded by pouring another glass of wine. A bigger one this time.

Chapter Sixteen

Beth wondered the same thing that Archie did about Gareth's call. Why now? What had happened to make him reach out?

"After I accepted his money to use for my down payment, Gareth ghosted me. First though, he made me promise that I wouldn't contact his wife. He threatened to tell my family that he was Ryley's father. I was stupid to tell him I hadn't told them about us."

When Archie didn't speak, she went on, desperate to get everything off her chest.

"Gareth coerced me, true. But I was the one who decided to keep my secret and his money. It was my choice to lie to my family." She dug her fingers into her scalp and lifted her hair in frustration. "We engaged in mutual extortion. I wouldn't contact Suzanne to tell her about Ryley and he wouldn't tell my family he was the father. Things got ugly fast. I'm as ashamed of my behavior as I can be."

She felt sick and found her hands clasped tight. "I have no idea why he'd want to talk to me now. You saw me shut off my phone. I could ignore him or change my number, but if there's good reason to contact me, then I need to call him back."

"Oh, there's a reason. But it won't be good." His gaze was steady, his voice grave without an ounce of judgment in it. "If you want, I'll be with you when you call. You don't have to do this alone."

No, she didn't. She had an ally in Archie.

Who'd have thought?

"Thank you." She reached for his hand. This time, she was the one who kissed knuckles. Then she turned his hand palm up and kissed him there, too, her tongue tasting salty skin and Archie. When she raised her face to look at him, she recognized the same want in his face that had taken over her body. Man/woman want. The kind of want humans had fulfilled for millennia.

Archie's hands went to her shoulders and pulled her to him, blind with need. This was real, she thought, as she followed his urging. Her mouth opened under his and the kiss he offered consumed her. Different from their other kisses, this one showed no signs of stopping, nor did she want it to. This kiss asked a question. "Yes," she whispered against his lips. "Yes."

"You're sure? I'll have no regrets in the morning," he responded with a guttural sigh.

"Will you?"

"No regrets," she vowed.

MORNING CAME TOO SOON, especially after one and half glasses of wine, but when Beth heard the thump of Ryley's feet in the room above her, she rolled out of bed. Tracking the direction of thuds, she knew the boys would be pounced on and woken any second now. She smiled as she scurried into the bathroom across the hall.

More thumps and boys' voices raised in happy morning chatter. Her heart felt light, and her body sang. Archie had wanted her to spend the night in his arms, but she felt the children should be eased into this new and different phase. They'd start with affectionate kisses. Casual touches and hugs would signal a change, too.

Some morning soon, they'd run into Archie's room and find her in there, too. With a couple of simple questions and answers they'd establish their connection. Jeremy and Duncan had already accepted her as a caregiver. This change should please them, and Ryley would forget that there'd ever been a time without Archie and the boys.

A man's shout of alarm told her that the horde had descended on Archie. She grinned into the mirror. The rush to get the children ready for the day began. Various wild animal growls and kids' squeals accompanied heavier footsteps as Archie played monster. He made his way to the upstairs bathroom, passing out orders to lift the lid and take better aim. Clearly, he was supervising the boys.

She laughed as she freshened up and combed her hair. Her heart light, she darted into the kitchen to start the coffee. Once the burbling began, she hurried back to her room to dress.

Footsteps on the stairs, light and heavy. Archie's voice asking Ryley if she'd made the coffee.

"No! Momma did!"

"Your momma is my favorite lady," he announced in reply.

"Me, too!" One of the boys agreed, quickly followed by the other one, shouting louder.

She'd confessed her worst choices to Archie and the world had not fallen in. He'd be with her when she talked to Gareth and together, they'd formulate a plan to deal with whatever his reason was for calling out of the blue. She removed the tags from her new capri pants, pulled them on and then tucked in her T shirt. Sliding her feet into new sandals, she headed to the kitchen.

The children sat around the square table. Cereal boxes and a carton of milk stood in the center. The scent of coffee woke up her taste buds and Archie held a mug to his lips. His eyes went wide as he took in her new outfit.

"Good morning," she said cheerily. "Everyone hungry?"

The boys cheered their agreement and Ryley stuck her thumb in her mouth and pointed at Beth's legs.

Archie grinned. "What are you wearing?"

She looked down at her body. "I went to the mall the other day. My skirts were getting wet in the surf. These are much better for beach walking." She lifted her foot to show him her bare calf and new sandals.

His expression of interest made her feel feminine and wanted. And first thing in the morning, too. Last night hadn't been a fluke or heat-of-the-moment thing. Remembering her decision to ease the children into this new phase, she stepped up and kissed Archie's cheek.

"It's no big deal, you've seen me in my sleep shorts and my tank suit." Last night they'd shared wine and kisses and much more. It had been deeply satisfying to be with him and her future filled with promise as she looked into his appreciative eyes.

"True, but mostly I've seen you in those long dresses," he blustered.

"If these clothes bind at the waist or otherwise make me uncomfortable, I'll be back in dresses in no time. So, look while you can," she responded with a cheeky tone she had never used in her life. Then she twirled so he'd get the full effect of her figure-hugging outfit.

Archie brought out all sorts of changes in her. She liked most of them, including her decision to dress for the beach. She felt young dressed like this. She'd been cautious in her clothing, convinced she needed to hide her body from the men she worked for and the women whose babies she minded.

In the end, her shields hadn't helped one bit.

When she walked to the counter to get down a mug for her coffee, she made certain to brush past Archie. He drew in a deep breath, and she swore that he held it.

She'd made Archie Jones breathless.

Imagine that.

AN HOUR LATER, WITH Ryley fully engaged in her favorite cartoon show and the boys at school and daycare, Beth had come back down to earth. When Archie parked the mini van in front of the door, she smoothed her palms down her thighs and mentally prepared for the call to Gareth.

Archie stepped in the door, and she walked straight into his arms. "Glad you're back. I'm calling now while I still have the nerve." She loved the way he smelled. His aftershave conjured the outdoors, clean and fresh. His arms around her made her feel safe.

"I'll be right beside you," he said as he held her in a bear hug. "Ryley's future is the most important thing."

She nodded. "Yes. But honestly, I doubt this is about her. I'm at a loss."

"The sooner the better, then. Maybe it's nothing."

"Maybe," she muttered. "Let's go into my room. We'll leave the door open in case Ryley needs us."

"GARETH." BETH TOOK a couple of breaths before saying his name. She'd expected to feel something when she heard him answer. She'd always liked the bass quality of his voice. But she felt nothing, not even dislike. Her nerves calmed.

"Beth, thanks for calling back."

"Sure."

"How are you?"

"Why?"

"Simple conversation. It's polite to ask."

"Is it?" She couldn't remember a time when he'd asked her how she was, not even when he was pretending to care. "Why did you call me?"

"How's Ryley?"

Surprised, she didn't respond to the question, but asked her own. "How do you know her name?"

He paused and she imagined him trying to remember that far back. "It doesn't matter how I know."

It rankled that he wouldn't tell her, but she wasn't surprised. He hadn't even contacted her when their daughter was born. She assumed he'd been busy forging a new beginning to his marriage. Ugh. She was relieved she'd dodged this bullet.

"Why do you ask about her now? You've been silent since before she was born."

"My younger daughter has developed asthma. I outgrew it, but she's much worse than I was at her age. I wanted you to know in case you see signs."

She blinked. "I'm sorry to hear this." She'd been fond of his children and this news distressed her for the child's sake. "Ryley's fine. Thank you for the heads up. I'll be aware." She'd gather all the information she could on the condition and be informed what to look for. "Is this an allergic reaction?"

"No, exercise can trigger an attack, so try to keep her from overdoing it."

"Not easy, she's incredibly active." Her little climber slash runner slash boy chaser. How could she get an almost three-year-old to slow down. Zero chance.

"Of course, she is. At her age, she's probably very busy." He sounded strained under the trite words. She forgot sometimes that even a distant uncaring father would have some experience with young children. Gareth wasn't an ogre, just selfish.

"Is there another reason for your call?" While she appreciated his warning, he'd only asked a perfunctory question that meant nothing. He hadn't asked if Ryley looked like him or anything about her development. How tall she was. How happy.

How could she have not seen the truth of this man?

"We're having problems again."

She paused for a beat. "No surprise there. You're a lying snake who manipulates people and circumstances." His wife wasn't much better, but she'd been exposed to Gareth for years and she had three children to consider. Knowing his true personality now, it was clear he would've fought tooth and nail over child support and made Suzanne's life miserable. "The counseling you went for was for show, right?" She didn't wait for an answer. "You never meant to change or work on your marriage."

Her stomach churned.

"If you're going to be like that, I'll let you go." His voice had an edge now. No longer smooth, he sounded agitated, and she understood. Gareth wanted to weasel his way back into her good graces by using what had worked on her before, her sympathy. When she didn't react as expected, he grew angry.

"I'm hanging up now," she warned. She heard him squawk in outrage before she disconnected.

She looked over at Archie, sitting on the corner of her bed. Putting her phone face down on her dresser, she smiled. "He called for two reasons. One was legitimate and the other was laughable."

This part of her life was over. Truly done. Her heart felt free at last of guilt and shame. "I'm glad we spoke. It helped relieve some leftover negative feelings." She recounted the call as Archie drew her in close.

The man was so warm. She sighed and soaked in the comfort, content after suffering for too long.

Her life was happy now. In a weird way she had what she'd always wanted. The most surprising thing about having a family of her own and a good man in her life was that she had it with Archie Jones and two children she'd only recently met. But the whys and wherefores meant little when the result was this wonderful.

Her attraction to Archie culminated in their time together last night and she couldn't be happier about the connection they'd made. Jeremy and Duncan were wonderful boys that she already loved. Could loving Archie be far behind?

Chapter Seventeen

M*onday*

They walked out of Ledger and Ledger Architects at six p.m. "For an initial consultation, that went well," Archie said as he took Duncan's hand in his. The boy had a tendency to chase wildlife if he saw any and there was a family of ducks waddling into a pond beside the office building. The goslings were still fuzzy and too cute to escape the children's notice.

"I was impressed with the plans and drawings I saw on the walls in their reception area." Beth swung Ryley up into her arms. "No ducks," she said to the girl.

"Jeremy, hang back here with us. Ducks protect their babies, and you don't want to be chased by an angry duck."

"Aw. Okay." He dropped back to walk beside Archie.

Addressing Jeremy again, Archie said, "Mrs. Ledger listened closely to you and your brother about what you'd like in the house. That was good."

"Yep. She's cool."

Beth nodded. "I agree. She made it clear that the boys would be heard and not ignored."

After the kids were in their seats and the doors to the van closed, Archie reached for Beth's hand. She squared up with him.

"I'm glad we all came together. I promise not to assume you'll go along with whatever I decide. This is a team effort."

"Thanks. I see more teamwork in our future." She nuzzled his ear but fell short of a kiss on the mouth. The boys had displayed a clear, loud, little-boy disgust at outright shows of affection. Archie hoped that secretly, Jeremy and Duncan were pleased.

"Let's have a treat for dinner. What do you say to a nice meal at the Sands? We can sit outside and look over the pool and the ocean," he suggested.

"That depends. Do they have a kid's menu?"

"I'm sure the chef can make whatever they'd like."

"Then I'll save my meatloaf for tomorrow's dinner."

"I love your meatloaf, but dinner at the Sands is more like a celebration." She'd told him she had one ready to pop into the oven. He opened the front passenger door for her, and she climbed in. Archie folded his forearms on the roof and studied her. Warmth rose in his chest as she got busy clicking her seatbelt into place.

Hard as it was to believe, he was in love with Beth. Utterly, completely in love. He wondered if she could see his heart in his eyes as he looked his fill.

"I like the sound of teamwork. I didn't have much of an example as a kid, but I only have to look at Bret and Karly and Jesse and Eva to see good marriages. My brother's made his life work in ways our parents couldn't." Not that he remembered his parents making any effort. He admired Bret and Jesse and couldn't think of better men to emulate.

"Except we're not married." The words were gentle but reminded him that anything less than a real claim meant that they had a tenuous connection at best.

"Right, we're not."

Her face looked shocked. "That was not a hint. I'm in no hurry to change things." She looked downright scared.

"Me, either. But you must admit I'm including you in decisions now."

"And you're doing a fine job."

When he climbed in behind the wheel, Beth had the kids singing a round of Row, Row, Row Your Boat which kept them entertained for half of the trip back to the island from Summerville. The song also meant there was no room for adult conversation.

While they sang, he mulled over what he'd learned about Gareth Monroe. Yesterday, after she'd told him about her phone call, he'd asked Beth for the man's full name. She'd given it without question, and he'd learned plenty about the jerk who'd disillusioned and mistreated Beth. Ryley was better off without Gareth Monroe in her life.

Archie doubted that the asthma story was true. Monroe had spent his life lying and twisting the truth to suit himself. But since Beth had made it clear she didn't want any more to do with him, he decided to spare her the details. She already knew the depths the man plumbed when it came to women. Telling her more would only make her dwell on him and Archie didn't want her to give Monroe another thought.

He and Beth had a bright future ahead of them. Why spoil it by picking at the past?

BETH WATCHED ARCHIE stride toward them, head up, eyes on her and the children. They'd demolished their meals and while the children had been eating ice cream, he'd left them to chat with his friend at the front desk. Janise had made a point of speaking with Jeremy and Duncan when they'd arrived, and it was clear she was someone they held dear.

Archie had introduced her to Janise, and they'd chatted amiably. She understood why the boys liked the matronly woman. She oozed motherly love and concern with her warm gaze and soft voice.

Archie had mentioned Janise as a woman who embodied all he wanted in a nanny for the boys. She'd made an impression on the three males when they were at the beginning of their lives together.

Beth made a mental note to invite her over for a meal sometime soon.

"Hi, all done?" Archie asked.

The ice cream dishes were empty, and Beth had seen to wiping Ryley's face, despite her protests that she was *all clean, Mommy!*

Archie held her chair out for her and as they strolled across the wide expanse of the patio, he took her hand while Ryley held her other one. Anyone who looked would see a happy family unit and Beth wanted that vision to be true.

They were happy as they were, of course, but she couldn't help but wonder if their future could be even more entwined.

"Would you mind if I moved some of my clothes and toiletries into your room?"

A broad smile bisected his face. "Brilliant," he said. "I'd love that." He pulled her into his side and pressed his lips to her temple.

A WEEK LATER...

"No more diapers. Imagine that." Beth shook her head in mock disbelief. She felt inordinately pleased with the accomplishment, because with the move to the motel, Ryley had regressed. Beth hadn't wanted to pressure her little girl and Archie had steered clear of the entire exercise.

"I think this calls for some girl time at the mall," she declared as she watched Jeremy clear the table. "Ryley could use new tops and bottoms since she's transitioned into regular underwear."

"Long as we don't hafta go," Jeremy said. "I hate the mall." He'd mentioned wanting money of his own and Archie had come up with a short list of easy chores. "I'll go when I get my allowance."

"Fine by me," Archie said. "We'll hit the pool after you get home from school and if you don't chase each other around the deck, I'll take you for a treat." He winked at Beth and the look of affection in his eyes warmed her. A man couldn't fake these feelings.

Since moving her things upstairs, they'd become more publicly affectionate, to the point that all their friends were now aware of their new status as a committed couple. She hadn't told her family yet, but she would soon.

After the call from Gareth, she'd felt happier than she had since she learned she was pregnant. She'd been relieved by a sense of closure, and excited by the future in store for this blended, extraordinary family. The end of Gareth meant a beginning with Archie, and she couldn't be happier.

He seemed content, too and had had some friendlier conversations with Celeste. Things would never be warm between Archie and his mother, but cordial was better than outright dislike on his part. He had mentioned that he'd returned his trust fund money to the family. That had been a kind of turning point. He'd made it plain that his business life was no longer tied to the Joneses. He was an investor, and far from the extravagant man-baby she'd assumed him to be. He sought out opportunities with up-and-coming industries and enjoyed great success with environmentally beneficial technologies.

Some day, she'd learn more, she vowed. He could probably use a good bookkeeper.

She had new friends in Eva and Farren and she saw a happy future for all the couples and the many children they were shepherding through life. Soon, Farren's secret would be out and there'd be a baby shower to plan.

Archie was helpful and easy to spend time with. Her heart sang when he touched her, and they reveled in each other.

Leaving with Ryley for their shopping trip, she stretched up to kiss his cheek. At the same time, he turned his face toward her. Their lips met and her arms looped his neck. When she pulled back, he followed and blessed her with another, shorter kiss.

At her knee, Ryley giggled. "Kiss kiss!"

Archie bent and scooped her daughter into his arms and kissed her cheek while Beth kissed the other one at the same time. Ryley giggled some more and kissed them back in turn.

"Have fun. I'll see you both later."

"Yuk!" said Jeremy.

"Never mind the comments," Archie said in mock seriousness. He winked at Beth. "Let's get you boys ready for your day." He eyeballed his charges and tapped their shoulders to get them moving. They thundered upstairs.

She looked around for the diaper bag, but realized with a grin that she wouldn't need to take it for much longer. Instead of diapers, the bag contained snacks, a change of clothes and underwear, and juice boxes. "I'm glad we got my car from my place. You were right, I'll need it occasionally."

"With three kids I'm surprised we made it this long without having it here," he replied. "I thought about buying you a minivan too but didn't want to assume you'd want your own."

She laughed. "No more assumptions. Woot! I like that. Looks like you've learned something after all," she teased. "I like my little runabout. It's perfect for me and Ryley."

As she buckled Ryley into the car seat, she marveled again at how her life had taken such a lovely turn. It was nice to walk away from the kitchen and the rush of getting the boys dressed. Duncan had his own style when he chose what he wanted to wear. He loved button down collars on his plaid shirts.

She could leave Archie in charge and have faith the boys would be fine. Co-parenting was different from nannying. As a nanny, she never would've been able to leave for personal time on the spur of the moment. She looked forward to one-on-one time with her daughter, then decided she could do the same with each boy, too. While the brothers enjoyed a lot of the same things, their age difference also meant some activities weren't suitable for both of them.

Archie would love her idea of having alone time.

It wasn't until she was on the bridge to Summerville that she noticed a familiar car behind her. *It couldn't be.*

But when she turned into the Summerville mall parking lot and the car followed, she was certain it was Gareth behind her. She parked away from other cars so they wouldn't be overheard by passersby and climbed out, making sure to stand a few feet from the car. A glance in the backseat told her Ryley was busy with a toy.

Gareth pulled in, parked, and climbed out. He looked rough, as if he'd been losing sleep. She expected to feel something as she faced him, but there was only revulsion where there once had been love. Or what she'd believed was love, she mentally corrected.

"Momma!"

She leaned down to Ryley's window and held up one finger to let her daughter see she hadn't been forgotten.

"Beth," Gareth said. "You look great!" His eyes traveled from the top of her head to her toes, making her feel exposed and uncomfortable. She'd worn her capris and a cheery linen shirt tied at the waist.

"What do you want, Gareth." It wasn't a question because she didn't care. Still, he was here for a reason.

"To talk, of course. It looks like you're happy. I'm glad to see it."

"How did you find me?"

"A neighbor of yours hadn't seen you around lately and had checked with others in your building. Old ladies gossip about young women, especially single mothers."

She didn't bother to point out how lucky she was to be single after making every mistake a woman could make with him. When she'd gone back to pick up her car, she'd given her location to a friendly neighbor who lived on the floor below hers. It must have been Mrs. Jenkins who shared the news of Beth's whereabouts. They'd chatted about Last Chance Beach because Mrs. Jenkins had fond memories of the island.

Maybe she shouldn't have been so forthcoming, but Gareth was out of her life, and she had a future to look forward to. She watched him carefully for a sign that he wanted to get close to Ryley or engage with her. He didn't look into the car.

"You're wasting my time and yours, Gareth. I don't want to see you. And I don't care why you want to see me."

His eyes turned mournful. A trick he'd used to make her sympathize. She hardened her heart. Her phone chimed for a call, but she ignored it.

"Suzanne's cheating on me again. This time it's her tennis coach. I don't know what to do to get through to her." He stepped closer and Beth sidled away from the car. She didn't want him to see Ryley. "You were a caring listener. There's no one else I can talk to. No one else understands what my wife is like."

"You two make your own messes. It's time you cleaned them up yourselves." She shook her head. "I can't believe I got sucked into your dysfunctional relationship. I told myself I could make life better for your children." She blinked as their faces swam before her eyes. *Poor kids.*

"You loved me once." He reached to touch her, but she avoided his move. "You can come back. Suzanne's leaving for good this time. I told her to go."

She shook her head. "You need to leave me alone. If you don't, I'll call a lawyer. I'll get a restraining order." She'd never known anyone who'd needed one, so wasn't sure what she'd have to do, but Archie would help. At the thought of him, her mind settled. She wasn't alone. She could depend on Archie.

But Archie was gone when she went home.

Chapter Eighteen

"Yes, Karly, tonight," Beth said the next morning as the children ate breakfast. "What I have to say must be in person. And the sooner the better." Next on her list was a call to her mom and dad. With Archie gone to Europe, she had time to deal with this important discussion. She wanted to come clean and tell her family everything about Gareth and her foolish mistakes.

After Gareth had left her in the parking lot, she'd watched him drive away, then climbed into her car. She moved it to the other side of the mall and parked again, making sure Gareth was nowhere nearby. She'd returned Archie's call, but her call went to voicemail. His message had been curt, and simply asked her to call him. Surely, if there was a problem with one of the boys, he'd have said more.

"I'm still shopping. Don't worry, I'll be home in time to get the boys." She kept her voice level so he wouldn't read tension in her tone. There'd be plenty of time to vent when they were together later.

Ryley had become impatient and wanted out of the car. She hoped shopping would take her mind off the disturbing meeting with Gareth.

After she'd found her daughter some new outfits and underwear, she settled at a table near the play area. While her daughter climbed around, she'd tried Archie again to no avail. Concerned, she'd headed home and found a dashed-off cryptic note.

He'd left for Europe to help a friend and would call when he knew more. That was it.

Archie had gone to Europe, leaving her in a state of distress when she needed him. Piqued, she hadn't bothered to text or call again until after bedtime.

She spent a lonely night in his bed after fending off the boys' questions about where he'd gone and why. They wanted to know which friend and what kind of help he was giving and why he had to go that far to give it.

All questions she wanted the answers to as well. She gave up leaving him messages at midnight.

And this morning, still without word, she was way past concerned and well into furious. He'd left her. What else could she think?

They'd played house and now he was bored with plain mousy Beth and had left for his next adventure. She wondered about the friend he claimed needed help. She knew for a fact that Archie Jones had few friends. He'd lost Keith, a friend no one else had known, and he had Jesse, who was as surprised as she was that Archie had left.

That meant the friend was a woman. Maybe she'd jumped to conclusions, but in her experience and with her knowledge of how the man liked to bounce from woman to woman, it wasn't much of a leap.

The fable of the scorpion and the tortoise crossing the swollen river came to mind. The scorpion had stung the tortoise and killed it. The foolish tortoise had expected the scorpion not to act like a scorpion.

Expecting Archie to change and behave like a man he wasn't, had only made her look the fool. But that was who she was, too. A woman easily fooled by hope, love, and dreams.

She'd love to escape to her home, but she had Jeremy and Duncan to think of, too. They needed her and she'd agreed to co-parent so here she'd stay.

A part of her had known this day would come.

She should welcome the knowledge that she was right. Why then, did the victory feel shallow?

And if Archie deigned to call, well, he could leave a message, because she was in no mood to hear his lame excuses for abandoning them.

KARLY FOUND HER THAT evening after the kids were in bed. She was tossing Archie's things into the study/cum bedroom. She'd decided as the only parent in the house she wanted the larger bedroom upstairs.

And stomping up and down the stairs had helped release her frustration. She couldn't drink or go for a long beach walk alone, or take a drive, which meant she stomped instead.

"Hi! You're here already?" She looked past her sister into the hallway and saw Bret standing with her parents. "And all together, too." Good, she had a lot to say, and she didn't need to say it twice. "Buckle up," she snarked. "We're in for a long discussion."

Her mom went through the kitchen finding drinks and snacks as they headed into the living room.

"First of all, Bret, have you heard from Archie?" At the confused shake of his head, she went on. "Neither have I. Not since I came home yesterday afternoon and found a note from him."

She passed it over.

"Europe? That could mean he's anywhere over there. Kind of vague, even for him," Bret said.

"Is this his usual way of ending things and moving on?" She bit her lip because she'd admitted she'd been in a romantic relationship with his brother and was now the scorned woman all in the same sentence. Their friends knew because they lived nearby and saw the relationship blossom, but her family lived farther away, and this was their first time hearing of it.

"No." Bret shook his head as he glanced at the note again. "This is not that." He passed the slip of notepaper to Karly, who read it and passed it to her father and mother.

Her father's face looked thunderous, and her mother's brows knit in confusion. "Where is he? He was totally committed to the children, and I saw the way he looked at you. Sweetie, the man's smitten and I don't think jumping to conclusions will help."

"I've been over this in my mind, and I agree he seemed committed to the boys, but it's been too long between messages." She no longer considered Archie "smitten." Not when he'd left her with no real explanation.

Her phone chimed. "It's a number I don't recognize, but it's very long."

"It could be from an international number. Country codes add digits," Bret said quickly. "It must be Archie." He sounded relieved as if he, too, had doubted his brother. "He buys new phones when he travels."

"I'll take this upstairs," Beth said and hurried to her newly acquired bedroom.

A groggy sounding Archie said, "Hello, glad I caught you before bed."

"Archie, what's going on? Where are you? Are you coming back?" the questions tumbled out before she could stop them. Worse, the fear in her voice was obvious and embarrassed her.

"Of course, I'll be back. I'm just not sure when." He cleared his throat. "Sorry, I'm just waking up. It's been a marathon."

"What are you talking about?"

"My friend Janise, from the Sands? She had an emergency and I'm helping."

"Oh?" What kind of emergency could a hotel front desk clerk have that would mean a sudden flight to Europe and why ask Archie for help with it?

"You sound funny. What's going on with you?" he asked.

"Nothing. What's going on with you?" She demanded, sounding like an angry pre-teen girl. She rolled her eyes. *Get a grip.*

"Let's take a step back." He sounded awake now. Alert. "Janise's daughter wanted a summer backpacking in Europe after high school. She's leaving for college in September."

Dread slammed into her. A young woman wandering Europe. Anything could have happened. Her heart clutched in fear. "Tell me."

"Apparently, she's fallen in with some protestors and they walked into a museum and tossed paint on a Rembrandt."

Beth closed her eyes. "Nothing violent?"

"Not yet. Janise asked me a few questions about various countries, and how best to approach the police for help finding her daughter. When I heard that, it seemed best if I came with her. I chartered a jet in case we need to hop around."

Only a man rich as Croesus would consider hopping around Europe in a jet, normal. "Why not tell me this before you left?"

"Interpol tells me this group could be heading down a dark path and taking Shandra with them. I wasn't sure what was happening before we left, just that Shandra was in trouble and scared. Janise was stunned."

When she didn't speak, he gave a long, troubled sigh. "I should have taken the time to fill you in. I'm sorry, Beth. But between Janise's fear and sketchy information and getting the jet arranged, there didn't seem to be time. Not when we had no concrete information."

"Where are you now?" She didn't mean to sound brittle, but there it was. She was disappointed that he thought running off without telling her the basics was acceptable. It wasn't acceptable.

"I'm in Lichtenstein. My friend said this is most likely where the group is headed. Whether Janise's daughter is still with them remains to be seen. We fell into our rooms and basically passed out. The poor woman hadn't slept in forty-eight hours."

"This is a lot to take in." Her mind whirled but her emotions around his leaving without a full explanation still sat front of mind. Her heart had taken a beating and her faith in Archie had faltered.

"I'm sorry I left you hanging, and I should have done better. How was your shopping trip? Successful, I hope. I'm also sorry I fell into my habit of not including you in decisions. But I believed you'd agree with my choice to help Janise however I can."

She blinked and held her breath for a count of three. "I would have agreed, absolutely. But you need to know I jumped to some conclusions based on my previous knowledge of you."

"Wait, you assumed I'd left you? Just took a flit on a whim?" His voice firmed. "You believed I'm capable of walking out on you? And the kids?"

She nodded although he couldn't see. "What was I supposed to think? Do you remember what you wrote on your note?"

"I said I was going to Europe, and I'd call when I ..." he trailed off.

"How much time do you think you need to find this girl?"

"If she'd answer her mother's messages, it won't be long. The police in Spain need to interview her and she needs to tell them what she knows about the group. I don't want to leave Janise alone until things are under control and she's seen her daughter."

"Does Shandra still have her phone?"

"We're not sure. I hope so. Janise is a wreck. She had doubts about this trip, and now she's blaming herself for letting it happen."

"Keep me in the loop. It's hard being here without knowing...well." She couldn't say her full thought. It was hard being at home without knowing if he'd ever come back to her. She had good reason to doubt him, despite his explanation.

Chapter Nineteen

This was worse than he thought. Beth sounded distant, angry, cold. It was unlike her. And she hadn't answered his question about her shopping trip with Ryley. He should call back. He checked the time. His day was just beginning, and Janise had said she'd be up by now.

He called Janise's room. "I'll order in for breakfast. What can I get you?" He took her order of toast and coffee, silently adding eggs, ham, and fruit for her and asked her to give him forty-five minutes. The flights had taken their toll on her and her worry had been obvious in her voice.

He wasn't used to juggling two women's concerns at once. But, with Janise sorted for now, he called Beth again. She answered immediately.

"How was shopping with Ryley?" he said by way of greeting. "You changed the subject."

"Gareth followed me to the mall."

"What?!" He paced the room, feeling a rush of fear that he'd never experienced. "Did he try to hurt you? Grab her? What reason did he give?" He had to get back home. NOW. His mind churned and bounced.

"He seems to think I should take him back. And no, he didn't grab Ryley. Didn't even look in the car window to see her. He's apparently told Suzanne to move out. She's cheating again." She sounded hollow as if reciting the events for the millionth time.

"I'm coming home."

"No, you're not. Please stay with your friend until you have answers. I can't imagine what she's going through."

"But you need me. I shouldn't have left." What had he been thinking? "I'll leave the jet here for her and fly home commercial. It'll be fine."

"No, Archie. There's nothing happening here that I haven't handled before. Besides, I have all the support I need. Bret and Karly and my parents are here with me right now. I plan on having an overdue discussion. And after they go home, Eva and Farren are only a few minutes away."

He frowned. She was right. Technically. But his heart said he needed to be there for her. "Are you sure?" He didn't need to ask what the discussion would be about. "I'll call more often and now you have my international number you can call anytime." He gripped the phone in his hand so hard he wondered if he'd crack the screen. He eased the pressure of his fingers. "Beth, are you *sure*?"

"Yes. If you came home, you'd be stressed about Janise and feel guilty for leaving her on her own. Now that I understand what you're dealing with, I'll be okay."

"But Gareth."

"Will not get to me. I know the kind of man he is, and he can't hurt me. Remember how I said he has no idea who I am now? His face when I told him to leave me alone was priceless. Should have taken a photo." Her voice edged toward humor. He could tell she felt lighter, less worried. The knot in his belly eased.

"Okay. I'll call again soon, and I won't wait until I have news to report. I'll call just to hear your voice." He should tell her he loved her, but the first time shouldn't be over the phone. No, he needed to be holding her, kissing her.

"You do that, and I'll be happy. And I'll be here waiting."

They disconnected and he tapped his phone on his chin. He wanted to leave for Last Chance Beach this minute, but he couldn't. The crisis at home had been averted.

Home. The word warmed him. Knowing Beth waited for him there sent heat to all the best places.

The food arrived just as Janise showed up. "I heard from her," she said as soon as he'd tipped the server and closed the door behind her. "Shandra. She's in France. A city near the border with Spain. It's called Perpignan.

"When the group said they were going to Lichenstein, she waited until they were asleep and went to the train station. She took the first train out of Barcelona. Didn't care where it was going."

"Good girl."

"Now that I know she's okay, I could wring her neck." Janise rolled her shoulders. Then tears gathered. "But all I really want is to see her, hug her. Then, I'll wring her neck."

"Jean-Luc will want her to give a statement. If she tells them everything she knows, she'll be allowed to go home. I'll vouch for her and if she needs to come back to testify or otherwise make an appearance, I'll bring her back myself."

"I don't want to know how you're friends with an Interpol Superintendent." She snapped her linen napkin open and placed it on her lap. "I'm suddenly hungry," she said with wide-eyed appreciation as her gaze roamed the table.

"I travel a lot, or, rather, I used to." He shrugged. "Sometimes, I'd arrange transport for people they wanted moved or I'd courier items that needed delivery. Nothing dangerous, but I helped where I could." He'd called Jean-Luc minutes after hearing from Janise about Shandra. His friend had been happy to help if it meant preventing something more serious than paint on a shielded Rembrandt. These were nuisance protests, but things could escalate quickly if not dealt with.

His tenuous connection to Interpol had meant he couldn't tell Beth anything until the issue was resolved.

"I hope Beth understands why I couldn't say much in my note. She was angry and upset with me when I first talked to her this morning. I called back and she's fine for now, but I'm glad we know where Shandra is and can get her home soon."

"I can't thank you enough for everything you've done. Flying me here, talking to Jean-Luc, arranging to get Shandra home. All of it. If it will help, I'll talk to Beth. I won't say anything about Interpol," she promised.

"I'll need the name of the place in France and Jean-Luc will have a local office handle her statement. And we'll leave as soon as we've eaten." He scooped a serving of light, fluffy scrambled eggs onto his plate.

"She said it's Perpignan and she's staying near the train station."

He called his pilot to have the jet ready to depart as soon as he could. After the call, he assured Janise that the city had a good-sized airport, and they'd leave for home as soon as they could. "Maybe as early as tomorrow."

Chapter Twenty

"Once we got to Perpignan, everything happened quickly. Turns out, Shandra had been observant and careful. While tossing some paint on a shielded painting had seemed harmless enough, what some of the group members whispered about frightened her later."

He'd been home for less than an hour but had got in just in time to help with bedtime. After settling the boys and Ryley, they'd met on the landing and spent some five minutes in a deep hug punctuated by wild kisses. Eventually, though, she asked questions. They'd settled on the balcony, side by side in their chairs, thighs touching.

"After the museum protest, they ran to a friend's apartment where Shandra charged her phone. After overhearing some of the members' plans, she turned it off and stuffed it in the bottom of her pack to save the battery. She understood she'd have to run. When her roommates fell asleep, she bolted for the train station."

"That's why Janise couldn't get hold of her. She'd turned off her phone. What were they planning to do?" Beth frowned, fascinated by the story.

"I'm not privy to that information, but whatever she told Interpol was important. She gave them names and dates and from that, they deduced a likely target. Sometimes terrorist groups recruit earnest young people who want to make a statement. Sometimes it's animal cruelty or child labor. Sometimes it's environmental destruction. Those things are important, and kids want to have their say, as they should. But their desire to do something, say something, means they're open to persuasion. Shandra may have saved some of her friends from getting in deeper."

He'd already explained what he could about his friend, Jean-Luc.

"All this means that your endless country hopping and moving around had served a purpose."

"You want to think that I had a real plan for my life before I got the boys. But I didn't. My movements and my money meant I traveled freely. A few years ago, that brought me to the attention of Interpol. They checked me out and one day, Jean-Luc approached me in Monaco. He needed to get a woman to Italy. After I talked with a man from a lettered US agency, and he confirmed Jean-Luc's identity, I agreed. This was casual and occasional."

"But it was enough that you could call on him to help with Shandra."

"Exactly. I'm no hero, so quit looking at me like that." Still, he wouldn't be a man if he didn't respond to the admiration in Beth's gaze. "And it suited Jean-Luc to help. In the end, everyone won. Janise and Shandra especially."

A gull took a bold chance and landed on the railing only three feet away. He cocked his head, looking hopeful.

"Sorry, no food out here tonight," Archie said. "But he's reminded me I'm hungry. Can we raid the fridge?"

"There's leftover lasagna." She stood and held out her hand to him. A simple gesture, this offered hand, but he dragged it to his mouth and kissed her palm in gratitude.

"I'm home," he said. "And I give you my word, that no matter what happens, I'll never leave you like that again."

"I was scared you'd never come back."

"I know." He rose and took her into his arms, his Beth, his love. Soon, he'd tell her, but first, he had to eat.

LATER THAT NIGHT AS they sat together on the sofa, she and Archie faced each other. The television volume was low, and the show forgotten as she shared the conversation she'd had with Gareth in the mall parking lot. "I was blindsided when I recognized his car behind me."

"Were you frightened?" Archie demanded, a dark gleam in his eyes.

"Not for my safety. But I didn't want him to connect with Ryley. I parked a distance from the other cars, and I stood away from her window praying she wouldn't kick up a fuss about getting out of the car."

"How was his demeanor? Did he do anything to scare you? Make threats?" The dark gleam had turned feral, and she glimpsed a man in full protective mode.

She huffed. "He launched straight into the 'poor me' mode that used to make me sympathetic. But I've had time to see the truth." She rested her hand on Archie's where it lay on the sofa back. "It's amazing that he'd think he could do what he did and still try his old tricks on me."

Archie looked at the television screen, then the floor. When he sighed, she understood he had a confession to make. "I had a private investigator look into Gareth Monroe."

"What? Why?"

"I wanted to know what kind of man you were dealing with. I wanted to be prepared if he came after Ryley. Or you," he admitted. "What did he tell you he does for a living?"

"Real estate development." He'd made a good living and had provided all the luxuries without complaining about Suzanne's indulgent lifestyle. She was often away for spa weekends or retreats with friends. Their annual vacations were lavish, and Beth had entertained the children every minute rather than have them 'pester' their parents. "He had an office in the house and another downtown where he had a building management company."

"The man is a slumlord. He buys older buildings that need work and evicts tenants. Some of them have lived there for decades. He claims the renovations will be extensive and that it will be unsafe for them to stay. When the building's empty, he paints the place. Nothing more. Then he jacks up the rents and gets new tenants. When they complain about the plumbing and heat, he ignores them."

"Lipstick on a pig," she muttered.

"What?"

She shook her head sadly. "It was what I heard him say. Now I understand he was talking about painting the buildings." None of this information surprised her. "What does it say about me that I didn't wonder more about his character?"

"It's not your fault. Gareth Monroe is manipulative in all areas of his life. His wife has known him for years and she went back to him. He fooled the marriage counselor, too. Don't blame yourself for being trusting and sweet."

"Sometimes it bothers me that he took a lot of that away from me. I'm different from who I was before him. I doubted you and your intentions with the boys. I assumed you'd leave the moment you got bored with us. And then, despite what I'd come to know about you, I didn't believe you'd return when you left your note."

"The note was vague and I'm sorry I couldn't get into specifics at that point. I didn't know enough about what we'd find when or if we found Shandra." He pulled her to him, needing the feel of her against him. Home had come to mean more than a place, more than the boys, and sweet Ryley. Home meant Beth and as long as they were together, they'd be home.

"I'm not the man I used to be either," he added fervently. "In that, we're the same. We've both changed. And it isn't a bad thing to be cautious with people, Beth. In fact, I'd say it's a strength." He touched her jaw with his fingertips. "And I've come to appreciate the quiet times with the children. These evenings with you are special, more special to me than you know. I'd do anything to live like this with you forever."

"Oh, Archie. I feel the same way."

"I love you, Beth. I love you for all that you are. I love you for making me a better man, for giving me what I never knew I wanted."

"I love you, too," she said through a quiet sob. "I thought I'd lost you." She smacked him lightly on the shoulder. "Don't ever make me feel like that again."

"Never. Never, my Beth. I have all that I could want, right here in Last Chance Beach. I think maybe Keith knew I needed those boys upstairs and he gifted me with all the love he'd worked so hard for."

"He understood you then as I do now. Love for you is all-encompassing and you give it freely and completely, without reservation." She blessed his lips with a feather light kiss. "And that's the best kind of love."

"The forever kind," he vowed.

ONE YEAR LATER...

Jeremy, Duncan, and Ryley grabbed their backpacks from the kitchen floor and headed out to the center court. Archie watched them go, their happy chatter warming his chest as it always did.

"Are you ready?" he asked, turning to see Beth as she completed her last walk through the house.

"I'm ready. We didn't leave anything behind." She came to stand with him, her arm encircling his waist. She held up a key. "I'll put this under the rock by the door in case someone else needs to live here for a while."

He hugged her to his side. "You never know who will need to regroup away from the world. The Landseer Motel is a perfect bolthole for people to hide in, while they figure out their lives."

"You told me once about how Grady hid here and emerged to a new life and love."

He nodded. "This place, this island, is special and I can't see living anywhere else."

"Anywhere you are, is home to me." She heaved in a deep breath. "It's time to go. I smell hotdogs." The Singles Fest welcome barbecue was already underway.

"Me, too."

They stepped out the door, locked it and placed the key under the rock. They walked the short length of breezeway and joined the Singles Fest guests in the center court. Farren waved them over to join her and Eva on blankets. Grady manned the grill while Jesse kept a watchful eye on everyone's children at the playground. He had his hands full.

Farren patted the blanket beside her. "Come, sit. You have time before you have to be at the new house, right?"

Beth sat with her legs to the side. She caught Archie's appreciative glance at her slim ankles and smiled into his eyes. God, he loved her.

Archie nodded. "This house is empty, and we'll catch up to the movers shortly, but we always have time for a picnic." His favorite way to enjoy a meal.

"My mom and dad are there to let them in," Beth explained. "They'll tell them where to place the furniture." She reached out in silent demand and Farren placed a pink-clad bundle of giggles in her arms. Beth cooed at the baby, scenting her head, jiggling the weight of her. She kissed the baby's forehead and got a toothless wet grin for her trouble.

"I'll get the hotdogs and then round up the children," Archie offered, wondering if Beth would share their news. He'd once thought three children were a handful, but soon there'd be four and he couldn't wait. His life had expanded to include friends and more family than he could've imagined. But a baby of their making was an incredible dream.

It had been a long time since he'd wondered what Keith had been thinking when he left his boys with him. But now? Now, he knew the fullness of family, of love, and how there was always plenty to go around. Keith had wanted him to have it all and he did.

Keith, you were right to make me a dad. Thanks, my friend. Your boys are in good hands with Beth and me. Believe it because I finally do.

The End

If you enjoyed *Make Me* and have ever found a wonderful romance by reading reviews, please pay it forward by sharing a few words about M*ake Me*. A review doesn't have to be long, or a retelling of the plot, just a few words on how you felt when you finished. Did you sigh at the end? Feel happy? Love the kids?

If you want to hear about exciting new releases and deals, please subscribe to *Bonnie's Newsy Bits* on my website. Readers can download a **free** short romance set in Last Chance Beach when they subscribe. All my romance titles are listed at https://www.bonnieedwards.com/

DID YOU KNOW? Last Chance Beach was created by a group of romance authors in 2020. We wanted to have a summer place where the living was easy and the romance perfect! We're mid-series now with lots of books available and more to come. You'll find sweet to steamy romance, some suspense, blended families, there may even be a touch of spooky.

Best of all, you'll be swept away to our lovely seaside town where all the endings are happy. You can find the series here: https://www.amazon.com/dp/B09S3BGDZ. Some books are also available at other retailers. Please check your favorite store.

You can also get updates and hang out with the authors and readers in the exclusive Facebook Group **Last Chance Beach Romance Readers**.

Other Last Chance Beach Romances

Masquerade Under the Moon – Kari Lemor
Island Treasure – Susan R. Hughes
Where Dreams Come True – Judy Kentrus
Beating in Time—MJ Schiller
You...Again—Nancy Fraser
Take Vitamin Sea for Love – Annee Jones
Solace Under the Stars – Kari Lemor
Make Me – Bonnie Edwards
Beacon of Thanks – Judy Kentrus
And more in 2024!

Don't miss out!

Visit the website below and you can sign up to receive emails whenever Bonnie Edwards publishes a new book. There's no charge and no obligation.

https://books2read.com/r/B-A-JXD-SRDQC

BOOKS 2 READ

Connecting independent readers to independent writers.

Did you love *Make Me*? Then you should read *Fake Me*[1] by Bonnie Edwards!

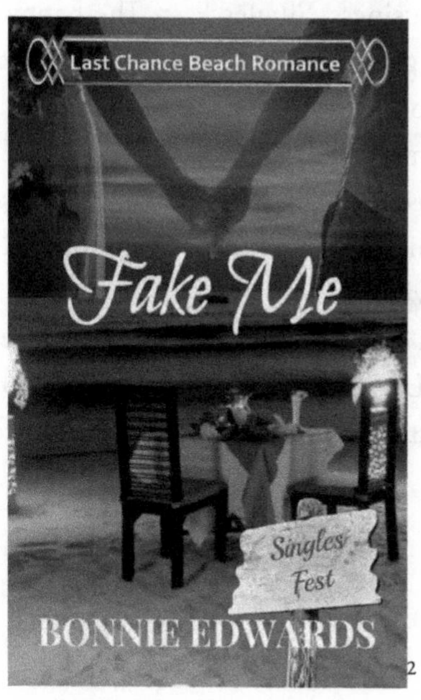

[2]

***How to fake out a meddlesome matchmaker - fake date the match*!**

International real estate broker Grady O'Hara, unkempt, miserable, and nursing his battered heart, is holed up in the Landseer Motel in Last Chance Beach. A first-class grump, Grady's appalled that enthusiastic sprite, Farren Parks wants him to open his motel to single parents looking for love. He suspects his sister has sent Farren to lure him into a romance. Again. The last one ended in disaster.

Farren expects him to tolerate children laughing, splashing, and squealing. Big no! Crowds of happy families? Bigger no!

He does not want a second chance at life. Or love.

---

1. https://books2read.com/u/47O8La

2. https://books2read.com/u/47O8La

Unless Farren agrees to fake date him to fake out his meddlesome matchmaking sister...

Grady soon plays handyman, painter, and business advisor to Farren's fledgling business, Singles Fest. The happy sound of children in the pool doesn't grate on his nerves as he expected. He sees parents making romantic connections that stir his heart.

But an old flame of Farren's has arrived and Grady wakes up to another looming loss if Farren gives her first love a second chance. The rival has brought his adorable kids to the motel. A rival who's clearly looking for a new wife...

FAKE ME is a standalone novel in a new line of contemporary romances set in Last Chance Beach, written by bestselling and award-winning authors who deliver something for every romance lover.

Also by Bonnie Edwards

Dance of Love

The Tinsel Tango A Dickens Holiday Novella

The Rumball Rumba: A Dickens Holiday Romance

The Winterland Waltz A Dickens Holiday Romance

Last Chance Beach

Fake Me

Take Me (and My Kids)

Make Me

Return to Welcome

Finding Mercy

Loving Logan

Craving Jake Return to Welcome Book 3

Claiming Shandy Return to Welcome Book 4

Christmas to the Max

Tales of Perdition

Perdition House Part 1 An Erotic Saga
Perdition House Part 2 An Erotic Saga
Rock Solid
Rock Solid
Parlor Games
A Breath Taken
The Tales of Perdition A Collection

The Brantons

Body Work
Slow Hand
Whole Lot O' Love
Rayder's Appeal The Brantons Book 4

The Diamond Series

Twinkle, Twinkle Little Thong
Diamond At Heart

Standalone

Long Time Coming
The Stone Heart
The Brantons A Collection
Thigh High

About the Author

Bonnie Edwards has been published by Kensington Books, Harlequin Books, Carina Press, and more.

With over 40 titles to her credit, her romances have been translated into several languages. Her books are sold worldwide.

Learn about more exciting releases and get a **free** romance by subscribing to her newsletter, **Bonnie's Newsy Bits** through her website.

https://www.bonnieedwards.com/

Cheers and happy reading!

Bonnie Edwards

Printed in the USA
CPSIA information can be obtained
at www.ICGtesting.com
LVHW041503130524
780142LV00009B/295